On a Black Blows Doom

A John Black Novel

Keith Soares

Bufflegoat Books

First print edition September 1, 2017
ISBN 978-0-9977707-0-4
Original publication date September 1, 2017

Edited by Christopher Durso.

This one is for my dad, Joe, and my sister, Dee.
Thanks for indulging me and my wild stories.

Images derived from
Four Horsemen of the Apocalypse by Viktor Vasnetsov (1887)
are in the public domain.

Also from Keith Soares

The Oasis of Filth

The Fingers of the Colossus *(Ten Short Stories)*

John Black

For I Could Lift My Finger and Black Out the Sun

If Only Every Moment Was Black and White

And It Arose From the Deepest Black

The Night Is Black, Without a Moon

On a Black Wind Blows Doom

The Black Eye of the Beholder (forthcoming)

In the Black Veins of the Earth *(forthcoming)*

Cloak of Black, Mantle of Sorrow (forthcoming)

Subscribe to the Keith Soares New Releases Newsletter

Get release news and free books,
including private giveaways and preview chapters.

Sign up at KeithSoares.com

Like Facebook.com/KeithSoaresAuthor
Follow Twitter.com/ksoares

PLEASE CONSIDER leaving a review where you purchased this book. Reviews are the best thing you can do to help an independent author like me, and even one sentence about your thoughts is enough.

Thanks in advance!

— K.

Prologue

"Johnny!"

Somewhere behind me, my mother screamed my name.

The lights of the deserted beach town, its odors and sounds, filled my senses. The rides and attractions of the boardwalk uttered their electronic music into the dark sky, while the scent of pizza and cotton candy failed to entice any takers on the abandoned strip. Still, it was bright, loud, and full of the smells we humans create in such excess.

In contrast, before me was only the rocky outcropping, the salt-tinged air, and the rolling sea, trailing off into the blackness of night toward a distant, unseen horizon.

Oh, and there was one more thing: Sol.

It was too much to bear. Too hard for me to ignore. "No, you're *dead.* I killed you myself."

He nodded. "The scriptures tell us that *on a pale horse rides Death.* Inescapable, by all measure. But is it really? After all, you're right, John. You *did* kill me. And that hurt. I will freely admit it." Sol shook his head once, quickly, and his mouth curved upward. He bared his gleaming white teeth but his eyes didn't smile. No, his eyes were feral, his intentions impossible to read. "My body was frozen, by *you*, John, and then shattered into a billion pieces, also by *you*, to be scattered in the wind. Quite honestly, I don't recommend the experience." He chuckled that smug chuckle. "But it is also said that *on a black wind blows Doom*, John Black. That day, the wind was indeed black. Doom was indeed in the air. I have returned, by will, by chance, or perhaps by fate, because there is a need for judgment. A last judgment for you, and for those with you." He nodded to the people behind me, those still on the boardwalk.

Mom screamed once more, and I turned, just enough to get a glimpse. Something was wrong. Something was very wrong with Holly. Before I could focus, I sensed Sol as he drew close to me, just over my shoulder. Fearful, I turned back.

"John, you've heard the phrase *Ars longa, vitas brevis*, correct?" His stale breath drifted over my face, overpowering even the briny smell of the ocean that filled my nose. Flakes of his still-changing flesh floated down to rest on my shoulders.

"What? No," I stammered. "Well, maybe. It's sorta familiar."

Sol gave a cocky smile, and I tensed. "I suspect you have, even if you currently find it hard to pinpoint any specific memory of the phrase. It's a bit of a bastardization, but it's Latin. It means *Art is long, life is short.*"

"And?"

"Only this, John. We began as mortals, you and I. In fact, thanks to your cleverness, my life has already proven to be short." He chuckled again.

Have I mentioned I hate that damn chuckle?

"Then how are you here, now?" I seethed. I had *beaten* him. He was *dead.* Even though a large part of me regretted the killing that seemed unavoidable with my powers, Sol's death at least gave me a small sense of peace. He'd directly and willfully attacked me, my family. He had kidnapped Holly. I didn't want to consider a world where Sol still roamed free. But what choice did I have? He was right in front of me. He was alive.

Sol put up one hand in a calming gesture and took a step back, relaxing his posture. He looked so strange, wearing khaki shorts and hiking boots. Not the stylish, Euro-hip look I was used to with Sol. He wore the clothes of Jake Weissman.

Jake.

Did he even exist anymore?

"And what happened to Jake?" I asked. This Sol was two men, somehow combined — one who used to be Jose do Branco, and another, Jake the Ranger. The first man had forced me to come after him, tried to force me to join him. Ultimately, he forced me to destroy him. The second had willfully brought destruction on so many, guiding those three giant monsters called Gorgols toward their maker. Toward my sister.

Sol furrowed his brow, considering, almost seeming to look inside himself. "It is an interesting situation, John. This body," he said, prodding at his ribs, "is predominantly Jake, although that may change in time, too. The mind, however… is *me*. Well, a part of Jake's mind is with me as well. His thoughts. They are a part of me. And in many ways, he makes — or I should say, *I make* — good points. Particularly about the Gorgols. I only wish they weren't gone. Your little sister is much more of a nuisance than I ever gave her credit for. I shall have to talk to her about it. Such *power…*"

Immediately my guilt about Sol's death — his first death? — evaporated. Head tilting downward, my eyes blazed at the man in front of me. "You go near my sister again and what happened to you last time will seem pleasant in comparison."

Another chuckle. "A *threat*, John? So unbecoming." Sol *tsked* at me, smiling. "But I must thank you."

"Why?"

"Well, as you no doubt saw, I was struggling. I admit that, as well. To return from death… Let us say it is not as easy as you might think. But I appreciate your help."

"What are you talking about?"

Sol inhaled, a teacher about to explain some simple concept to a toddler. “When you attacked what remained of Jake Weissman, when you exploded your energies into him, into me, you did me a great service. You blew away the last controlling vestiges of him. Other than the residuals of his physical form and some basic thoughts and memories, Jake Weissman is dead. And *I* am alive. So, in a way, John, you both killed me *and* resurrected me. Thank you.” He bowed, smiling. Maybe he even meant it as some form of appreciation. But to me it was the most mocking thing anyone had ever done. And I had been mocked a lot growing up. I was sort of an expert.

“Johnny!” Mom called, and this time I couldn’t ignore her.

Below us, on the remains of the boardwalk, I saw an unbelievable sight. My mother stood next to the wheelchair inhabited by my sister for so many years. A wheelchair that was suddenly empty.

Holly was *standing*.

No, that’s not quite right.

Holly’s body was in a standing position, but she almost appeared like a marionette, held up by strings. She was a few inches above the wood slats of the boardwalk, high enough that her toes dipped downward into points. Her arms drooped, her chin tilted toward her chest, her jet-black hair hung limp around her face.

It was a face that seemed empty.

“What are you doing to her?” I demanded, turning back to Sol.

He *tsked* again. “Me? I’m afraid that I am not behind your sister’s current condition, John.”

Holly had created Gorgol Alpha, a 200-foot-tall indestructible monster, but when it was needed most, Holly had opened a window and forced Alpha to disappear through it. She made the monster out of nothing, then unmade it, back into nothing. Or did that window lead into Holly herself? Had she consumed the giant creature?

Her body pulsed with an energy that I saw, heard, and felt, yet I wondered if it was there for everyone. Could my mother see it? A sort of light radiated from Holly. She was a ghost, a shadow, an angel — a dark, glowing, floating vision from Heaven.

I reached out with my mind. *Hol? Holly? Are you okay?*

No response.

Holly, you're worrying me. You're worrying Mom. Are you okay?

Still nothing.

I stretched a probing tendril from my mind toward hers, trying to connect, like I had done with her so many times before, like I had done to so many others as well. But there was nothing to be found. No beacon, no life force, not even static where something should have been. Just emptiness.

And I felt *him* doing the same. An unmistakable mental tendril of Sol's also searched for Holly.

So I intercepted him.

Stay out of my sister's head.

I pushed backward, toward the source of the thread, forcibly. Not deadly force, but a shockwave of warning. The connection broke and I opened my eyes.

Below me, Holly's light fluttered and went out. The sense of her energy flicked off like someone had thrown a switch, and her body fell to the boardwalk like a pile of dropped beach towels. Still, where that energy turned off, something else turned back on. I could feel Holly's presence again. Had she returned to normal?

She landed in a heap of unguided legs and arms, head falling forward onto the wooden boards, and Mom rushed forward to help.

I turned around with a fire in my gut, low but present. If the fight had to continue, then so be it. I had beaten him once. I would, somehow, do it again.

But Sol was gone.

PART 1

— *famine* —

1

Believe it or not, the next 11 months were blissfully low-key. No monsters, no helicopters, no mass destruction, no unexplained behavior. And no Sol.

I even had the chance to celebrate turning 16. And the biggest surprise of all? Mom got me a phone. No more mental-push-stealing cellphones from strangers. Can we all say *huzzah*? So that was pretty badass. Plus, Carrie threw me a little party by getting some of my friends together: Bobby, Steve, Tom, and a few of her girlfriends to even things out. We had pizza and watched two movies.

Steve and Tom, true to form, relentlessly hit on two of Carrie's friends, Hayden and Aliania. The two girls were opposites. Hayden was petite with close-cropped dark hair and smooth, sepia-toned skin, while Aliania was blonde and curvaceous.

Despite Steve's incessant nerdy jokes, Hayden was the kind of person who could see the best in just about anyone. I'm not sure if she was really into him, but she was just so nice, how could you blame him for trying? It also didn't hurt at all that she was super-hot.

And Tom kept telling Aliania that her name was "absolutely beautiful." I was pretty certain he wasn't really talking about her name. Still, he must have asked her half a dozen times if her name was borrowed from a goddess or an angel or a Caribbean island. She laughed and blushed, flipping her long locks in a way that did nothing to stop Tom's compliments.

Meanwhile, to one side of the room, Bobby sat talking with a stylish and confident girl named Marcia. They seemed to be having an engaged discussion about places they'd like to travel. Marcia, being half-Korean, noted South Korea as her first choice, since she had never actually been there herself. It seemed at times like a game of one-upmanship, each of them trying to come up with some more exotic and somehow *better* travel destination for the list. Still, while Bobby smiled and chatted, I never got the feeling he was hitting on

Marcia. At least, if he was, it was nowhere near as obvious as the other two.

I had a moment when the incredible weirdness of it all took hold of me. I mean, when I turned 15, I was sitting in my Aunt Cindy's station wagon, at a park in the desert, about to fight Sol to the death. (Well, what I *thought* was the death.) Turning 16, I sat on the couch with my girlfriend eating pizza and watching movies. Crazy, right?

One of the movies we watched was about a motley group of superheroes called together to save mankind. Bobby and I shared a glance and a smirk. If only the entire fate of the world could be neatly decided in a hundred and 20 minutes, give or take.

As I see it, movie superheroes consist of three types. First, there are Suit Heroes, the kind where roughly 99.78 percent of their power comes from the outfit, giving no real sense of specialness about the person inside. Better hope the suit doesn't break down or you'll end up with a pretty average dude in a funny costume. And if you're going to make the argument that the superhero must have incredible ingenuity to make the suit in the first place, I think you're essentially equating them to fashion designers with advanced electrical-engineering degrees. Was that your intent? Sorry, I'm biased. I felt silly enough wearing the simple black mask Pip gave me. I can't imagine my embarrassment if I had to walk around town in a full-on metal suit.

Then you have Particularly-Good-at-One-Thing Heroes, like the guy who's excellent with throwing stars, or the woman who can do those amazing flip kicks. I could see where these people would be helpful in many real-world situations, but compared to the others, they seem hopelessly outgunned. I think the other two types of superheroes keep Particularly-Good-at-One-Thing Heroes around just so they can try to relate to the common man. To seem more human.

And finally, we have Actual Superheroes. These are the people that have something completely different about them that makes them superpowered. It's not a suit that can be taken away, and it's not just some excessive training in one thing. Actual Superheroes are the real deal. The only problem is that sometimes you get one that's so powerful you start wondering why they don't just mop the floor with everyone else like they should.

Naturally, I find myself most interested in Actual Superheroes — the ones whose power runs through their blood. Since that's, of course, where mine is. And nothing, not a single thing, can ever take that away from me.

Or so I thought.

I have a feeling that I'm coming off as arrogant, and if so, I'm sorry. Having to live with power inside every single cell in my body, it's hard to relate to a guy who's especially good with a two-handed axe, or a woman who creates an uber-powerful armadillo suit.

All right, I admit it. In private, I would totally love to have an uber-powerful armadillo suit. And, in a pinch, I would really like to be able to turn to the dude with the two-handed axe and shout, "You're up!"

The other great thing about having nearly a year off from being a hero is that I had time to simply chill out. I don't mean laze around on the couch, though I did my share of that. I mean time to try to get a handle on all that rage and bloodlust that had been getting out of control. Sol's reappearance got me a little fired up, but in general my final moment with Gorgol Alpha — where I fully intended to give my life to stop the creature from getting to my sister — took pretty much all that bad stuff out of me. I mean, afterward I became a complete pacifist and the rest of this story is about how I helped old ladies cross the street and tutored children in math. You do know I'm being sarcastic, right?

Yeah, the fire was still inside me. Anger and fear and rage and passion. Everybody has that stuff. It's whether you let it take over that matters. I finally felt like I could hold all of it in check. Although I hadn't actually tested that theory. It could be that checking one's rage was a lot easier when one was eating pizza with one's girlfriend. I'm no social scientist. Pardon me if I don't have the stats on all this.

Holly, who was rapidly approaching her teen years, was getting tall, although she was still about the same in terms of speech and mobility. Mom had to buy her the next size bigger wheelchair, and it was oddly emotional when we decided to get rid of the old one. I mean, it was silly to stress about a chair, especially when Holly didn't so much fit into it anymore, but you grow attached to things. And I had ridden the darn thing to outer space, so there's that. You never forget your first outer-space wheelchair. Trust me.

At least Holly hadn't repeated the whole float-around act since we'd left the boardwalk. In fact, everything with Holly felt *normal.*

And then there was Pip. Would you believe she went public? Yep. Unmasked and all. Crazy. The world learned that Red Hope had a real name: Phillipa "Pip" Siva. Did you just stop and say, "What the heck? I didn't know her last name was Siva?" Very good! You're paying attention! Maybe more so than me, because I didn't know it until they interviewed her on TV. Good friend, huh? I mean, not knowing her last name was probably lower on the list of terrible things than when I cut off her arm, but it was definitely in second place. I'd spent so much time *thinking* I knew her that it never occurred to me how wrong I was and how little I knew.

As for her name, it didn't much matter. The TV people only wanted to call her Red Hope anyway. And of course, they bugged her about Yellow Fury (Bobby) and Black Sword (me). Asked her when we were coming back, where we went. What we ate, did for a living. Did we work out? What zodiac sign were we? And the most burning question of all: Where did we get those powers?

Pip lived in the city, not all that far from the park where Sol and I had our little throw down that one time. She volunteered to help police and rescue efforts from time to time, which resulted in a lot of grateful folks willing to support her daily life. On one occasion, she stumbled upon a limo that had been blocked into a dead-end alley by two other cars. Men with guns were trying to abduct the daughter of a wealthy businessman, so they could extort a huge sum of money for her safe return. Pip saw to it that the girl was never touched, and the would-be kidnappers had a *very* bad afternoon that lead to a lengthy jail sentence. As a result, the businessman considered himself forever in Pip's debt. Basically, if she asked (or even if she didn't), her every need was paid for in thanks. Plus, the interview circuit earned her enough money that she bought a condo in a high-rise with security. Pretty funny that a superhuman needed security, but at least it kept away the wackos and zealots. Because there were a lot of those.

The seemingly endless Gorgol origin theories finally died down. Mostly there was a sort of global lament that no one was able to keep a sample of Gorgol flesh for study. How was that possible, given the size of the beasts? Well, I had never hung around long enough to witness it, but apparently a few hours after they died, the Gorgols just fizzled away into thin air. Nobody could come up with a rational explanation for why that happened, but I knew. They came from nothing. Made sense they'd go back to it.

Even Jake Weissman got his share of attention. And he wasn't even around anymore. A bunch of folks started calling themselves "The Way of the Ranger" and said they were awaiting his return. Keep waiting, folks. When Pip revealed in an interview that Jake had been on some kick about the Gorgols coming to avenge the earth, it at least gave the Way of the Ranger people a focal point. Maybe they started a recycling program or something.

And what about Bobby?

The whole Pip-goes-public thing was hard on him. I mean, if it were just up to him, he'd have gone public in a heartbeat, follow her lead, follow her to the city, too. But he knew that if he did that, it would take maybe 35 seconds for someone to figure out that *I* was Black Sword, and then my peaceful little life would shatter like an icicle falling off a skyscraper.

I appreciated that Bobby was a good enough friend to stay undercover in order to protect me and my family. But I didn't know if it could last. He never brought it up, never asked me for permission or anything. But I knew he had a thing for Pip, and I knew he had a crappy home life. His parents remained narcissistic assholes, not that you're surprised.

All he had to do was stop caring what it would do to me, Mom, and Holly, and Bobby could solve two pretty big problems all at once.

Still, it turns out that Bobby wasn't the one who shattered the quiet. It was a woman. No, two.

Eleven months of blissful peace and quiet was what I got, and then it ended. Well, it's not like I expected it to last forever.

2

Her name was Dr. Naima Ramadi, and she was a psychiatrist in a city only about 75 miles west of my hometown. She was several things I'm not: female, adult, highly educated, a medical professional, a parent, and… well, at least one other significant thing.

Naima was Lebanese by heritage, although she had never so much as planted a toe on Lebanese soil. Not for lack of desire. Her parents were more concerned with her integration and education to bother with other aspects of her cultural upbringing. She was an only child, and as such was afforded both the huge benefit of being the sole focal point of two wealthy parents and the loneliness of growing up with only confusing adults to talk to about daily issues.

I'm going to stop for a second. I can feel your thoughts — I'm magical like that. *Who is this Naima, and why should I care?* Well, duh. You can guess the answer. She developed powers. But wait. They aren't what you think.

By the time I first heard of her, Naima was in her mid-forties. She was divorced and had one child, an eight-year-old son named Sharif. Her husband apparently couldn't deal with the requirements of Naima's job as an associate psychiatrist at the state university's Emergency Psychiatric Evaluation Center, a place they called "E-pec" for short — stress on the "e," definitely not pronounced "epic."

So she solo-parented and she worked long hours. Not a great combination. Like my own mom, she had to rely on the kindness of neighbors and the help of for-hire agents. Even in the best scenario, this, as I have witnessed, can give a parent heart palpitations. Leaving a kid, especially a kid having special needs, with what amounts to a stranger… well, it's stressful.

My story is complicated. It's hard to be one of the most powerful humans on Earth and not have other people stir the pot of your life. Naima did. So I need to tell you about her, even stuff before I knew her. All of this happened well before I'd ever heard her name, but it's important shit. Sorry. I know, I know. Language.

Naima was working one particular late afternoon when a woman was brought in. The event itself wasn't all that remarkable. People were brought in all the time. Sharif, her son, went to an after-school program in the rec center adjacent to his elementary school, so he was fine until 6:30 that night, or even later if she called her neighbor for a favor. That meant Naima had at least an hour to work with the new arrival and get her situated.

The woman was tall, strongly built, and as blonde as they come. Scandinavian, perhaps? Yeah, you're right. It was Margrethe.

Margrethe, the Norse God of Vengeance. Or at least a pretty close approximation. She was back.

In body, at least. Mind? Maybe not. She'd been found in a city square, ranting about things *they* had done to her. You know, aluminum-foil-hat conspiracy theories. This was, I suppose, the remainder of my effect on her brain, my lasting mental *push*.

Piecing together the history of Margrethe is like reading tea leaves; it's only as accurate as you believe it to be. When she attacked us and ripped off the car door, we were way out west, coming out of the mountains. So, months later, how the heck did she get to some city less than 100 miles from where I lived? Your guess is as good as mine. But, since I'm the one doing the typey-typey here, I think it was the beacons. She eventually was drawn east by our beacons. By my beacon? Yeah, probably. I did sort of erase Margrethe's mind. That might have been a good reason to find me.

But I don't think she did it consciously. I mean, first, I hit her pretty hard, blanked her mind pretty good. Second, when she was initially brought in — Naima can attest to this — Margrethe really had no idea who or where she was.

She was just mad.

It took three large men to get her gently strapped onto a gurney, and even that was a small miracle. If they'd been trying to hit her rather than just restrain her, I'm pretty sure her body would have been doing some serious sluicing, and who knows where that would have led. In a way, it's a good thing. I have a feeling Margrethe would've been spending her remaining days in a government lab if people had realized what she could do. Thankfully, they were pretty slow and methodical about it, and her cells didn't act up enough for anyone to suspect.

I mean, we lived in a world where Gorgol fights had been a televised sport and Pip was a celebrity. Margrethe would have drawn a whole lot of interest, if only people had known.

Anyway, she was restrained but still upset, writhing about and yelling things like "Give it back!" or "Get out of my head!" So, of course, to your typical psychiatric ward staffer, Margrethe didn't seem even slightly unusual.

Except for one thing.

They weren't going to sedate her. As a rule of thumb, Naima and her staff wouldn't even restrain someone unless there was an obvious need to do so. Margrethe was physically imposing and acting in an aggressive manner. She was strapped down mostly so they could keep her in one place long enough to deal with her. But she still wouldn't calm down. Shortly after they rolled her into a room, they thought they could leave her alone for 30 seconds. Margrethe started rocking her entire body back and forth, and ended up toppling the gurney onto its side, with her still attached. The same three big guys had to lift her and the bed back to an upright position, and at that point, Naima decided the tall blonde woman was a potential danger to herself or others — a Code Grey. First they tried oral medication, but Margrethe spat it out and almost bit the orderly's finger. Naima instructed a nurse on her staff to inject a sedative and inform her when the patient had calmed. In the meantime, she went off to check on others under her care.

It didn't take long for another orderly to come find her. "Doctor?"

Naima looked up from the chart she'd been studying to see Raul staring at her with a strange and unreadable expression. Raul was six-and-a-half feet of muscle, which might make you assume he was deficient mentally. Not so. He was taking night classes to become an RN, and sometimes Naima would quiz him on various medical details. She had an amicably antagonistic relationship with him, taunting him if his responses were off-base. To Raul's credit, she couldn't remember him ever answering a question wrong more than once, despite her attempts to trick him. She was used to seeing a glimmer in his eye when he knew the right answer to her question, which made his current expression even more unsettling. "Yes? Is something wrong?"

Raul grimaced. "I… I'm not sure, but could you come take a look?" Naima nodded and followed him back to Margrethe's room. There, her psychiatric nurse, Mark, sat puzzled next to the bed where Margrethe continued to struggle.

"Mark? I thought you were going to sedate her," Naima said.

"I tried," he said, holding a hypodermic needle at eye level for her to see. "Watch." Mark stepped into position beside the gurney and attempted to insert the needle into Margrethe's flesh.

Her skin resisted. No matter what he did, Mark couldn't get the needle to penetrate, and as he applied more pressure, he only succeeded in snapping the needle in two, spilling the liquid sedative onto the floor where it joined the detritus Naima immediately recognized as Mark's prior attempts. "What in the world…?" Still, she was a pro. She didn't think Mark was incompetent — far from it, actually — but she also wasn't ready to give in. "Let me try."

Mark shrugged and prepped another needle. "At this rate, we're going to waste a lot of drugs."

"I'll be careful," Naima said. Her eyes remained locked on the patient as she approached with the new syringe. Standing next to the bed, she was acutely aware of Margrethe's imposing size, particularly because the blonde woman continued to jerk back and forth. Wordlessly, Naima nodded toward Raul and Mark, and they reached out to hold the patient still.

Once they latched on, Naima touched the skin of Margrethe's arm with her free hand. Later she told me that there was some sort of unusual tingle, not unlike touching the housing of a running motor, feeling the energy inside. It was strange, but not strange enough to give her pause. She brought the needle to touch Margrethe's skin.

And it slid in easily.

Naima pressed the plunger and the medicine was delivered into the patient's bloodstream. She glanced at the two men with a confused expression. In minutes, Margrethe had calmed. In a half-hour, she was asleep.

"I have no idea how you did that," Mark said moments later, cleaning up the mess of his failed attempts.

Dr. Naima Ramadi could only smirk. "Neither do I." What had she really done? Given a simple injection. From her point of view, she didn't understand why Mark hadn't been able to do it. Shooting the sleeping Norse giant a last look, she shook her head, confused, then left to check on her other patients.

3

Carrie told me about the rather harrowing drive home from the dentist office with her dad, the day that Gorgol Alpha trashed half of the town. She gave me all the details; her initial, frightening realization that a giant creature was so close — she even mentioned how afraid she was for *me* — and then the frantic push through jammed streets, trying more than anything just to escape. It was surreal listening to her describe the radio play-by-play of Black Sword and Yellow Fury's face-off with the monster, since of course that was just her telling me what someone else told her about what I had lived through. Does that make sense? I hope so, because it hurts my head.

It dawned on me that I would have to be more careful with my outward public appearance. I mean, yeah, I wore the black mask, and so far that was sufficient, but the rest of my attire was just, you know, me. And here's the thing about having a girlfriend: I started to realize how often I wore the same thing. I mean, it's one thing if I hang out with Bobby a dozen times in my *Force of Will* movie t-shirt, but if Carrie started seeing it over and over, and then — God forbid — I wore it one day when I had to be international superhero and man of mystery Black Sword, well, she was going to put two and two together. Heck, my neighbor, Mr. Morrison might recognize that.

As it was, I wasn't inherently good at keeping vital secrets from someone I cared about. There were about 60 times each day when I almost told Carrie everything. Usually by accident.

"Hello…?"

I shook my head.

"You there, John?"

Uh oh. I zoned out again. Carrie was looking at me funny, snapping her fingers.

We were sitting in my room. The door was — get this — closed. I know, right? After all that crap for closing *her* door. Kinda hypocritical, but who was I to judge? A beautiful girl was sitting in my room with the door closed. I decided it was in my best interest not to debate.

Mom was pretty cool about the whole thing. I guess she was beginning to embrace the idea of me as an adult. Or, you know, at least I was somewhere on that pathway. Still, a side of me thought Mom probably let me get away with murder because I had superpowers, had saved the life of her daughter, fought and beat giant monsters, and generally got all my homework done on time. Either way, I wasn't complaining.

It was probably a good sign that I could zone out while Carrie was around. I mean, if I was always worried about what to do or say in front of her, that wouldn't be good, right? Then again, if I was basically a zombie while she was around… crap, dating was confusing and hard.

"Present and accounted for, sir!" I said, idiotic salute and all.

Carrie tilted her head back, looking straight up, perhaps asking some divine power why she tolerated me. Yet there was a slight upturn at the corners of her mouth. Amusement. Good. "Are you ready, or are you just going to sit here and daydream?"

Ready? Oh yeah, right. "Ready."

"Really, John?" Carrie looked down.

So did I. Directly at my bare feet. "Shoes! Just gotta get shoes on. Two seconds!" I ran to find a pair of shoes.

"It never takes two seconds," she scoffed.

Fine. It was longer. Maybe three minutes. But you know, I was close. After a brief chat with Mom about when I would be back, Carrie and I left. We were headed to a basketball game. More specifically, to Carrie's kid brother's basketball game. His name was Michael MacGregor Jr., but everyone called him Mack. He was eight.

If you, like me, presumed that eight-year-olds would play basketball on an appropriately scaled-down court, then you, like me, would be wrong. Sure, the basket was a bit lower than the normal pro height, but other than that, it was a regular basketball court. Also, it was night time. That was weird. Eight-year-olds playing on a full-sized court, after dark. Okay, clearly I should expect some pretty amazing play, right?

I think they could have swapped the basket for a large trash can at each end of the court, and we still might not have seen more than five total shots made.

Final score: 4-0. After four laborious quarters of play. And, to top it off, technically each team made a basket, but technically, you're not allowed to shoot into your own hoop. Hence, Mack's goal — yep, it was him — was an own-goal, thereby doubling the opponent's score. And no, they didn't show mercy. There was mocking a-plenty. I think I even heard parents chuckling. Not cool, basketball moms and dads. Not cool.

If you've ever been to a basketball game, you know that they sound a horn at the end. Usually the auditorium is relatively quiet, except for the random squeaks of sneakers and pings of the ball bouncing off things. Then, suddenly, the gates of hell open and this horn sounds, a soul-eating tone. And I don't mean that it was any kind of special horn for this particular game; this sound happens at *every* basketball game. You've been there. You know it.

Game over. We lost. Mack was responsible (poor, Mack). But the end product was this: It was time to go home. I got up.

"Where are you going, John?" Carrie said. "Bathroom?"

I paused, confused. "No, uh, I was going home."

Carrie laughed and rolled her eyes.

I stood, confused. "What?"

"We talked about this. Twice."

"What?"

She sighed. "This is a *tournament*, John."

I tried to remember or understand. Nothing. "And?"

"We have another game," Carrie said.

"But… they lost."

"That doesn't matter."

Of course. A tournament where losing doesn't matter. Why didn't I assume that was the case?

So we sat through another game. Mack scored again.

I'm not even going to tell you who the points counted for.

* * *

Carrie's parents drove her brother home but let us walk. It wasn't far. The elementary school was sort of the hub the neighborhood revolved around.

Still… on the way, there was something weird.

A man, standing on a random street corner. Head tilted down, sharply to one side, like it hurt. He was tall and thin, swathed in dark clothes, his hair a disheveled mass of dirty brown. I couldn't see a single detail of his face, even as he moved toward us with the distracted air of someone checking his phone or daydreaming.

Or lost.

The evening smelled of honeysuckle and sounded like crickets, and there, among all this normal peace, was this guy. I had to walk Carrie right past him to take her home. And I felt something.

I believe, firmly, that this had nothing to do with my powers. It was just normal human intuition, if you can call something like this normal.

Something was wrong with this guy.

As we passed, I did something unnatural. I reached out with my mind.

There was a buzz, like bees, echoing in my head.

It reminded me of Jake Weissman, in a way. And it wasn't about power. As far as I could tell, the man partially blocking the sidewalk before us was 100-percent USDA Grade-A normal human. But the static on his channel wasn't all that different from what I sensed from Jake/Sol. Was this what it was like to touch insanity? The sense of it shocked me, simultaneously making me feel a deep sorrow for what was happening in this man's head, and giving me an extreme case of the willies.

I'll be blunt. It scared me.

I cut the connection and took Carrie home as fast as possible.

4

I couldn't wait to tune in. Banner Productions, those kindly folks who had offered me a bunch of cash as long as I didn't mind selling out my family and soul, were about to unveil the catch of the century. The "real" Black Sword and Yellow Fury were set to be interviewed on live TV. I asked Mom to make popcorn.

It was going to be awesome.

And yet, I admit I was a little ticked off. No, not in a rage. I was trying to keep that crap under control, remember?

But who were these imposters? I mean, I was torn. I really wanted them to be top-notch, quality imposters, people I could look at and say, *Oh, yeah, that guy could* so *be me*. You know, people like incredibly hot young celebrity movie stars, or internationally recognized champion athletes. Essentially, my doppelgängers. On the other hand, if they were too good, what would I do with that? Would I have to *prove* to the world that *I* was Black Sword? I mean, you know, if I was telling anyone.

So there was a curious benchmark I was looking for. Someone sufficiently skilled and cool that I was okay with the viewing public thinking that person was me, but at the same time plausibly insufficient for the role.

It was a lot to ask.

Thankfully, Banner Productions was not averse to phoning it in. Honestly, I hope I meet their version of "Black Sword" one day. He was hopelessly ridiculous. I loved it.

Possibly the best part was that Mark Simeon, that uber-suave, ultra-cool, excessively smarmy producer, was the one handling the interview. The guy who tried to talk me into a deal. I was relishing the idea of watching him squirm when his efforts fell apart.

They had to fall apart, right? I mean, he had the wrong guys. People would recognize that. Wouldn't they?

No, of course not. As absurd as Banner Productions' version of Black Sword appeared to me, I guess other people actually *believed* him.

It was horrible.

I had wanted to reveal myself before. To Carrie, so she would know the truth. To the world, so I could stop hiding. Heck, it had taken me time to even tell my mom. But I knew what going public would mean: a lot of unwanted scrutiny and attention. Not just for me, but for my family. For Holly. The lights and cameras. The yelling and the mobs. The seizures she would invariably have. I couldn't. But the idea lingered.

I digress. Back to the TV show.

First, the pros: Mark Simeon had clearly been careful making his selections and considering the visual details. Plus, it was dramatic. No in-studio interview on a couch by a desk. Nope, that would have been way too tame for superheroes.

They did it on a rooftop. Oddly, this was a fairly spot-on bit of guesswork by Banner Productions, as Bobby and I had experienced our fair share of important moments on rooftop. I couldn't tell what city it was — maybe the capital — but of course they did it at sunset, for dramatic lighting.

A couple of helicopters circled the roof, their blinding spotlights sliding back and forth randomly, creating lens flares and alternating pools of light and shadow. As Mark Simeon stepped into view, mic in hand, his hair rippled in the whirling air.

He began his introduction, dramatically intoning the importance of the event. "For the first time ever on live television, you will hear *directly* from the superhumans known only as Yellow Fury and

Black Sword, a Banner Productions exclusive…" As he spoke, two figures stepped up in silhouette behind him.

For a millisecond, I was on edge to see who the superheroes were. Then I got a hold of myself.

Oh, yeah.

"But first!" Simeon shouted. "First, the heroes must *prove* themselves! We need to know these two are who they say they are, am I right, my people?" *My people* was Mark Simeon's extraordinarily arrogant way of addressing his audience.

Behind him, the helicopter spotlights zigged and zagged, and I would swear smoke machines were fired up to billow new clouds into the swirling air. The two shadowed figures stepped forward, finally into the light.

And then there was the first commercial break. What a buzzkill.

A few minutes later they were back. And essentially, Mark Simeon set the stage *again.* This went on, padded with video footage of the real me and the real Bobby fighting the real Gorgols, for a couple more breaks. I yawned.

Finally, around the halfway point of the show, the overhyped demonstration fight finally happened.

I mean, they did a great job, at least on the surface. Had I not known any better, and with the mask on, I would have sworn I was looking at *me*. And Bobby, as well.

But the thing is, it was me and Bobby like nothing had changed. Like no time had passed at all. It was us in our clothes from the fight with Alpha, dressed the exact same way. Somehow, probably from poring over video, they had even made masks that looked identical to the ones Pip made. And of course, Pip herself was public, so I suppose they could have even taken measurements. Suffice it to say, they nailed us, but it was time-machine us. Us from before. The us the world knew, from video.

No one else knew that subtlety. The world probably assumed I woke, ate, slept, and woke again in those clothes, wearing that mask. Not so.

"All right, you guys — what can you show us to prove you *are* Yellow Fury and Black Sword?" Dramatic music swelled. The two dark figures nodded, and then, in obvious synchronicity, they faced each other and began a slow circular movement. A real live superhero duel.

They slid and moved. Did they sluice?

Nope.

But they moved fast. Interestingly, the camera seemed to anticipate their moves, sliding out of their way, accidentally enhancing the drama of their movement.

Accidentally.

Ha.

Later on, when Banner Productions was accused of using special effects for the fight sequence, they claimed their camera operators had simply been "caught by surprise" and needed to "repeatedly dive and dance out of the way."

Of course, I didn't need the accusation to know it was a lie, and I didn't need to think about the second lie that was offered in defense.

They pulled out all the stops. Blurred movement, dramatic angles, shots that made normal human acts seem super. Almost.

Finally, the farce of a superpowered fight ended with Mark Simeon himself jumping into view waving his hands. He stood with the two masked superhumans atop the tall building, waves of air and light swaying over them. "Enough! Enough! We believe you!" He laughed, sounding giddy in a prepackaged way, almost enough to sound convincing. But to me, not quite.

Commercial time came again, and both going into it and coming out, the footage of the fight was replayed in slow-mo with filters and effects added. *Nice work, live production crew. Very effective.*

Once the show returned, Mark Simeon waved the two fighters closer, and they came to him, like beckoned dogs. "All right, fellas. We're here on live TV — the world is watching. Will you take off the masks? Will you show yourselves?"

The two feigned hesitation. First one acted as if he would reveal himself, then the other would interrupt. Mark Simeon cajoled them both. More clips were shown.

And there was another commercial break.

Finally, the moment was nigh. The sponsors had shown their ads and time was running out. Fate and/or the allotted 60 minutes required that something must happen.

As the lights of the city twinkled all around them, Black Sword and Yellow Fury finally stepped forward and reached for their masks. After so long, and given the tremendous amount of stress it caused me, it seemed like a complete letdown. Not just finding out that *they* weren't *us* — because of course they weren't — but just the whole movement seemed stilted and lame.

Together, their masks came off and they blinked at the camera.

They looked nothing at all like Bobby and me.

In fact, if I were to say they looked like anyone, they looked like *each other*.

In my living room, my mouth hung open as I watched. Holly bobbed in her chair, amused or annoyed or both. Mom scoffed and muttered indignities under her breath.

On screen, Mark Simeon asked the question on so many minds. “Who are you?”

The older one, the bigger of the two who was supposed to be Bobby, smiled. “I’m Joe.”

“And I’m Jimmy,” the other one — me — said.

Joseph and James Richardson, those were their names. The two who pretended to be Bobby Graden and me. What a pisser.

“You’re *brothers*?” Mark Simeon said.

The bigger one nodded. “Yep.”

And then TV-me smiled. “What can we say? Power runs in our family.”

5

Every day, Dr. Ramadi did her rounds. Margrethe was a patient of some importance to her, but not the only one.

The main thing that kept the big blonde woman on Naima's mind was that there was no easy diagnosis. Oh, and no one knew who she was.

Margrethe had some form of significant memory loss, possibly dementia, although it worked in an unusual way. They called her *Jane Doe VI*, which was the traditional unknown female name of Jane Doe, incremented for each one they'd ever encountered, meaning E-pec had seen five previous mystery cases. None had remained unidentified for more than four days. Margrethe was Jane Doe for more than three weeks.

From Jane Doe VI's own mouth they learned that she had been bouncing from shelter to shelter, getting some meals, finding places to sleep. But how she had arrived at such a life was a blank slate. She couldn't tell them anything about who she was or where she came from prior to a few months earlier.

Margrethe wasn't destined to remain lost. First, the world kept records. Although she had gone off the grid once she connected with Sol, the fact of the matter was that she had a previous life. A driver's license, a job, bills to pay, credit cards. Second, she *wanted* to come back into her mind. When she was calm and reflective, she would ask Naima and the rest of the staff to help her — to do whatever was necessary to recover her memory.

So Naima began the process of trying to find out who Jane Doe VI was, while simultaneously considering options to help her patient. She thought an MRI would be worthwhile, to assess the current state of Jane's brain, but the blonde woman could be delusional and was prone to fits of rage in uncomfortable situations — something called a *catastrophic reaction.*

The E-pec didn't have MRI equipment, but it was located on a university hospital campus, just a short walk from another facility where skilled technicians operated the large circular scanners daily.

"Jane, you understand that we'll take you in a wheelchair to another building, then you'll need to lay down on a moving bed and be very still while the scan is done?" Naima watched her patient's reaction, gauging her level of comprehension.

Margrethe nodded. She sat in her room wearing the same standard-issue faded green cotton shirt and pants that every patient wore. The room smelled faintly of ammonia and, under that, the less desirable smells the ammonia tried to mask. The smells of patients who had significantly less self control than their lost Jane Doe VI.

"And you understand that the machine will be above you and around you, and it will make strange noises, but at no time will it harm you or even touch you?" The doctor did her best to look reassuring.

Margrethe nodded again, but Naima noticed a slight flicker in the blonde woman's eyes. Still, the doctor thought the MRI was necessary. Raul brought in a wheelchair and helped guide the patient to sit. She wasn't strapped down. After three weeks in the E-pec, the staff had begun to think they could trust Jane Doe VI, or at least deal with her mood swings.

Once she was settled in, the orderly rolled Jane Doe VI down the hall as Naima walked beside the chair. Given her status and time constraints, Naima certainly didn't need to be present for the MRI, even though she had a general fascination with the scans, the slow reveal of the brain's folds and shape.

Her mind wandered as they headed toward the door, planning the rest of her day. She knew Raul had everything under control, so despite her interest, she would see them to the exit and that would be that. She pushed the glass door open, holding it to allow Raul and Jane Doe VI to pass.

At first, everything was fine.

"Hey, doc," the female clerk at the front desk called out. Her name was Clarice. She was an older woman, dark hair and dark skin, a little round, always friendly. Naima paused, still holding the door, as Raul pushed past with the wheelchair. "We got a ping on your Jane Doe there." Clarice nodded toward the pair leaving the building.

"Really?" Naima said.

"Yeah, apparently her name is Margaret Vit."

Naima bobbed her head in acknowledgment. "*Margaret*, huh?" She started to turn toward the door as it began to close behind Raul.

"Oh, wait," Clarice said, checking her monitor. "Not Margaret, looks like her name is *Margrethe*. I guess she's all exotic or something."

At that moment, bright sunlight touched Margrethe's skin and her face, nearly blinding her eyes. She heard her name, and she *remembered.*

Shoving the wheelchair backward into Raul as she propelled herself forward, the big blonde woman sprang back to life and ran. The Norse God of Vengeance raced into the lush open lawn that filled the gap between several buildings on campus, dodging people as she tried to get away.

Raul gasped from the impact but caught himself. He was admittedly surprised, but not *completely* surprised. He'd been an orderly too long for that. Within a moment, he was running to catch Jane Doe VI.

The lawn was crisscrossed with walkways, allowing the medical staff to make their way to various wards and buildings. It was busy that afternoon, with more than two dozen people witnessing Margrethe's attempted escape.

Each one of the bystanders would later be asked to recount their tale, multiple times to multiple people with forgettable government suits and forgettable government personalities. Probably each one of the witnesses later regretted whatever random sequence of events led them to be there that day, if for no other reason than the fact that telling the story would consume many hours of their life.

Margrethe zigged but Raul zagged, and he caught up to her.

It didn't matter.

As Raul dove to wrap his large arms around her, Margrethe's body *sluiced*, sliding impossibly and bending unnaturally to avoid his strong arms. Raul tumbled to the grass, wide-eyed and gasping, but with enough sense to follow the roll into a crouch.

But the sluice had really happened.

Everyone saw it.

Everyone had seen it before. On TV. From me, Bobby, Pip, even Ranger and Alpha.

Everyone knew what it meant, by that time.

This woman, this large blonde woman, had *powers*.

"Margrethe! Stop!" Naima called from the door, but Margrethe kept moving.

Raul's eyes followed her movement and he gauged a second attempt, flinging himself forward. And once again, Margrethe sluiced. She ducked away from him and continued running.

Dr. Naima Ramadi, still holding the door open for no one, finally realized she had been watching the whole scene motionlessly. She shook herself into action, running into the grass to help her colleague. "We're just trying to help you, Margrethe!"

Raul was quick and athletic, already pouncing for a third attempt to regain control of the patient. Margrethe sluiced again, this time back toward the E-pec building. The doctor closed the distance. She was a good mother and she doted on her son, but never once did she think of him or even her own safety as she rushed in to help. Perhaps she did take her job more seriously than her family. Perhaps her ex-husband was right. Raul rose to try once more. “Gently!” Dr. Ramadi pleaded.

As Raul’s arms reached to surround Margrethe, the patient’s body contorted in a way no human possibly could, and she slid toward Naima. Strangely, as the two closed in on one another, Margrethe’s sluicing seemed to slow down, like her body was flowing through thick mud. Instinctively, the doctor reached out to try to stop her patient. Two of Naima’s fingers brushed Margrethe’s skin.

And instantly, the sluicing stopped. Left standing in an awkward position, the patient fell over, and Raul quickly grabbed hold of her.

Naima crouched with one hand on her patient’s arm, feeling a tingle vibrating between their skin, something distinct and bizarrely electric. The woman, once Jane Doe VI, now Margrethe Vit, no longer fought. Instead, she simply lay upon the freshly cut grass, staining her light-green cotton shirt and pants with the lawn’s deeper green.

Someone gasped.

As Naima looked up, she saw people — some she even knew — looking at her as if she were an alien life form. Their eyes flicked back and forth from the patient to the doctor, unable to determine which was more strange: the woman with the superhuman powers, or the other woman who had seemingly made superhuman powers go away.

6

A chat notification blinked on, then another, and another. Checking my phone, I expected something from Carrie. Boy was I wrong. It was Pip.

I hadn't had my phone for too long, but, of course, it'd been long enough already to have exchanged approximately 48 quintillion texts with Carrie. No, you can't read them.

But this was new. This was Pip. *How the hell does she even have my number?* I thought. *Oh yeah. Bobby.*

I checked the message.

game changer
need to meet up

A game changer*? Really?* That seemed unlikely. I mean, we had seen megalomaniacal whack-a-moles trying to *take over* the world, delusional dingbats trying to *save* the world, and giant monsters that didn't *belong* in our world. What sort of game changer could there really be?

Wait. Sol.

It had been so long, I had almost allowed myself to forget he was out there. It had to have something to do with Sol.

I wrote back.

S?

I assumed she'd know who I meant. There was a pause. Then the buzz of my phone as a new message appeared.

NO
NEED TO MEET UP

YOU ME AND B

Well, geez. Calm down. No need to yell.

So I texted Bobby and he confirmed. We needed to go to the capital. Pip had something important to tell us.

But, of course, there was a catch. How were we going to go see her without being seen ourselves? Pip was internationally known superhero *Red Hope*. A somewhat sizable group of her fans rabidly followed her every move, including a contingent that camped out at her apartment building around the clock.

The building had security, but Pip could fix that, make it so we could pass by the guards without fanfare. Still, if the two of us waltzed in to see her, it wouldn't be long before the news channels started speculating. And that would lead to renewed interest from the press. Which meant scrutiny. Which meant photographers and reporters calling out our names.

And all of *that* would lead to two things I really didn't want, not one bit. First, pain for Holly; she just couldn't take the commotion. The seizures would return. Plus, it probably would mean the end of things for me and Carrie. I was finally at a place where someone liked me for me, *and* she was a beautiful, smart, and funny girl. The last thing I wanted to do was let her know who I *really* was. A freak show. What do you think am I, nuts? Don't answer that.

So we'd have to figure out how to meet privately, and the onus for that was squarely on Pip. No one was watching me or Bobby. It seemed like everyone was watching Pip.

But, you know, she did have those fancy powers and all. *Push, push, push*, she made her escape. After all of the little mental suggestions she made, I imagine her adoring public thought it was a pretty tame night, with no sign of their heroine. Or maybe they believed she came out and did the cha-cha in the middle of the street riding a rainbow unicorn. Who knows what she pushed them to think?

Little did they know she was across town.

We met on a rooftop, of course. Pip picked the building and the time. Being 16 at last, we drove to the capital city. Not me — I didn't even have my learner's permit. Having the ability to fly made driving lose a little of its luster, I have to admit. But, with Bobby at the wheel, we did drive, and we did it almost legally. I say *almost* because, although he actually had his driver's license, Bobby still had to push his parents' minds to ignore the fact that he borrowed their car. And technically he was on a provisional license, which meant he was only supposed to drive to and from work or school.

So we agreed we'd just have to call it a work trip.

How did Bobby convince his lazy, self-centered parents to let him get a license? I honestly have no idea. I have a hard time believing Mr. or Mrs. Graden actively did much of anything for him. Maybe it was so they didn't have to bother taking him places. Maybe they wanted him to run errands. Maybe he pushed their minds. Probably. Man, what else did he push them to do? I should stop thinking about it.

We made it to the capital without incident. In fact, we didn't even *see* a cop until we were downtown, and there, the police seemed like they had more important things to worry about than Bobby, the provisional driver. The biggest problems we faced were parking and walking across the street. Seriously.

First, Bobby circled and circled trying to find just the right parking spot. There were plenty available, but all of them required parallel-parking skills that, frankly, Bobby didn't have. Eventually, we lucked out when someone drove out of a spot at the end of a block, allowing Bobby to simply slide in rather than worry about all the angles and adjustments necessary for parking between cars. We were suburban kids, folks. We came from the land where parking was ample and the only meters around were on the side of your house for electricity.

After the utter boredom of waiting for Bobby to find a good spot, I was eager to get across the street to the building where Pip was, assumedly, waiting for us.

With Bobby just behind, I stepped off the curb mid-block and poked my head out into traffic. Hey, I looked both ways — I'm not saying I'm a slave to the rules, but when you cross a street downtown, it's in your best interest to look both ways. Still, we got in trouble about it. A tinny amplified voice blared at us, "Walk in the crosswalk, please! Are you trying to get hit by a car?" It was coming from the speaker of a black-and-white police car parked just to our left, the officer inside broadcasting as he casually sipped a coffee.

"*To protect, serve, and ridicule*," Bobby said as he smiled and waved. We obediently shifted over to the crosswalk at the corner, looking pretty sheepish. Chastised five seconds after we arrived in the big city. What better way to advertise that you don't belong, right?

Well, I suppose it was better than being hit by a car. We'd already done that routine, and once was enough.

Across the street, I doubled-checked the building address, just to be sure. You know, anything I could do to look out of place. Inside, we rode the elevator up to the roof. I couldn't help feeling a sense of déjà vu about another rooftop. My life felt like a series of important events strung together on rooftops. It made me nervous for what Pip was going to say. The bell dinged and the elevator stopped to let us out. We went down a hall and opened a door cleverly labeled ROOF.

Pip was there waiting, leaning against a giant, thrumming air-conditioning unit. She waved casually as we approached, eyeing us in a way that made me uncomfortable. No other salutations. I half expected her to be wearing a full-blown superhero costume, mostly because I hadn't seen her in person for some time and her TV persona had become larger than life. Thankfully, she still seemed down-to-earth, wearing faded jeans and a grey, fitted t-shirt.

We came to a stop, shoes crunching down on the gravel surface of the flat roof. For a moment, I wondered how and why human beings put gravel on their rooftops. I shook my head. Some mysteries of the universe would have to remain unsolved. The sun was beginning to set behind us, and the din of the city seemed to come from everywhere, although it was muted slightly by the fact that we were several floors above it all. The air even smelled cleaner from so high up, free of the street level's odd mix of dusty, industrial cement tainted by an undercurrent of cloying, greasy grime.

"Trio Supremo has reformed at last," Bobby said, making a dramatic flourish with both arms to virtually encircle us.

I grimaced. "We sound like a pizza special."

"You need to stop with the team names," Pip said sternly, although I could tell she truly found Bobby to be amusing. That was just their pattern; he made lame jokes, and she pretended to be annoyed by them. The slight curl on one side of her mouth was the dead giveaway.

Bobby nodded and gave a tilt of his hand, a gesture of mock deference. "How have you been?"

"Good. The attention can be annoying, but it's not unbearable. Actually, it's kind of cool most of the time. I think you'd like it." Pip looked a Bobby in a way that made it clear there was something more behind what she said. "You?"

"Same old," Bobby said with a mischievous grin. He donned a fake accent that might be called Stereotypical Trust Fund Kid. "Classes at the Snoot Academy are going smashingly, though Dean Bricklayer has *really* been on my case about getting posters made for the upcoming ice-cream social. We all know how that can be, amirite? Back at home, the folks are as *amazing* as always —." Suddenly the accent fell away. "Nah, my folks suck, but that's nothing new."

Again, the slight upturn at the corner of Pip's mouth betrayed her amusement. "The city's a great place to live," she said. "Everything you need is nearby. And, they would appreciate you here. You would be welcome." The statements hung in the air like damp towels after a shower, heavy with the dirt they tried to wipe away.

Bobby stood quietly for a moment. "All right, then, what's the big secret?"

Pip blinked, shaking something off, then turned to me. "You guys know I can't call or text with anything too important, right? I mean, I'm doing that for you guys. Trying not to lead the world right to your door."

"Thanks," I said. One word, but it meant a lot more.

"Okay, so what's the *game changer*?" Bobby asked.

Pip became serious. "Have either of you heard of Dr. Naima Ramadi?"

Bobby and I did the look-at-each-other-confused act.

"I thought not. And you won't, either. Not through any normal channel." Pip paused, and a long silence ensued.

Bobby turned on his snooty fake accent again. "All right, well, splendid chat. Thank you *so* kindly for the invitation. Wonderful to see you, dearie, though I guess we'll be running along." He pretended to turn away.

Pip just shot him a look. "The reason you won't hear about her from any normal channel is because she's special, and because the government knows it."

"What the heck does that mean?" I asked. So Pip explained. About Naima and her patient, the Jane Doe who became Margrethe. Just hearing that name made me sweat. If Margrethe was back in the picture, that meant there were at least two superpowered humans who probably wanted to kill me. I was thinking about how either she or Sol could show up any day. And apparently I had missed Pip's point.

"Don't you guys get it?"

"Get what?" Bobby said.

"She has power! Naima — she's like us, but she's the *opposite of us*!"

"I totally don't understand what that means."

Pip sighed, throwing up her hands. Then she spoke to us like we were children, like we needed some serious 'splaining. I thought it was funny, but Bobby seemed a bit offended. "When she gets close, your powers start to fade away," Pip said. "Like, they're still there, but less potent. Then, if you're really close, or she touches you, the power is completely wiped away."

I shook my head. "Hold on. You're saying this doctor woman can make us *normal*, just by being near us?"

"Well, I would have used the word *powerless*, but yeah, I guess you're right. When Naima's around, we're just *normal*."

"How do you know that?"

Pip looked at me, then Bobby, with a wide-eyed, serious expression. "Because I've met her."

"Really? Where is she?"

"Well, friends, *that* part is a secret." Pip smirked.

I was getting kind of sick of the runaround. "Can we just cut to the chase?"

"Sure," Pip said. "Margrethe has power like us. Naima somehow has the ability to cancel out our powers. The government took them both — it was the perfect coincidence for them: the chance to study a person with powers, while having control over those powers. With Naima around, Margrethe is a straight-up normal human being. But…"

"But what?" Bobby asked.

Pip was being coy again. "I doubt those government stiffs will be able to keep Margrethe much longer. If they even have her still."

"You just said they had the perfect coincidence — a way to make Margrethe behave. How could she get away?" I said. But in the back of my mind, a small spark of fear flared. *If they can capture Margrethe, have a way to keep her docile, who's next?* Pip must have read my mind. Which I realized later was distinctly possible.

"Think about it, boys. The government stumbled into the perfect way to control and study people with power. People like *you*. Or, for lack of a better example, people with power they could actually locate with ease. Meaning *me*."

"Oh shit." Bobby eloquently stated what we were all, at that moment, thinking. "So what did you do?"

"I broke Naima out. With help. I personally didn't get too close. My security detail has become loyal, you could say. And they happen to have pretty amazing resumes. Black-ops shit. Covert. Can't tell you about it. Anyway, they got her out. The government even had Naima's kid in custody, a boy named Sharif. Bastards."

"Isn't that illegal?" I asked.

"What I did or what they did?"

Good question. I picked one. "Um, what you did?"

Pip shrugged. "Is it illegal to steal bread if you're starving to death?"

"Technically, yes," I replied.

She pointed at me. "Yes. *Technically*. But what's *right*?"

"So where is she? Is she here? Are we going to lose our powers?" Bobby sounded both excited and terrified. Funny how we had come to rely on this strange gift, this strange curse, that we'd inherited at random.

"Nope." Pip smirked again. "Not here. But you better believe I know where she is. Mother and son both. In hiding, thanks to yours truly. But the question, gentlemen, is this: Now that we know Naima can take our powers away, do we sit around waiting for someone to use her against us, or do we all — the three of us, together — need to *do* something about this woman, permanently?"

"You mean *kill* her?" I asked, timidly.

Pip snapped toward me. "What? Jesus, John, no. Man, you can be dark sometimes."

"Then what?"

"That," Pip said, "is what we're here to discuss."

7

We headed home, fairly confident that the trip out of the city would be as uneventful as the trip in. Not quite.

As he drove, I noticed Bobby was quiet. His eyes kept flicking to the rearview mirror often, like he was afraid someone was behind us. Or maybe *afraid* isn't the right word.

"What do you think about this woman, Naima?" I asked, trying to break the silence.

Bobby shrugged, but that was all. No words.

I sat in thought a moment, the buildings crawling by in the steady traffic, alternating bands of light and dark reflecting on the windows. I remember being impressed that Bobby could navigate the streets without breaking out in a sweat. Although I suppose city traffic was tame compared to some of the things we'd seen.

Seemingly from everywhere, and completely at random, horns blared. Horns. Why? What good did it do to honk a horn? Some of the side streets were at a standstill. The horns simply added music to the panorama we crawled past, the frozen processional.

"Pip," I said. Not a question.

"Yeah, of course," Bobby said.

"And she knows?" He nodded. "What does she think?"

"Hard to tell." More silence. In the car, that is. Outside, horns a-go-go.

"Do you, you know, think there's any hope?"

Bobby curled up one side of his mouth, taking another peek in the rearview. “Like I said, it’s hard to tell. Her dad, well, he was a bit of a jerk. You’ve seen how, I don’t know, *standoffish* she can be? That’s because of her dad.”

“But he died, right?” I knew he had. Cancer. She told me.

“Yeah. I don’t think that makes it any better.” Bobby turned left and we were just about out of the city. Only the last few blocks of rundown buildings stood between us and the highway back home. “No real closure.”

I started to nod. I knew something about a lack of closure with a parent.

Before I could even react, Bobby slammed on the brakes and we skidded to a stop behind a yellow taxi.

In the middle of the road, first one of the cab’s rear doors and then the other flew open. From the driver’s side, a woman leaped out of the car and stormed off, obviously angry. She was in her mid-twenties, dark hair, dressed in a conservative tan skirt for some city job I’d probably never understand. From the other side of the car, a man appeared.

If the woman looked angry, the man topped her. He was furious, flushed red face accenting his dark, puffy sideburns. Quickly, he rounded the back of the taxi to chase after the woman in the tan skirt.

“What the —?” Bobby muttered to no one. I felt the same, although I remained quiet. City life was weird.

Sideburns was taller, and his longer legs allowed him to reach Tan Skirt before she could even get to the sidewalk. He grabbed her elbow and swung her around. Mouths opened and closed like pissed-off fish gulping for air. She tried to pull away, he held on. The cars around them, wanting nothing more than to make progress in the lane they unfortunately occupied, blew their horns in an attempt to encourage something to happen. Once again, horns did nothing. The two stood in traffic, arguing.

It was awkward, and yet we couldn't look away. I mean, people argue. That doesn't make one person right, or another wrong. And some people argue in public. But, with the taxi doors still sitting wide open and two lanes of traffic at a standstill, this argument felt *wrong*. It was out of place, excessive.

I watched Sideburns' fingers, big and meaty, digging into the flesh at Tan Skirt's elbow. She pulled away again, but he held strong. I looked up and noticed she was crying.

Here's the thing. I have no idea what they were arguing about. I don't know if he was wrong or right, or if she was. Or neither. In love and war, there isn't always a right and wrong. I only knew that what was happening at that very moment was wrong. And might have been on the verge of getting a whole lot wronger. Is that a word? Whatever.

"Bobby, we gotta do something," I said.

As if my words shook him out of a daze, Bobby looked my way and nodded. "Okay, but what? I didn't bring my mask. Did you?"

One shake of my head and we knew that wasn't an option. There was no point in sneaking around if we were going to jump out in the middle of a downtown traffic jam and start demonstrating superpowers in our t-shirts and jeans. “I can just *push* him to cut it out.”

“Do it,” Bobby said.

So I reached out, toward Sideburns, just a tendril, not trying to make him aware that I was even there, certainly not trying to hurt anyone, but trying to flip a few switches in his mind, convince him to calm down and discuss things rationally.

I couldn’t find those switches.

There were three minds I had touched in my life that didn’t seem right to me. They belonged to Walter Ivory, Jake Weissman, and the random dude Carrie and I bumped into on our walk home. One went crazy and died. The next was pretty messed up, and I guess was sort of dead, too. The third, I don’t know. Jury’s out. Never saw him again.

Sideburns’ mind was like feedback from a guitar amp. Loud and unruly. Almost painful to me. I looked for ways to calm him down, but amid the drowning noise, I struggled.

“Johnny?” Bobby asked, seeing my furrowed brow.

I didn’t respond, or if I did, it wasn’t with words. Maybe a grunt.

“*Johnny*?” Bobby asked with more urgency. “What’s going on? Take care of the guy and let’s go, okay?”

I grunted again. “Working on it.”

Bobby reached out with his mind to help. Then the two of us were stranded in the front row, just in front of the blaring speakers, at the

Sideburns' Distorted Insanity Rock Show Extravaganza. We both tried to find something, anything to latch onto, to calm the man down.

I dug deeper. Where other minds, to me, appeared to be complex tunnels and pathways, this one was just static and noise. I couldn't find a proper path, and every time I thought I did, the noise slid me around until I couldn't tell where I was going in the first place.

Finally, I thought I'd found my way, just walking through the dark, eyes eventually adjusting. I thought I could make out a path…

And I guess that's about when Bobby got a different idea. Enough with the subtle approach. Using his mind more like a club, Bobby simply knocked hard and the guy passed out, melting down to the pavement. Tan Skirt pulled back at first, then crouched down, confused by what had happened. A delivery-truck driver got out to help Sideburns. Somewhere in the distance we heard a siren. It was time for us to leave.

The cabbie in front of us got out and pushed both doors closed, then after a moment's hesitation did the right thing and pulled over to wait for the police, so he could give whatever statement he could.

Meanwhile, Bobby and I shared a glance as if we both suddenly had migraines. Or maybe our ears were still ringing from the unexpected show. I felt nauseous, coming back from that fluid landscape of noise to the world of structure and rules. It was a bit like trying to stabilize your walk after getting off a particularly crazy roller coaster.

"That was a tad odd, huh, Johnny?"

"You could say that," I said, rubbing one temple.

8

Sol was always present, somewhere in the back of my mind. If I tried, I could forget about him for long days and weeks on end. But he was always there.

I had come to feel the thorns in my cells, the very source of my abilities, were both a blessing and a curse, like a virus I'd been infected with. Sol was sort of the same way. Minus the blessing part. He was just a curse. And thankfully he wasn't in every cell in my body.

I know now that I shouldn't have let him go. Sometimes it's just too easy to do nothing, even when you know *something* has to be done. Inertia. My body was at rest, and was tending to stay at rest.

The short story is that Sol ran off to a big city in the Midwest — one of those places where the skyscrapers look even more impossibly tall because they're surrounded by so much *flatness*. There, he used his abilities to take up residence in a penthouse suite atop the largest of the buildings, a monolith called Babilu Tower, standing 108 stories high. And yes, I thought *Tower of Babel* when I first heard the name, too. Maybe Sol was trying to reach Heaven. Maybe Sol thought he was a god.

Anyway, the building made Mount Trashmore look like an anthill, and even would have dwarfed Gorgol Alpha by hundreds of feet. Sol must have bought into the old idea that bigger is better.

So what would Sol be doing living in a skyscraper? Good question. Remember those knuckleheads, the Way of the Ranger? The people who followed Jake, simply because Jake was someone they saw on TV and had an agenda they thought they understood? Yeah, well, those folks were sort of *desperate* for something real to do. Sol found them, at least a few of them, and he began to work his magic.

In short order, he convinced them that he *was* Jake, which, while technically true, didn't mean that he intended to become Earth's Next Champion like the Way of the Ranger might have been hoping. Whatever. Either enough people were lemmings just because they wanted to be lemmings, or he bent all of their minds. Either way, it didn't matter. People started following him. First a few, but soon dozens.

And they changed their name to the Way of the Sun.

Back in Sol's new penthouse, the growth of his flock meant that he was quickly running out of space. A push here and there convinced the other tenants and owners, some of whom had been in Babilu Tower for decades, to vacate — move on to some other digs. This left more and more of the building for Sol to occupy, which of course, he did. Not everyone who followed the Way of the Sun moved in with Sol like the tower was some big compound of lovebirds, but a whole lot did.

If you're a clever sort, right about now you're wondering, "Yeah, but how did he *pay* for all this? Even if he made his direct landlord *believe* he had paid when he hadn't, someone up the chain would have noticed things were amiss." You're right, oh clever you! Sol was better than that. In a way, Sol became the world's biggest, saddest grifter.

He got a patron. Well, honestly, he stumbled into having a patron, but it amounts to the same.

One of his Way of the Sun lemmings happened to be Kellie Steward, daughter of zillionaire Rami Kol and his wife Lana Steward. She had everything going for her: looks, money, heredity, influence. Did I forget to mention intelligence? Nope. When future generations study Kellie Steward, I have the distinct feeling they will discover she was the first human being to operate with absolutely no brain. She was that dumb.

Anyway, Kellie saw Ranger, that is, Jake Weissman, on TV and was hooked. The dude *rode monsters*, for Pete's sake. Later, when Pip explained Jake's motivations on TV, Kellie Steward became the Way of the Sun's major financial backer.

It took Sol about 13 seconds of being tapped into the organization before he realized he needed to meet Kellie. I have no knowledge of that meeting, other than to say Sol came away financially independent. And a certain "Ms. K. Steward" became the tenant of record for multiple floors atop Babilu Tower.

The penthouse was Sol's to do with as he wished.

But let's get back to me.

I mean, that's sort of what this is all about, right?

There was a person, this Dr. Naima Ramadi, who could make my powers go away. *Go away.*

That became a rather enticing concept.

I mean, don't get me wrong. Being superpowered, in principle, was awesome. Fly about, super-strength, dodge bullets, yadda yadda. However, in practice, it had brought me to some of the most gut-wrenchingly awful moments of my life. My father's death. My sister's abduction. Confrontations where I was 100-percent certain I was about to die. Some seriously unpleasant shit.

And on the other hand, there was Carrie. She was great, and she was utterly, blissfully, wonderfully normal. She liked me. Just plain old me. Not Black Sword, not the superhero. Me. She was, in fact, utterly, blissfully, wonderfully unaware of my superpowers.

That meant I had a chance.

Maybe I could live a real life, a sort of post-superhero life. Maybe Naima could help.

And if she could help me, she could help Holly.

Naima could save my family from this curse.

Here was my logic, for what it's worth. I had seen the thorns in my blood, the things that gave me power. Jake had transferred some thorns to Alpha, also via blood. That meant you could transfer powers, by blood.

And now Naima could turn off these same powers.

With a sudden and complete sureness, I believed that Naima's blood was the antidote to mine. Get a little sample, get it into my bloodstream, and, *whammo*, John and Holly Black are normal kids again.

Honestly, I became obsessed with the idea.

I just didn't realize I wasn't the *only* person who wanted to use Naima to erase my powers. Take me out of the superhero game.

Someone else had the same plan. But it had nothing to do with wanting me to live a normal life.

9

"Nice shirt," Carrie said.

"Huh?" I said.

She just pointed at me.

I, being male, didn't understand. There was a pause. She tried to give me time to figure it out, but that was like betting on a three-legged mule in a hang-gliding competition. Okay, fine. That analogy makes no sense.

Finally, she clued me in. "Your red shirt…" Carrie put one finger to her lips, faux thinking. "I feel like I've seen it before."

See? I told you I needed to be careful. Guys never notice if you wear a shirt 18 times. In a month. But girls?

I realized suddenly that I had probably worn the same red shirt the last time I'd seen her. With palpable fear, I worried I that had worn it the time before that, too.

Crap.

"Um… sorry?" I smirked, a hopeless grimace indicating clearly that I was a lunkheaded fool.

Thankfully, Carrie laughed.

"It's fine, John. But, you know, maybe next time wow me with something different."

Okay, sure, Carrie. Wow *you. With my wardrobe. That sounds easy.*

We were sitting at the coffee shop, and no, I hadn't successfully assimilated into the java culture. What I had done was learned to find one thing I could stand: iced coffee with what my grandmother would have called a "pyramid" of sugar. It wasn't a reference to shape. She used "pyramid" liberally in place of the words "a lot." I'm pretty sure she meant "myriad," but even that didn't make a ton of sense. I learned a long time ago that grandma got grumpy when you corrected her. And when she wasn't grumpy, she usually was willing to buy ice cream. So when she would say things like "Did you hear Uncle Bob just came into a *pyramid* of money?"... well, it didn't make sense on several levels, but we all knew what she meant. Still, if I smiled and played along... ice cream.

So, there I was with my iced coffee, stirred full of a pyramid of sugar, when I suddenly swallowed the wrong way and started coughing. I don't mean subtle *Pardon me, I'll be all right in just a moment* coughing, I mean full-on *Someone do the Heimlich!* coughing. I nearly spritzed Carrie with iced coffee.

Why?

Because of the shirt.

My *red* shirt.

The one I had picked up off a clothesline, the day I had... done a few bad things. You know, just killed Gorgol Sigma. And, oh, chopped off Pip's arm. All of which was broadcast on live TV.

Back then, I needed to get rid of my old grey shirt and go *incognito*. I swapped that grey shirt for what *was* a brand-new (to me) red one. The red shirt Carrie had suddenly taken an interest in. Because I had worn it too much.

Damn.

There's no way she knows, I thought. And that was a reasonable thought. I mean, I had picked up the shirt *after* the fight, and *after* I had made all those reporters and helicopter pilots go to sleep. So there was no way anyone but me knew where the shirt came from, right?

Nevertheless, the thought — the possible connection — caught me off guard. Hence, the massive coughing fit.

"John, are you okay?" Carrie said, leaning in and touching my arm. I tried to speak, but more coughs came out. I was lucky that it was only coughs. There's that moment when someone's coughing and maybe *they* know they aren't going to suddenly die, but no one else does. Carrie looked at me like that.

And suddenly, the coughing stopped. Not subsided. Stopped. My cells — correction, my thorn buddies — had apparently decided all this coughing nonsense had run its course. Some part of my throat sluiced, hopefully only *inside*, and I was immediately fine.

That was weird.

Carrie pulled back. Not in fear, but surprise. And something else. Her eyes flicked down to my throat, just for a second.

"I'm… I'm fine, thanks," I stammered, looking away.

"Don't scare me like that," she said, taking a sip on her fancy drink.

I thought that was the end of it.

You know, me thinking things are done and good is a bad idea. I have a pretty terrible track record with that particular thought.

We finished our drinks and got up to leave, and I absolutely should have left well enough alone. Of course, I didn't. "I'll be sure to wear a different shirt next time, Carrie," I said with a sheepish grin as I held the door for her.

She paused, right in the middle of the doorway. Customers were ahead and behind, coming in and going out, so it was odd that she would stop that way. She looked at me with a sparkle in her eye that I could only describe as strange. Or knowing.

"I think I've seen every one of your shirts by now, John Black."

10

You may remember my (not Uncle, not Cousin) Marcos. Or maybe you don't. Heck, maybe I don't. He wasn't my uncle. He wasn't exactly my cousin, unless you use that term like some people do to define basically every extended member of your family.

He was a guy that was supposedly in my family on my mother's side. He had given me some advice once — *Strike where the water will be!* — that worked so well I chose to ignore how bizarrely convenient it was. Otherwise, I might have found it fishy.

I never did any digging on Marcos. My mom firmly believed that we were family, so who was I to judge, but honestly for all I knew, Marcos could have been pulling off the most elaborate scam in history to get free food and drinks at our family reunions.

Screw it. He was a good guy and he gave me some good advice. If he stole a few steamed shrimp for the trouble, I'm okay with that.

(Aside: I think Marcos really is a family member. I think.)

(Second aside: I'm kidding! Geez! Marcos is my definitely related on my mother's side. By blood. Through marriage. Twice removed. Or something. But definitely. Can't you guys take a joke?)

In any event, Marcos and I saw each other again. And again. After that first time, when he gave me some advice on fighting "bullies at school," there was a long gap, but one afternoon, the day after my shirt incident with Carrie, he just showed up again.

Mom was at work, Holly was still at school, and I had just stepped in the door from my bus ride home. Believe it or not, I had pulled out my algebra homework and was actually contemplating doing it. Or maybe having a grilled cheese. Or possibly having a grilled cheese while watching TV. But seriously, I was thinking I'd get to that algebra.

Until Marcos knocked.

The front door creaked a bit as I swung it wide. "Oh, hi, Uncle —" He tilted his head, just slightly. "Sorry… *Marcos*," I said.

"John," he said with a shallow bow. Who does that? "You're looking well. Things going better at school?"

I laughed. When I had last seen Marcos, I was about to fight 200-foot-tall monsters I believed were from outer space. This time around, my biggest immediate issue was when to start my homework. "Yeah." I laughed. "Yeah, things are a lot better."

Marcos grinned, his white teeth in stark contrast to his tanned skin. Behind him, Mr. Morrison was making none-too-straight lines in his yard with a blaring red lawnmower that made the entire neighborhood smell like oil and gasoline. Well, those plus the raw pungent smell of cut grass. Same thing happened every time he dragged the old metal monster out of his garage. "That's good to hear," Marcos said, ignoring the din of Mr. Morrison's deafening plant-beheading machine. "You know, if you wanted, I could teach you some basic moves. Self-defense." He held his palms up. "No charge, no strings attached. Start and stop whenever you want."

It was weird. It was an out-of-the-blue offer, which was weird enough. But the really strange thing was that I was interested. After all the battles I'd been in, I still felt I had next to no idea how to handle myself. Pip had tried, really hard, to jam as much knowledge of sword fighting into my head as she could in a couple days' time. And I still wore my double belt (Bobby was nice enough to locate the two pieces under the roller coaster after I had let them go during my final almost-confrontation with Gorgol Alpha). But in hand-to-hand fighting, really there had just been my couple of smackdowns with Bobby. And at least for some of those, he was my friend and unlikely to put a serious hurt on me.

So, while I had no desire to jump back into the world of superpowered fighting, I figured a little learnin' might do me some good.

Besides, like most of your average nerds, I always had a fascination with the martial arts and imagined myself whipping out an amazing roundhouse kick on random occasions. Maybe I could actually learn how to do it.

"Sure… that'd be cool," I said. Then something struck me. An idea, that is, not a physical thing. "On one condition."

"Name it," Marcos said.

"No sparring."

He frowned. "That is a strange request, John, when learning self-defense. Without sparring, a certain level of realism is removed from the training."

"Understood. But that's my stipulation." I gave him a firm look, crossing my arms.

"Very well, as you like it. But you must trust me that when I teach you moves and patterns, they will mean something, even though I will not be able to demonstrate this through sparring."

"Okay, fine." We shook hands. Like men. Like equals. It was cool.

"When shall we begin?" Marcos asked. Glancing over his shoulder, I saw Mr. Morrison begin another death-row sentence for his overly tall grass.

I thought about my algebra homework, waiting for me. "How about now?"

This time it was Marcos who laughed. "No time like the present, eh, John? But no, neither of us is ready. And I bet you have homework…" Dang, he was good. "You know that I teach martial arts, not as my primary job, but evenings and weekends?"

"Um, no. Well, yes. Sort of." I shook my head. "Sorry, what I mean is that I knew you did it a lot, and I assumed you were a teacher. But I don't know what you do for a living or when you teach."

Marcos made a forgiving gesture. "All is well, John. How would you know these things? By day, I am but a simple accountant at a large firm headquartered off the interstate. You know where all those nondescript glass and steel buildings stand in rows, with their big lit-up logos on top?" I nodded. "Pretty boring crap."

I guffawed. Hearing the normally serene Marcos call something *crap* was too funny. He smirked, humoring me.

"But my passion is martial arts, specifically taekwondo. So I would be most pleased to teach you, but the best place to do so will be at the studio where I work. And you must dress appropriately, of course."

"I get a karate outfit?" I was probably salivating.

"No." He shook his head and I was immediately crestfallen. "In karate, practitioners wear a *gi*. You will need a *taekwondo* outfit, though I'd prefer if you called it by its proper name: *dobok*."

"Okay, then I get a *dobok*?" I looked at him sideways, trying to make sure I was speaking correctly.

"You do."

"Is it cool looking?"

"It is."

"Yes!" I did a little fist pump. You would have, too, admit it.

All that remained was to determine the details: when, where, and how often. We came up with Wednesday evenings, when he had an off day from teaching class. The *where* was his studio, of course, but I needed the address. And *how often* was decided as once a week, at least to start.

* * *

Marcos was a pretty great guy. Knowing our family situation, he not only didn't charge me for the lessons, he also picked me up and dropped me off.

Wednesday night of the following week, he knocked at our door again, precisely at 6:30 pm. I had made sure to eat dinner early so I'd be ready, then proceeded to mill about for 20 minutes trying to figure out what else I needed. I felt like I *needed* something else. Clothes? No, he was providing a *dobok*. Money? Nope, free. What did I need? I couldn't put my finger on anything, and eventually realized that I didn't need anything. The only thing I had to bring was *me*.

So when I got in his car and we started driving, I felt strange. I felt completely unprepared, and yet I knew that I was as prepared as I possibly could be. I tried rolling my neck and stretching my arms, even wiggled my fingers, as we drove. He told me the ride would be about 15 minutes, one way. And then he let me do all this foolish stretching for a good 10 minutes before he finally spoke.

"John, you'll do fine," Marcos said. "This is only the first session. I won't overdo it. Promise."

I sighed and dropped my hands into my lap. "All right, sorry. Just… what am I going to learn first?"

"Nothing," he said.

"Nothing?"

"Precisely."

"Okay, well, I'm confused."

Marcos glanced over at me as he drove. "John, the first thing you will need to learn is to *unlearn* everything else. You need to forget who you are, so you are ready to really embrace what I will show you."

That sounded preachy. I'll admit, I got a little worried at that moment.

Until Marcos chuckled. "But unlearning everything will take time. So tonight, maybe we'll just get you suited up, try out some basic stances, and maybe a punch or a kick. *Maybe*."

Unlearn everything. I knew from that moment forward that Marcos's offer to drive me to and from lessons might have had an ulterior motive.

For 30 captive minutes a week, he could help me *unlearn.*

11

Information is a disease. It can't help but spread and be spread. Especially when that information is about something completely and utterly bizarre.

You know, like people with superpowers.

What I mean is, Margrethe's strange story spread, despite a serious attempt by the government to keep it quiet. After all, they hadn't had *one of us* to study before.

Remember, Sol confronted and beat the military head-on. Bobby and I had been more stealthy about things in general, drifting in and out of the public eye. Pip was completely public, but that made her pretty much hands-off for the men in suits. Take her for some months-long experiment and her fans were gonna notice. And the others, Petrus, Margrethe, even Holly. No one really knew jack about them.

So when reports started circulating about that a woman on a hospital campus who had *moved* the way Red Hope moved, the way Yellow Fury moved, the way John Black moved — sorry, I mean Black Sword. Well, people talked. And when people are talking, in whispered hushes all over town, all over the country, even shadowy government threats don't stop that. It might keep things to a dull roar, but it doesn't stop the talk.

Then the story bounced around — there was a woman who could do *those things*, the things the superpowered folks could do. She did it right there in front of people. Ears listened. Clever ears heard more.

A really clever pair of ears, hearing this story through untold numbers of intermediaries, daisy-chained across the country in an epic game of telephone, heard something even better.

Sure, there was a superpowered person — Margrethe. But, more importantly, there was someone else.

Someone who *stopped* Margrethe. Without a major show of force, or a big battle. Someone stopped Margrethe with a touch.

I tried to imagine Sol hearing that news. It must have scared the crap out of him.

Someone could take away his power.

And *that* was what he absolutely had to investigate. Had to follow every lead. Find out where that person was, in a way no law-abiding person could.

Sol, I presumed, needed to find Naima. And then he needed her dead.

Or else she was a threat, a bigger and more direct threat than me or anyone else. I might fight Sol, try to stop him, but Naima could just walk into a room and shut him down. That, my friends, was significantly more problematic for a megalomaniacal douche like Sol.

And had I simply *thought* of that sooner, perhaps I could have prevented what happened.

My phone rang. It was Pip. For a moment, I stared, not sure what to do. Why didn't she just text me? Finally, I realized it might be something really important, so I tapped the button and stammered a half-hearted, "Hello?"

"They're being followed. I need your help," she said, without preamble.

"Who?"

"Naima and her son. Sharif."

Shit, I thought.

"You can say that again," Pip said. Well, maybe I hadn't just thought the word after all.

12

There was a knock at the back door. Not the front door, too conspicuous.

I opened it carefully, like some member of an underground revolutionary army, covertly meeting in a safe house to plan a people's revolution. Momentarily, I thought we should have set a password. Let that be a lesson to you in your daily life. Agree on your secret-meeting passwords in advance.

Pip slipped in, and my eyes darted left and right, scanning the backyard for infiltrators as I slowly closed the door. As soon as the latch clicked, I realized how stupid I must have looked.

She's got superpowers, dummy. If people had seen her, she'd just push their minds to make them forget, I told myself. *Oh yeah,* dummy*? Then why did she sneak in the back door*, I counter-argued. *Touché*. Foiled by me again. I was a formidable opponent for myself.

I turned to see Pip staring at me. "Hi," I offered, one hand weakly raised.

"Howdy," she replied. "Ready?" I nodded and led Pip into the kitchen where everyone else was already waiting. Mom and Holly, plus Bobby — who noticeably perked up when Pip walked in the room.

Pip and I sat, filling in the empty spaces at the kitchen table. I had the urge to roll a map out, like a true revolutionary. Perhaps speak with a French accent. And there should have been cigarette smoke. Lots of smoke.

I think I watch too many movies.

"Pip, good to see you again," Mom said, formally. Stiffly. Holly smiled. At least we'd been able to overcome the general awkwardness of having a former abductor and abductee in the same room. Once Pip and Bobby helped defend Holly and Mom from Gorgol Alpha, a bit of forgiveness was permissible.

Out of the blue, a small black spider crawled onto the kitchen table. Mom swatted it with one hand. "Ugh, sorry. That's the third one I've killed this week." She gave an awkward smile. Maybe having bugs in the house was a knock on her capabilities as a mom. Or something. Mothers are used to being people of great importance and influence in their own households. And my mother was at the table with four of the most powerful human beings on the planet. That must have been weird. To put it another way, I don't think it was the bugs that were bugging her.

I was about to speak when I saw Holly twitch. Just slightly, but I had years of training looking out for odd signs and triggers when it came to my sister. The twitching didn't continue, so I just socked it away, thinking I'd keep an eye on her.

"I won't beat around the bush," Pip said, leaning over the table. With her plaid shirt and rough jeans, she looked the part of the revolutionary leader. Involuntarily, I leaned forward, too. "I'm pretty certain Naima and Sharif are being watched, and that means it's the government or Sol. I seriously doubt it's the government, and I don't know how long I can keep them secret if it's *him*. I need your help. We have to *do* something."

"Why?" Mom asked. Of course. She was the only one there without superpowers, the only person for whom Naima's draining touch meant nothing.

Pip was rankled. I don't think she ever cared for being questioned, and since she was the big celebrity of our bunch, I suppose her patience had dwindled. "I don't know what John's told you, but Naima can take away our powers."

"I know that much," Mom said, sliding past Pip's attitude with grace. Parents. Am I right? Mom had her own type of superpowers. I know one thing for sure. If Mom were the one with powers, we'd all just be following her lead. We practically were anyway.

Bobby spoke. "Sol can't have Naima just floating around in the world. It's too much of a threat to his power. More than even us. He can *fight* us. He can't fight her."

"Okay, but how do you know she's being watched?" Mom asked.

"I broke her and her son out of a government detention facility, and I set them up with an apartment in the city," Pip said. "Naima provided a decent alibi of a recent divorce, needing to get away. They're in a pretty densely populated neighborhood, pretty transient, too, with enough new people around that a couple of strangers don't stand out. I helped them get food, clothes. Naima was talking about getting Sharif into a school. The biggest problem was a job. Naima is a psychiatrist. She certainly couldn't just go apply for *that* job anywhere. And, of course, if she did, they'd want references. And as soon as she did all that, she'd be back in government detention, getting prodded and analyzed like a prized pig at the state fair."

We sat silently for a moment. Everyone at the table had a vested interest in not having superpowered people become the focus of intense government trials.

"But she's not arrogant about it," Pip said. "She's willing to do *whatever* she has to, to get through all this. If that means flipping burgers, she'll flip burgers. But any job means giving your name, address, tax ID... Or fudging all that and living as someone you're not."

"So does she go by an alias?"

Pip nodded.

"How'd you do that?" I asked.

She shrugged. "I know a guy."

I looked sideways at Bobby, Mom, and Holly, but it was clear Pip was done answering that line of questioning.

"And what tells you she's being watched?" Mom said. "By Sol or by the government? I still don't quite get it."

"I saw a guy."

Mom twisted one corner of her mouth. "That's it?"

Pip shrugged. "Maybe. But he was paying attention to her building. And I've seen him more than once, when no one else knew I was there." She gestured into the air. *On rooftops... or flying.*

"Was there anything specific about this guy?" Bobby said. "How do you even know it was the same guy? You said it yourself — there are a lot of people in the around where she is."

She thought for a moment. Then she pointed to the inside of her wrist, like a doctor taking a pulse. "He has a tattoo of the sun, here."

Bobby raised an eyebrow. "Okay, that's probably gonna narrow down your pool of suspects. I'll give you that."

"How do you know it's not a government agent? You said you broke her out," Mom said. "They'll obviously want to get her back."

"I seriously doubt it's the feds. I have some connections, you know, now that I've gone public and all..." Pip's face flushed and she looked away.

Bobby didn't take his eyes off Pip. "How are *you* not in government detention, getting tested and analyzed?" he asked.

"Well, going public made me *too* public. I think it's too hard to grab me without making a scene."

Why didn't I think of that? Maybe going public was actually a good *idea.*

And that's when Holly stood up.

That can be a rather unexpected move from a person who's been in a wheelchair most of their life.

I had forgotten to keep an eye on her, the way I told myself to just moments before. The twitch must have returned, and then it must have turned into something worse.

Holly floated in the air, as if someone had put a coat hanger into the shoulders of her shirt and hung her up to dry in front of us.

"Holly!" Mom shouted, standing and reaching her hands out for her daughter.

At the same moment, I quickly reached out with my mind. *Holly, what's happening?*

I don't like this talk, Johnny. No *Hi* or anything friendly. Just business.

Okay, why? What's upsetting you?

I don't know if I like this person. Naima.

Why not? I looked at Holly and she met my eyes. A single tear fell down one of her cheeks.

"What's going on?" Mom pleaded as she reached for Holly. It almost looked like she was holding Holly up, but really she wanted to pull her back down. "John?"

"Just a minute, Mom," I said. Bobby and Pip were standing as well, all eyes on Holly.

The floor shuddered. The walls shook. Dishes and glasses startled to rattle and clang in the drying rack. “Uh oh,” Bobby muttered, and I quickly shushed him.

Holly, I sent to my sister. *Why don’t you like Naima? You don’t even know her.*

I know what she can do.

Okay. And?

She can take this away, Johnny!

What? Our power?

Yes! Don’t you understand?

I didn’t quite understand, but I knew Holly was hurting. I rounded the table, coming to her side. *What do you mean, Holly?* Her face was just inches from mine and her eyes bored holes into me.

Johnny, if this woman takes away my power, I’ll never be able to talk to you again.

And suddenly it all made sense. For me, if I lost my power, I’d just go back to being a normal, boring kid. For Holly… different story. She’d be trapped in her own head all over again. I sighed heavily with the knowledge and pressed my forehead against hers, trying to comfort her.

After a moment, Holly drooped slowly back into her wheelchair, like the air had been let out of her.

13

Of course he got himself on TV again. Sol was far too self-centered to stay in hiding forever.

It was a huge scoop — the man who had once taken over the governor's mansion and thwarted all attempts to expel him was now back after a prolonged absence.

At first I didn't understand. Until I remembered that no one else knew where Sol had gone.

That he'd been dead.

The secret interview — Sol was a known terrorist, after all — took place in a posh business office, all marble and leather and sleek dark wood. Conveniently, the camera faced away from any windows that could identify where they were. I know now that they were right there, in Babilu Tower, in Sol's sort of home base. Not tucked away in some cave in Afghanistan, or buried among the mysterious trees of Mirkwood. Sol was hiding in plain sight.

He smiled, blinding white teeth contrasting against his deeply tanned skin. His dark hair was perfect. His cornflower-blue shirt immaculately pressed. As the interview began, he crossed one long leg over the other, casually, showing off loafers that I assumed were Italian leather. He didn't wear socks. Who does that? Who doesn't wear socks?

"I want to note up front that — by our guest's request — this interview is live and capped at one hour. So let's get into it. With me is a person I'm sure needs no introduction, and in fact, I find it hard to give him one. He is known simply as *Sol*. Because we are limited in time, why don't we just get to questions? I think the first thing everyone will be anxious to hear is, where have you been?" The interviewer, an equally sharp-dressed man with dark chocolate skin and stylish black-rimmed glasses, tried to match Sol's comfortable poise. They each chuckled a bit. Yeah, Sol chuckled. I shuddered.

"Stephen, that is an interesting question," Sol began. I guess the interviewer's name was Stephen. Sol said it like they were old friends. "I have not merely been *out of the public eye*, so to speak. No, I have been doing something much more interesting, that no man has done before. Save one or two, depending upon your religious persuasion."

Sol was like a fisherman, calmly holding the baited line. Waiting. Stephen bit. "And what was that?"

"I died. And now I am returned."

Stephen, clearly not ready for such an outlandish statement, paused. But he was a pro — look it up in the book — he was going to get the interview done professionally. He carried on. "Well, you look perfectly fine to me. Healthy and alive. So, changing the subject a bit, a lot of people —"

Sol cut him off. "Perhaps you do not comprehend the complexities of what I am saying to you, so allow me to spell it out more clearly. I was dead. My living tissue was shredded from my body, cast away into a hundred thousand pieces and gone. I took my final breath and went forth into the great unknown, the final frontier that we call death. And yet, here I sit before you. Returned."

"You're serious?" Stephen said.

"Quite," Sol said calmly. You could see the interviewer considering asking another question, maybe two. He opened and closed his mouth, unsure, simply making that repeated movement until something happened. So Sol continued. "In the late summer of last year, I experienced the culmination of life." *That's one way to put it, you jerk. I killed you.* "There was a great and terrible storm, one that would no doubt devour any mortal soul, and I found myself in its midst, unable to break free." *Oh, nice, so I'm not even part of this story?*

You don't mind my interjections, do you? Sorry.

"Where was this? Where did it happen?" Stephen asked.

"*El desierto de las tres manos*," Sol replied. "The Desert of the Three Hands."

Stephen glanced to one side. There was a pause, presumably as someone did some research. Stephen held one finger to an ear. "Okay, yes, there was a *devastating* sandstorm in that region last year."

"Correct." Sol nodded.

"Tell me about your experience there. Help us understand what you went through." Stephen had resorted to TV interviewing 101. Appear empathetic.

"Stephen, what I am about to tell you — to tell the world — is humbling." Sol paused for dramatic effect. I believed Sol was humble about as much as I believed he was a penguin in a human suit. "I faced an adversary in the desert, and I failed." He hung his head slightly, just enough to appear moderately contemplative.

"Who was this adversary?" *Good question, Stephen. See? I knew you were the right man for the job!*

Then I froze. Sol was about to say my name on national TV.

That's it. Cat out of the bag. Shit hitting the fan. Mustard off the hot dog.

Get ready, me, I thought. *I'm about to be famous. Like it or not.*

I gulped. Did I want this? Could I live like Pip? Make it work?

Oh no. What's Carrie gonna think?

I jumped up to grab the remote and turn off the TV. Pretty rational. I mean, if I didn't *watch* Sol say my name, then it didn't *happen*, right?

"John, what are you doing? Leave it on! I'm watching this," Mom said, distracted in her focus on the charismatic Sol despite all that had happened between us.

My shoulders drooped. *Here it comes.*

Sol smiled for the camera, adding a tinge of wistfulness to his demeanor. Such a performer. "Actually, Stephen, you know my adversary quite well. As do your viewers. He is called *Black Sword*."

There was a huge gasp. After a moment, I realized it had come from me.

"He didn't say my name," I muttered. I was half-crestfallen, half-elated. Mostly confused. Sol's smiling mug in the camera suddenly became extraordinarily personal. He was looking *at* me.

Stephen the Interviewer blinked, pulling his glasses down momentarily to wipe at his eyes. "Are you telling us that Black Sword, the superhuman who killed those creatures, the Gorgols, some months back, *also* killed you? I thought you said it was the storm."

"It was the combination of the two." At least there, Sol told the truth.

"And you died?"

Sol nodded.

Stephen asked a series of follow-up questions, trying to get more detail about what had happened in the desert, but Sol was elusive. Or at least coy. Finally, the interviewer changed tactics. "What was *death* like? We hear so many stories — out-of-body experiences, bright lights, choirs of angels. What was it like for you?"

Sol thought for a moment, most likely another rehearsed act. "It was nothing. There was *nothing.*" Stephen, and perhaps the entire world, considered the ramifications of such a statement. "Until… I inhaled. A great, painful, blessedly life-giving breath of air."

"But, there was nothing in between?" Stephen asked.

Sol dipped his chin slightly. "Just as you say. Or at least, that is my recollection. But there was one thing."

"What?"

"A sound. I remember a sound. Like a million tiny voices, talking all at once. Like static on a radio, or feedback. Perhaps…"

"Perhaps?" Stephen echoed, trying to pull the next words out of Sol.

"Perhaps it was the voice of God," Sol said.

Stephen seemed unconvinced. "Isn't it possible you merely passed out for a time? Maybe you were knocked unconscious?"

"No. An astute question, Stephen, but I fear I have not explained myself fully. I was literally *shattered* in that sandstorm, torn apart, strewn into the wind. I was, wholly and completely, *dead.* My body — how might you say it? — was *blown to bits.* And when I returned to life, I was someone else entirely."

"I don't understand," Stephen said, tapping a pen to his lips. As if he were actually taking notes or something.

Sol gave him a pitying look. "Stephen, I thought you would have realized by now. When I came back, I returned as the one you call *Ranger.*"

"Ranger?" Stephen raced to come up with rational questions for a topic he clearly found irrational. "He was pretty well covered by the news media, and he didn't even look like you. And now he's missing or in hiding."

"Stephen, I grow tired of your failure to grasp the simple truths of what you see. *I* am Sol. I died. *I* returned as Ranger."

"Then why are you Sol again now?" *Touché, Sol. Excellent question, Stephen*, I thought. *Why?*

"Because I am different from you, from the man who was Ranger, from Black Sword, from any other living soul. I have an unrelenting *need* to *be*. Not a desire. A need. My will *overcomes*. I have become *eternal*."

There was a prolonged silence, as Sol's eyes smoldered with fiery energy. The camera zoomed. His face filled my view.

From offscreen, Stephen spoke. "Then, what's next for you? What else is there? If you can die, and return, then…"

Sol's eyes, so large and deep, squinted with a spiteful intensity. "You understand that we are all creatures beholden to fate, yes? Of course. Fantastical stories often hinge on prophecies and mysticism, yet the real world is rarely so preordained. But fate? Ah, fate. Fate waits for us all. Fate is not the train attendant, shepherding you aboard. Fate is the *rails*. The inescapable certainty that you go where it decrees." The interviewer nodded, one of those practiced TV nods that you can tell means *I'm not really listening to you.* Sol saw it, too, and he leaned toward Stephen, getting so close as to startle the other man back to focus. "Though I have proven that death cannot hold me, there is something else I must do. And two things I must have. All three of these things are like planets in orbit, circling around the same, single need."

"And what's that?"

His mouth curling into sneer, Sol chuckled again. "Revenge."

14

Carrie seemed distant, which was unusual for her. If anything, Carrie was normally very much present. Admittedly, we weren't talking. We were doing homework at the kitchen counter in her house, her mother down in the basement, padding away on a treadmill with the TV blaring some report on the day's stock-market activity. Pretty boring stuff.

Treadmills crack me up. Although I am keenly aware that not everyone is self-ambulatory — my sister, for example — walking or running is sort of a basic human concept. And then you create this large, complicated machine so that you can walk or run but not go anywhere. I'm sure the cavemen would look at smartphones and television and airplanes and be amazed, but if they got a look at a treadmill, I believe they'd just shake their furry heads and think we were all mad.

Anyway, Carrie and I were alone. But something felt off.

"Everything okay?" I asked.

Carrie was busy looking at the ceiling. She blinked and tilted her head down toward me. "What? Oh yeah, fine."

"What are you thinking about?" I asked.

Be careful with that question, friends. It's five words that open a can of worms. You never know what you're going to get when you ask that question. People's minds are complex, confusing balls of constantly exploding synapses, blasting forth the most off-the-wall scenarios and ideas imaginable. Which possibly explains why Carrie's two-word answer took me completely and utterly by surprise.

"Black Sword."

"Huh?" For a moment, I had no idea if she meant *me* or not. If she was calling me by that name.

"You know, the hero."

Okay, phew. Not me. Well, Black Sword is *me, but it doesn't seem like that's what she meant.* "What about him?"

She smiled and looked away, blushing a little. *What's this?* "Nothing."

"Come on," I said, nudging her gently on the arm as if I could physically coax the answer out of her.

She shook her head, tossing her curls of red hair around in a way that was mesmerizing. "Who do you think he is? Where's he been all these months? Why hasn't anyone seen him?"

I sat quietly. Of course, I had an answer for every one of her questions, but I could hardly tell her that. *Oh, Black Sword is me, and I've been mostly been hanging out with* you *for the past several months. I haven't been putting on a mask and fighting monsters on TV recently because, frankly, there aren't any monsters to fight. Now, want to go get ice cream with me?* See? That would be awkward.

I looked at her carefully, and once more saw her gazing off, distant and thoughtful. And something powerful and odd and interesting and disturbing dawned on me. "You have a crush on him, don't you?" I said.

This time she came back quickly, getting overly defensive. "What? No way. Shut up!"

I didn't know how to feel about it. She absolutely seemed to be daydreaming about Black Sword. My girlfriend was daydreaming about another guy. Even though that guy was technically me.

"I don't even know what he looks like. Though I bet he's cute," she said, looking at me sideways with her big dark eyes.

She's messing with you, John, my man. That's what I told myself, but what did I really believe? *No way. She actually has a thing for Black Sword. That's like cheating on me, isn't it?*

Cheating on me, with me. I shook my head. What a mess.

"I wonder what he looks like, under the mask," she said, eyelashes flittering, making my heart do the same.

"He…" I started. "I…"

"You what?" she asked, leaning in close.

I almost said it. I almost shouted *I'M BLACK SWORD!*

Carrie was so close, all I could see was her face. "I…" I couldn't. I wanted so much for Carrie to like me for me, not for some superpowers. I didn't want to mess that up. "I have no idea."

Somehow, I wasn't convincing. "Sure about that?" she said, her nose practically touching mine.

"Hey! Homework!" Carrie's mom suddenly called out from behind me, coming up the stairs. Abruptly, Carrie pulled away, flipping a page in her chemistry textbook.

I grabbed a pencil and started writing something in my notebook. "Oh hi, Mrs. MacGregor." My voice almost cracked from nerves.

And I realized I was trying to write with the eraser end down.

* * *

My girlfriend had a crush on someone else, and even though *I* knew it was me, she didn't. And that made me upset.

I felt like I was living in one of those Shakespearean plays where everyone pretends to be someone else and everything gets confused.

Or maybe it was just a sitcom.

Later the same day, Bobby knocked on the door, but when I answered, he wasn't his usual easy-going self. "Hey Johnny. Can I come in?" His voice was flat, no energy.

"Since when do you need an invitation?"

"Heh," he clucked. Not a laugh. Just an exhalation of sound.

What the heck is going on with everyone today? I thought.

Rolling my eyes, I followed Bobby to the living room, where he plopped down on the couch. I did the same, grabbing the controllers and the TV remote.

"Hey, before we play a game, can I ask you something?" Bobby looked serious. Bobby almost never looked serious.

"Okay."

And then he got quiet.

Why do people do that? Say they need to ask you something and then get quiet? It's counterproductive, to say the least.

Finally, I guess he worked up to it. "Johnny, I want to leave."

"Leave what? My house? You just got here."

"No, not your house. *Town.* I want to get out of this town, for good."

"Did something happen at home?" I asked. Bobby's self-centered, lunkheaded parents were good at being disconnected from his life for long periods of time, until they decided it was time to reconnect and mess things up.

"No! Well, yes, but that's nothing new."

"What?"

"Eh, you know, same old. Mom accused me of taking $20 from her wallet, then she threw a fit about it for like two hours. Once Dad heard, he lost it, too."

"Did you take the $20?"

"Of course. I'm 16 and unemployed, and I have to eat, you know?"

I laughed and so did he. It was good to see some of the tension dissipate. "Did you admit it?"

"Of course not. Let them think it was gremlins, for all I care."

"That's it?"

Bobby's head rolled around on his shoulders, like you do when you're just exhausted by it all. "No, Johnny. That's not it. It's everything. Every day. My parents truly and completely suck. You know this. It's never going to change. Today was just a minor bump in the road compared to everything I've gone through with them."

"And so you want to leave town?"

"Yeah," he said, looking me in the eye. Serious.

"Where would you go?" I thought I knew the answer. I didn't think I'd like it.

Bobby dropped his chin to his chest. "The city. You know."

I nodded. *Pip*. "She said you could?"

He tilted his head to one side, smirking. "Yeah, we talked about it."

"Moving in? That's pretty serious, isn't it?"

"Well, it's not *quite* that. She has two bedrooms. I'd get the other one."

"You're 16, Bobby," I said.

"What are you, my mom? I mean, if I had a mom that actually gave a crap about what I did."

"Exactly. Well, I do. You're 16 and you want to leave home?"

Bobby turned to me. "Johnny, we have superpowers. We've fought giant monsters. We're not going to follow the typical path most people follow. I don't ever plan to go to college and get a desk job. Why would I? For me, this is what I have to do."

"I see. But what about, you know, *going public*?" He knew I had a vested interest in the next words he was going to say.

"I'd like to say that I won't, but I don't know how to stop it. If I'm *there…*"

"Someone will see you. And they'll put two and two together." But that wasn't all they'd put together.

"I know," Bobby said. "And I realize that means they'll find you."

I leaned back, pressing into the couch. "Do you have to, Bobby?"

"Yeah, Johnny. I can't live here like this. Not anymore. Not knowing that it could be different."

My mind raced. Everyone would find out. Find out Bobby was Yellow Fury. And then everyone would know about me. “Can you just wait a little bit? For me? Please?”

Bobby sighed. “Until what happens? When will it be okay for you?”

“I don’t know. But come on. Just a few weeks? A month?”

Bobby looked down at his hands in his lap. “I guess I’ve been here this long. What’s another month?”

“Really?”

“Yeah, but you’re going to need to get ready. After a month, I’m doing it.”

“Okay, okay. Thanks, Bobby, really. But…”

“But what?”

I looked around the room. Just a living room. Just four walls, a couch, a TV. And all the hours and hours we’d spent together. “I’ll miss having you come around here, you know?”

“Don’t get sappy on me, Johnny,” Bobby said, trying to be tough, but suddenly needing to wipe at his eyes.

15

"Who the hell are you?" my mom said from the other room.

I was asleep. Those words woke me.

And then a man's voice replied, something low and grumbly that I couldn't make out. There was a thump and an *oof.*

I leaped out of bed, grabbed for the doorknob. In two seconds, I was entering the bright lights of the kitchen.

There, I saw a scene from a movie. My mother, the normally docile and polite Andrea Black, held a 10-inch carving knife, daring the bearded man in front of her to move. With her other hand, she cradled her abdomen in a strange way. *What the hell? Is Mom hurt?*

On the counter beside them, my mom's phone and mine sat side by side. *That's not where I left my phone. Is this guy a thief?* I shook my head, once, quickly. "What's going on?" I said, blinking to adjust my eyes.

The distraction was enough. The man, a tall, burly guy with curly dark hair, wearing a dusty blue jacket and stained work pants, jerked forward.

As he did, I saw a tattoo on the inside of his wrist. A ball with stylized flames circling it. The sun, of course. *The Way of the Sun. Here?* I thought.

He grabbed my mother's wrist and the knife fell free. She clutched herself tighter with the other hand and winced.

Human history is littered with people making exceptionally bad decisions. On this particular day, whoever the fellow in my kitchen was, he'd broken into the wrong damned house. Instantly, the fire within me kicked in. He was attacking *my mother*. No. Just no. Fire turned to rage in a breath. I guess I hadn't beaten my demons after all.

I moved with astonishing fluidity and speed, thrusting into the guy's throat and knocking him to the ground. My attack was part physical and part mental, although the mental part was physical as well. I used my mind to enhance the blow, sending him sprawling. In other words, I roughed him up pretty good. On the floor, he looked stunned.

Do not break into a superhuman's house. Just don't.

Turning, I wondered about my mom. Did she find any solace in the fact that I could do these things? I mean, has she been sure the whole time that I would come save the day? Because, otherwise, having a stranger in your house would probably be considered rather terrifying. I glanced over at her, as she held herself in that strange way. The bastard had grabbed her pretty hard. What else had he done? Standing over him, I gestured like I would hit him again. Not too superpowered, not trying to break anything. The fire was already subsiding. He cowered beneath me.

"You okay, Mom?" I asked.

She nodded, but her expression was pained. "He pushed me and I hit the corner of the countertop. That's all." She gestured at the arm still wrapped tightly against her midsection. Her face showed worry. "John. He saw you." Her eyes flicked from me to the man on the tile floor. The man who was very much awake, and, although rubbing his pained neck, clearly was taking in everything he was seeing.

Yeah? So?

Oh, right. I just demonstrated pretty clearly that John Black was *one of those.* One of the superpowered people. In my house. On my street. In my town.

Now what?

Kill the guy and dump the body. Yup. Gotta do it.

Does that sound extreme? I thought maybe that would be extreme. But I considered it.

No, of course, there was the other way. *My* way. Change his mind. Erase what he'd seen. I had done it with Margrethe.

And she came back, I thought.

What did it matter? In a month, Bobby was moving to the city, and the world would begin the process of finding out exactly who I was. I supposed all I had to do was make the guy forget for a month. It had been longer than that with Margrethe.

"I'll fix it," I said to my mother.

As the man sat there staring at me, I reached out with my mind, just a tendril.

And I froze.

Sol.

The very first thing I found in the man's mind was Sol.

"Who the hell are you?" I asked aloud.

The man said nothing. But he started to smile.

That old fire, that old anger I had, it blazed up for a second time, like it had never left. I knew it was never going to leave me, and that all I could do was try to control it.

But, right then, I didn't really want to.

“Tell me who you are.” I raised one hand menacingly. “I don’t have to go easy on you, you know.”

The man’s grin widened, showing yellowed teeth through the long curls of his mustache and beard. He laughed, a short, guttural laugh, turning his wrist out to show off his tattoo. “I am the Way of the Sun.”

And then he lunged upward.

Not at me. At my mom.

She screamed and jumped back. From down the hall, I heard Holly shout, “Mommy?”

I didn’t move. There was no need. With a thought, I froze the man, pressed him against the hard, cold floor.

I thought about what Sol had said on TV. *Revenge*. Suddenly, I realized what it could mean. *He’s going after my family.*

Locked in place like a fox with its foot in a bear trap, the man glowered at me. He was raving, with spittle dotting his lips.

In a way, that made my job easier. If the man had seemed normal, I might not have wanted to do it.

But I did.

I erased his mind.

Mom got the car. I wanted to go, but she insisted I stay with Holly. She seemed oddly determined.

And like Margrethe before him, Mom dropped the man off at the bus terminal with a wave.

* * *

"What now?" Mom asked when she returned. It was the middle of the night, but Holly and I sat awake, waiting for her to come back. Mom still held her stomach with one arm, trying to do it nonchalantly so we wouldn't notice.

I shook my head. "Well, the truth is that Sol isn't going to quit. The last few months were nice, but everything is changing. And Mom?"

"Yes, John?" she said, the picture of motherly comfort tainted by the strain on her face. She was in pain. And I knew what I was about to say could shatter our comfortable home life forever.

"Soon, people will know who I am."

She nodded, face expressionless. "I was afraid it would happen some time."

"And?"

"And what, John?"

"It's going to ruin all of this, our lives. Your life, Holly's. Mine. And Carrie…"

Mom put an arm around me, leaning in to kiss my forehead. "John, if Carrie breaks things off with you because she finds out who you are, then you don't need her in your life."

"I know, but…" I *didn't* know. Or didn't want to think about it. I was gaga for Carrie and no amount of rational thought was going to make the prospect of our split any better.

"But, John?"

"Yeah, Mom?"

"If you've already decided that will happen, you're selling Carrie a little short." I looked into her eyes and knew she was telling the truth, as she understood it. I hoped she was right.

Johnny?

Yeah, Holly?

If people find out about us, that's okay with me.

Yeah? What about the cameras, the lights, the flashing and shouting?

It's okay. Up until now, I've just been the girl in the wheelchair.

You're not just that, Holly.

I know. But that's what some people think. Don't forget, Johnny. I can touch minds, too. And besides, I wouldn't mind showing off a little power.

A feeling hit me. An emotion? A color? Something. It was raw, and shaky. Like something about to crawl out of the ooze and come to life.

What does that mean, Holly?

Sorry, nothing, Johnny. I just mean that I won't mind people thinking of me as something more.

Okay, Hol.

"John?" Mom asked, and I looked up. "What do we do now?"

I thought, scowling. "Okay. If Sol's coming to us, we need to have a plan, to be on the same page."

"Okay," Mom said.

"And I think we need to find this person, Naima, and fast. Before Sol does." *I know you don't like that idea, Holly*, I sent to her mind.

I don't, Johnny. I don't like that idea at all.

I know, Hol. But if she can turn this off, wouldn't you rather she was on our *side?*

I guess, Johnny.

"You don't think he can use her…?" Mom asked.

"I don't know what he can do," I said. "But I don't want to wait around to find out."

16

It was gone. The power. All of it.

The thing I remember most was that it didn't just leave, like turning off a light. It faded as we got close, like losing track of someone in fog.

"Johnny?" Holly said, her voice pleading.

I turned to her and saw the fear in her eyes. *It's okay, Hol.* I sent the thought with my mind, but it was pointless. Near Naima, my thoughts remained in my own head. I tried to connect my mind to Holly's, but there was nothing. And I mean *nothing*.

It wasn't that I couldn't find the path anymore, it was that there were no paths of any kind. I can't explain it. It would be like sitting in the cockpit of a plane and realizing there was no sky. You ain't gettin' anywhere, friend. Might as well jump out and walk.

We met up in an abandoned warehouse on the outskirts of the capital. The space was large, dark, and empty, with the sweet, sickening smell of decay billowing around us like a cloud. Mom pushed Holly as we approached Pip, who was standing beside the dark-haired woman and her son.

Holly's expression became even more complex, almost compressed, until she looked terrified, trapped. "Mommy?" she said. Mom crouched down, trying to comfort her, but the effort made Mom wince. Her run-in with the kitchen counter still bothered her. I went to Holly as well, pressing my forehead against hers, the way I had done so many times before. But this time… although they were separated by a mere half-inch of flesh and bone, our minds remained apart. I couldn't talk to my sister.

Bobby broke the ice. "I'm Bobby Graden," he said, extending a hand.

Dr. Naima Ramadi took his hand and introduced herself, and her son. "Please, call me Naima." Then we all just sort of stared at each other for a minute or two.

"Um, nice to meet you?" Bobby added finally.

Naima smiled. "Are you… *Yellow Fury*?" Bobby blushed and nodded. Naima turned to me. "And Black Sword?" I just rolled my eyes. "Wow." Naima was short and thin, but not overly so. Her skin tone was notably darker than mine with an olive tint to it. The shape of her eyes made me think of almonds, and the color of those eyes seemed out of place — light, almost glowing, in contrast to her dark skin and even darker hair. Naima's hair probably was long, but she wore it pulled back in a tight, business-like fashion, keeping it out of her way. She had a nose that was a bit too large, with a slight hook, but not unattractive. On the contrary, it was a striking feature that probably made her better looking. You know, for someone my mom's age, that is. She was dressed in a copper-colored blouse that shimmered slightly, and a tasteful black skirt.

Meanwhile, I looked down at my crappy green t-shirt, rumpled dark jeans, and stained sneakers. So there was one more thing Naima and I didn't have in common: style.

"You're pretty much the only person on the planet who knows who we all are," Bobby said with a grin. "Well, except for *us*."

We stood in a loose circle around Naima and Sharif — me, Mom, Bobby, Pip, and Holly in her chair. Sharif, a bony kid half my age, seemed intimidated, and stood partially behind his mother. I guess he wasn't all that keen on strangers anymore, perhaps since government agents took him captive and he had to live on the run. Which I could completely understand. I don't remember him saying a word — he was a quiet kid who looked a lot like his mother, but with close-cropped dark hair and ears that were too big for his head.

"Told you guys," Pip said. "Weird, isn't it?"

"You could say that." I looked at my hands, flipping them over like they'd betrayed me. The thorns were still in there, right? They had to be. What was it about Naima that made them go silent?

Or…wait a minute. Did she kill them?

No, that was impossible. Pip had been around this woman, and still had her powers afterward. It was just a proximity thing.

"Is it true?" Naima asked, almost timidly, hardly wanting to make eye contact. We were the superhumans who had destroyed giant monsters. But now we were simply *human*. And she did it to us. She must have felt a rush of great power.

Maybe simply being human is a good thing, I thought. *A normal life…* I pondered it a moment, like a dream. It was easy, in her presence, to think of what it would be like. If I could make it permanent.

But was everything really gone? I tried to reach out with my mind. Make contact with Naima. Nothing. To the side, some broken shards of cinder block were strewn on the warehouse's dusty floor. I tried to lift one with my mental powers. Zippo.

I saw Bobby's face, and Pip's, and realized they were probably doing the same thing. Trying to use powers that didn't exist.

Bobby poked one finger at the flesh of his forearm. "Can we…?" he started, then clammed up, like he was afraid to say something.

"Can we what?" Pip asked.

"Can we *bleed*?" Bobby asked, in a hushed tone that nevertheless seemed to bounce off the unforgiving walls of the empty warehouse.

It was a question none of us dared to answer.

Beside me, Holly twitched. *She doesn't like this one bit*, I thought. "Hey, let's try something," I said. "Um, Dr. Naima?"

"Just Naima, please," she said. Her voice had no hint of an accent, except for when she said her name. The way she pronounced it seemed natural in a way that it didn't coming out of my mouth.

Something must have been growing within Naima. In her first encounter with Margrethe, it had taken touch. Later, Pip said you had to be very close to her. Now, was her sphere of influence growing? When would it stop? What if it never stopped? Could she alone rid the world of superpowers? "Okay, sorry. *Naima*, can you and your son walk back toward that door? I want to see how far away you have to be for us to, you know, get our powers back."

"Sure," she said, looking down at her son and touching him on the arm, gently prodding him to step back.

At first, there was nothing. Then…

She got five feet away, and I heard more than felt a tingle, somewhere inside me.

Ten feet. It was like shaking the pins and needles out of your foot after it had fallen asleep.

Fifteen feet. I tried reaching out with my mind, to my sister who was still shivering in her wheelchair, looking down, her black hair fallen in front of her face. I still couldn't reach her mind, there was something there, but it was static, impossible to clear.

Twenty feet. *Holly?* She either couldn't or wouldn't respond.

Twenty-five feet. A cinder block near us jiggled and started to rise off the ground. Bobby grinned. Apparently that was his test. *Holly?* I tried again, still failing to get a response.

At about 30 feet, Naima and Sharif were close enough to touch the door. They stopped, looking back at us expectantly.

As if an explosion came from within her, Holly leaped out of her chair, her body flung into the air with an unseen force, to hover in front of us with her arms high like a dark and terrifying ghoul raised from the dead. An unbearably loud screaming cry rang out, not real sound, but in my head. For a moment, it obliterated any other thought or action.

A sphere of force emanated from my sister as she hung before us. It expanded with lightning speed and slammed into the walls and ceiling of the warehouse. It hit Naima's body, then Sharif's, and pushed them against the door, jarring it open and tossing them outside into the brightness of the alley.

And then the building pulsed away from us in a surreal spherical shape, then collapsed back upon us, its old bones unable to sustain the strength of the invisible force within.

Mom! I thought through the pain in my mind.

I didn't fear for me, or Bobby or Pip or even Holly. We had power once more. The building would try to crush us and fail.

But Mom was just a person.

My mother was about to die.

No! I used my own powers to send a second wave of force after the first, and with it, I caught the falling walls and ceiling, holding together the old supports, bricks, and girders in a curving, impossible shape around us, my mental powers straining. To each side, I saw Pip and Bobby working their magic in similar ways, seeking to aid me in holding back the tide of heavy objects trying to smother us all. Together, we held aloft the debris. Something that looked like the world's strangest igloo hovered above us.

For a moment, all motion ceased. The shell around us came to a sort of equilibrium — we held it, and for the moment it stopped falling. But we were trapped. We stood within the dome I had created, but we knew it couldn't last forever. I had control, but if I tired, or even flinched, what would happen?

Mom would die.

Pip sprang to life first. "We need to get *her* out of here!" She looked around, not sure what to do, until suddenly she aimed herself toward the space where the door had been. And she *pushed.* Slowly, a tunnel began to form, cutting through the debris. Bobby stepped beside Pip to help, aiming his abilities into the same tunnel, extending it.

Finally, light. The tunnel reached the alley behind the crumbling warehouse.

"Go!" Bobby yelled to my mom. "You need to go!"

But Mom wouldn't move. "Not without her!" she yelled, pointing at Holly, who was still floating in the middle of our makeshift dome.

Grimly, Pip nodded. I could see sweat beading on her forehead from the exertion of her powers as she walked to where she could reach my sister. All of my energy went to keeping the ceiling from collapsing. Pip put a hand on Holly's leg, not pulling or guiding, just touching. "Holly, your mother needs to get out of here, or else she could be hurt, maybe even killed. So we need you to come down now, to go with her."

Nothing happened.

And then, almost reluctantly, Holly descended, sliding back into her chair, her energies swirling away like leaves in a fall breeze.

Mom and Pip exchanged a look. "Thank you," Mom said, spinning Holly's chair as quickly as she could and pushing through the tunnel Bobby still held open. Her movements seemed stilted, probably a residual from her injury in the kitchen. Just as I was wondering if Mom was hiding something more than a bump or a bruise, she and Holly broke into the light, then turned back to look down the dark tunnel to where Pip, Bobby, and I stood amid the frozen form of the collapsing building.

And that's when I let go, and we were crushed by brick, block, dust, and steel.

PART 2

— *conquest* —

1

Yes, we lived, but damn, it hurt.

And there were two tricks.

First, we needed to get out of what remained of the building without being spotted.

And second, where the hell did Naima go?

After our bodies sluiced back to their normal shapes, sloughing off debris along the way, we crawled our way out of the rubble as quickly as we could. We found my mother and sister not far from where the door used to be, tucked into another alley to avoid some of the smoke and dust and random falling objects.

"Did you see her? Or the boy?" Pip asked, breathless. Mom shook her head as she wheeled Holly into the open space, bouncing the chair awkwardly over chunks of brick, wood, and metal. Pip scanned the area, but there was no one to be found. Then she pulled out her phone. The screen had been shattered by the collapsing building, but somehow it still worked. After a moment, she jabbed at the phone in frustration. "She isn't answering."

"Guys?" Bobby asked.

No one answered.

"Guys?" he repeated. "We need to roll. We just crushed an entire building. People will be coming to check this out."

"Agreed," Mom said. "Come on."

We started moving, with her in the lead. As her son, I was used to following her, something I had done for pretty much my whole life. Then the complete *strangeness* of trailing after my mother, when I was superhuman, while she pushed another superhuman, and while two other superhumans trailed behind, through a city we didn't know — well, it all kind of hit me. Not all powers are the same, my friends. You don't need to be superhuman to be a super human.

"We've got to get to the car, assuming it didn't get too damaged," Mom said, not bothering to turn around. "I've got to get your sister away from here." In the distance, sirens began to wail.

We weaved between buildings, trying to remain unseen, until suddenly we came upon a huge green trash truck. It was shaking its big metal arms over its shoulders like a boxer celebrating a KO, tossing the contents of a dumpster into its vast rear compartment. The driver, an older black man with a stubby cigar tucked into the corner of his mouth, saw us approaching. "What the hell?" he said, teeth still chomping on the stogie.

Of course, I thought. *Red Hope just appeared. That'll surprise most people. But that means it won't take long for him to figure out who Bobby and I are, either.*

I went to push the man's mind, but Pip beat me to it, leaving him humming a tune as we whisked by.

Rounding the next corner, we saw the van parked on the street among countless other cars. People were beginning to gather in the streets, drawn to the unexpected excitement of something newsworthy. Little did they know, it wasn't just some old building falling down after years of neglect.

Pip stopped running. "I better stay back," she said, pulling into the shadow of a doorway.

Bobby looked conflicted, and for a moment I thought he would stay, too. But, in a way that was more powerful than any signed contract, we were friends and we had a deal. He honored it. "I'll call you later," he said. Pip responded with a barely noticeable nod, fading out of view.

And so, trying to look as nonchalant as you can when you're covered in rubble, appearing from an alley near a collapsed building, and casually walking to your car with an also-dusty girl in a wheelchair, we loaded up and drove off. Luckily, despite the fact that in the not-too-distant past every one of us had been tabloid news fodder, the building's self-destruction was simply too interesting for anyone to pay us much mind.

Final score: our team, zero. Naima and Sharif, um… two? Wait, that makes no sense. Anyway, they were gone. Oh, and I guess the building scored a point or three, as well. Okay, fine, this was a bad time for a sports analogy.

* * *

Back home, things were a mess. Not collapsed-building messy, but darned close.

"Someone's been here," I said, perhaps the most obvious statement ever made, looking across all of our worldly possessions that had been tossed about, ransacked.

Mom looked at me, Holly. "Kids, you know what this means, right?"

"Um, yes?" I offered. Then there was an uncomfortable silence. "All right, no. What does it mean?"

"I means we can't stay here anymore. This house isn't safe. After that *man*… and now this? We need to leave."

She was right, of course. But where would we go? What would we do? I stepped over something that had been smashed on the floor. My videogame console. *Really, assholes? Whoever did this… now it's personal. Those were my games. I won't forget this.* A man has to have enthusiasms, after all.

Finally, we had reached the top of the cliff. Jump or die. This was it. There was no turning back. Sol had played the hand for us. We couldn't stay at home and continue to pretend we were a normal family. We had to go *somewhere.*

We had one choice to make, really. Only one.

Go public.

Or hide.

"We can go back to the city, to Pip," Bobby said. "She'll have room for us all, at least for a little while, until we figure something out. We'd all be safe there, together. Let's just get back in the van and go. Now." Bobby sounded almost relieved.

"Don't you need to tell your parents *something*, Bobby?" Mom asked.

Bobby just shrugged. What was there to say? Mom knew all about Bobby's relationship with his parents. "They'll figure it out once the world knows who we are." He laughed, but it was tinged with something. Disappointment, sorrow, maybe bitterness? "The funny thing is, they'll probably want me back once they know who I am."

"Mommy?" Holly said, looking concerned.

"Yes, dear? What is it?"

Holly just shook her head, looking at me.

What's the matter, Holly? I sent to her.

I don't want to leave home, Johnny. I like our house. And I don't want to live with Pip. She's all right, but I want to live here.

I told Mom and Bobby what Holly was saying to me. Mom leaned down and hugged her. "Holly, Sol will just keep coming back here," she said. "We've got to do something."

Just for now, Hol. Just until Sol is gone. I promise, I'll take care of him for good this time. I promised it, but I had no idea if I was lying or not. How could I put a true end to someone I had already killed once?

Holly was quiet. Then finally, her head nodded, just slightly. *Okay, Johnny. We can live somewhere else, just until Sol is gone. But I don't want to live with Pip.*

Some things about my sister were just like that: black and white. Maybe there was no specific reason, but she wasn't going to budge. Or maybe she had a really good reason and I was the one slowly catching up. At that moment, it felt like the latter. "I think Holly's right about one thing — we shouldn't live with Pip." Bobby was crestfallen. "At least not all of us." I nodded toward my mother. "You, me, and Holly can find some other place."

"What for?" Bobby asked. "Why not stick together?"

"Because if Sol decides to really come after us, not just send his goon squad, I don't want to make it so easy for him to find us."

Bobby nodded. So did Mom.

"But where?" I asked, having no idea the answer.

"Marcos," Mom said, nodding. "I know he'll help us. And quietly."

Of course. Marcos. Well, at least my rides to taekwondo practice with him would be shorter, huh? If I ever got to do that again.

Johnny?

Yeah, Hol?

I just want to spend some time in my room before we go. In case...

In case what?

Her eyes were intensely focused on mine. *In case I never see it again.*

* * *

We packed what we could. Bobby even went home to get things of his own. Did he tell his parents anything? Better yet, when he walked out with a suitcase, did they even ask where he was going? I thought about asking him how it went when he returned, but from the look on his face, I knew to leave it alone.

A couple of hours later, the van was loaded and it was time to head out. Wistfully, I stood in the driveway, looking up and down the street, the place where I grew up. I turned toward the house, really looking at it for maybe the first time.

Funny how that works, isn't it? Finally looking at something you've seen every day of your whole life. Our house was small. The shutters probably needed paint. The driveway was cracked. The grass was too long in spots, dead in others. The row of bushes to one side of the front door was an unkempt mess, probably hadn't been trimmed in years. And yet, it was *my* house. *Our* house. I wasn't ready to leave that place, or my town.

Leave town? Oh crap.

That's when it dawned on me. I couldn't go anywhere without talking to Carrie first. "Mom?" I said, walking inside.

"Yes, John?"

"I can't go yet." I found her as she was about to walk into Holly's room.

Mom was absently holding one arm across her stomach. In the other, she held a canvas bag that she slowly filled as she walked around the house, a last effort not to forget something. "What's the matter?"

I smirked sheepishly. “Carrie.”

Mom nodded. “Of course. You’re right. You can’t just up and run away from that girl. She cares for you. Go talk to her. We’ll leave when you get back.”

“Thanks, Mom.”

I started to turn, but my mother opened the door to Holly room and gasped, dropping the bag and spilling its contents all over the floor. I rushed to her, looking over her shoulder and into the room.

And there, in the middle of the floor, Holly sat in her wheelchair.

She was covered in spiders.

Black, pulsing things, their tiny legs pumping as they crawled over her lap, up her arms.

I expected to see a look of horror, of revulsion, but on her face Holly had a completely different expression.

She looked embarrassed.

2

"Hi," I said, not knowing what else to say. How to start what would no doubt be the strangest conversation I would ever have. And might have the worst outcome.

"Hi, John, what's up?" Carrie smiled. I wondered if she'd still be smiling when I was done saying what I had to say.

If it had to be over, I wanted the ending to at least fit the beginning. Something about the symmetry made it better, in my mind. That's why I had asked Carrie to meet me at Jeremiah Underly Park, at the same table where we had our first date. No checked tablecloth or basket of snacks this time around — just us.

"Carrie, I have something I need to tell you," I said.

That's a loaded phrase. Perhaps *the* most loaded phrase of all time. *I have something to tell you.* I'm pretty sure no one ever said that and then followed up with *The kitty litter needs cleaning.* Those were words of import. Of significance. Of sudden and irreversible change.

I swallowed, hard.

This was it.

No, let me emphasize that.

This was *it*.

No. That's not enough.

This was *IT*.

I was about to tell someone that I had powers. What would she think? Would she shun me like the freak I so often felt I was? Or had the TV exposure changed things? Had seeing me, the others, operate, and become unwitting celebrities, changed the game? Were superpowers acceptable?

But I didn't think about any of that.

I remember it clearly.

I thought about one thing.

One.

Thing.

Only.

Don't pee your pants.

I repeated it like a mantra.

"Okay, what is it?" she said.

That snapped me back to reality. It was time.

"I need to tell you something," I repeated.

Carrie rolled her eyes and sort of batted her lashes at me. That wasn't going to help one bit. "We've established that, John. Spit it out." Then she pulled back. "Wait. It's not something bad, is it? About you, or your mom? Or Holly?"

I waved my hands. "No, no. Nothing like that. It's just…"

"Just *what*, John? Now you have me worried." Her forehead wrinkled up and my heart rate increased.

"Okay, well, don't worry. Well, maybe…"

And then Carrie punched me in the shoulder. Or she tried. My shoulder sluiced, just enough so she missed. "Ugh, I keep forgetting you have the double-jointed thing," she said.

"That's just it, Carrie. I don't. I'm not double-jointed." My mouth was suddenly dry. Not just dry, but arid. There was a desert in my throat. I didn't know if I would be able to keep talking.

"What are you saying, John?"

I had to do it. But I could only manage three words. "I'm Black Sword."

Carrie was utterly quiet. Still.

Say something, I thought. Though I'm not sure if I wanted Carrie to say something or me to break the awful, stifling silence.

"Did you hear me?" I finally asked.

Carrie nodded. "Yes, John. I heard you. But… are you just saying that because you think I have a crush on him?"

"No! Of course not!"

"Because I do, you know."

Now, what the heck was this? Carrie was just messing with me. "You what?"

She leaned closer. Curls of red hair fell around her face as she spoke. "You heard me. I have a crush on Black Sword. I have for some time."

"How — how long?" It was all I could think of to ask.

This time she definitely batted her lashes, just inches away from me, so close I could smell the sweet, floral tones of her perfume, mixed with the warm and human scent of just *her*. "Oh, I don't know, John Black. Just about as long as I've known *he* was *you*."

And that's about when I realized how much of a transparent fool I had been.

* * *

She knew. She knew for some time. How? Mostly, she was just paying attention.

But it was the t-shirts that did me in.

I asked her if she thought other people knew, too. She said she doubted it. She only put the pieces together after we had been dating for months. Like I said, I only had so many t-shirts. She saw the same ones time and again. Eventually, the random replay of some news footage of Black Sword overlapped with something I was wearing. She just put two and two together. Plus, of course, she well knew when I had been around and when I was harder to find. Mild-mannered John Black's disappearances meshed far too well with the appearances of superhero Black Sword.

I felt kinda stupid.

"The mask was pretty effective, though. I mean, it took me quite a while to figure it out. Even still, I wasn't sure until that day you were choking, and your neck just sort of—" She made a zig-zagging gesture with her hands. "I thought to myself, *Oh yeah, he's double-jointed.* And then I had to stop myself. Because even if your *shoulder* was double-jointed, your *neck* certainly wasn't."

"Why didn't you say anything?" I asked.

"Me? Why didn't *I* say anything? Don't you think *you're the one* who should have said something?"

"Well, uh…"

"Allow me to finish that thought for you. *Well, uh, yes, Carrie. You're right. I should have been honest with you and told you.*"

She was right.

"I'm sorry, Carrie. It's just, you know, sort of the craziest thing ever. So I was a little worried about how you'd take it."

She squinted, looking me in the eyes. "You thought I would freak out, didn't you?"

"Sort of."

"Well, I have to admit, I did kind of freak out, once I knew," she said, giggling.

"That's okay," I said. "When I realized I had powers, I kind of freaked out, too." And then I had to tell her the whole story. Like pretty much everything, all the way back to the snow and the car and Bobby and Walter Ivory and all the crazy crap about Sol.

"Oh my God. He's your *nemesis*," Carrie said when I finished.

"Ugh, don't say that. It makes him sound so, I don't know, *important*, or something."

"Isn't he? I mean, he's a superpowered madman, who pretty much seems like he's intent on killing you. That's what he meant in that interview, right? The one about *revenge*."

"Probably. I don't really want to think about that right now."

"Why?"

"Because that's the other thing I needed to tell you. My family and I are leaving town. I guess we're sort of going into hiding. And…"

“And what?”

“And I’m not sure when I’ll see you again.”

Cue the swelling music, turn on the gauzy filters. Carrie hugged me, tight, and for a long time. Sure, she asked where we were going. But I couldn’t tell her, right? Wouldn’t exactly be a secret then, would it? I just told her we wouldn’t be too far away. I did confirm that I wasn’t moving to Norway or anything crazy like that. Besides, have you ever seen how scary those massive cliffs they have are? The ones that tower over inlets from the sea? They call them *fjords*. Fjords? How is that a word? I’m not sure I can trust a group of people that puts a *j* after an *f*.

In the end, of course, I promised that I’d be back.

No one would ever figure out we were heading to live with Marcos. Just like no one would ever figure out who Black Sword was, all on her own.

3

Marcos lived 45 minutes from our home, alone, on a tree-lined suburban street pretty far from the other houses despite their almost identical appearance, in a McMansion that was far too big and empty for him, lined with echoing bedrooms.

In other words, the perfect place for a retreat.

The miles hummed by underneath the car, and at first I tried to nap. Then I realized I needed to know something, bad. I didn't sit up. I was in the front passenger seat and figured I would keep up the illusion that I was asleep, to let my mom drive in peace. Especially since I didn't know what I was about to find out. Holly was behind us, in the center of the van.

Hol?

Yeah, Johnny?

What's up with the spiders?

Silence.

Hol?

Nothing.

Holly, come on. We're gonna be in the car for a while. Just tell me.

Her voice blared in my mind. *I'm strong, Johnny!*

What do you say to that? What should I have said to my sister, confined to a wheelchair for so many years through no fault of her own? A person who had suffered through abduction, a girl who had been robbed of a normal life?

That was it.

I always thought about *my* normal life, and how it had disappeared because of my powers. What about Holly? It wasn't even the powers that took away her sense of normal. If anything, the powers were the only thing that promised to bring it back.

You are *strong, Hol. Always have been. Stronger than anyone I know.*

Don't do that, Johnny. It makes me mad.

Do what? I asked.

Talk to me like that, like I'm just a little kid. I'm not a little kid anymore.

Patronizing you? You mean that?

She grunted, out loud. I don't think me correcting her word choice was the best idea at the moment. *I don't know what* pa-tro-ni-zing *means, Johnny! Cut it out, I mean it!* She had missed out on so much, my sister. But I didn't feel sorry for her. She was right. She was strong. Shake-the-world strong. Make-giant-monsters strong. What was I in comparison? A guy who used a belt as a sword.

Holly, I'm not talking down to you. I mean it. You're amazing. You've done things I don't think I could ever do.

Then why?

Why what, Holly?

Without warning, the car lurched, catching a little air before settling back to the road surface.

"Whoa! Sorry, guys!" Mom said. "Must have been a pothole I didn't see coming."

I knew better. That wasn't any pothole.

Why what, Holly?

Why are you *so famous? Why is Bobby? Why is Pip? And Sol, too!*

I'm not famous, Holly.

Give me a break, Johnny. It's just a matter of time before people know you're Black Sword. *And Black Sword* is *famous.*

I stayed quiet. Holly was in a mood, and I didn't know what to say or do to help her out of it.

Why not me? No one even knows I exist! Or cares.

The car hopped again, a smaller blow this time. Did Mom know it was from Holly? We weren't speaking out loud. Hard to say. I doubt it.

Soon, Hol. That's all I can say. Soon. Someday really soon, people are going to find out about me, and Bobby. And then, it only makes sense that they find out about you.

Whatever. Then she was quiet again, for a minute or more.

Hol?

When she next spoke in my mind, her voice sounded different. Maybe excited, happy? Or maybe… a little arrogant?

Can you do this, Johnny?

I felt a tingle by my left hand, and then a tiny black spider crawled up my arm.

Suddenly it made sense.

Horrible sense, but sense.

Hol, did you just make *this spider?*

She didn't respond, not with words.

She giggled. A *giggle* in my mind.

And another spider appeared, on my right arm. That second time, I noticed the little flash, the little hole in the universe that opened and closed with a feeling like an abnormal tickle. Not a flash of light, per se, but a flash of power.

Just as Holly had made giant monsters, she was now making tiny spiders.

Holly *made* them. Out of nothing.

How?

Stop, Hol. Mom will see.

I don't care.

I sighed, mentally. You know what? Sighing with your mind is just weird. *Mom doesn't deserve this, does she, Hol? She doesn't need more on top of everything she's already got. If you want to be mad at me, okay, go ahead. But then let's have you and me talk about it when Mom's not around, all right?*

You brought it up, John.

Wow. When was the last time my sister called me *John* in one of our private conversations? Probably never. That could only mean one thing.

She was pissed.

And at that moment, I realized, point-blank, one really important thing: Nothing — not her condition, not her wheelchair, not her powers, and certainly not me — was ever going to stop my sister from growing up.

Which meant that she wanted the same thing everyone wanted at her age, the same thing *I* wanted at her age. To be empowered, to have the right to choose and do things for herself, even if sometimes those things were mistakes. At least they'd be *her* mistakes. Just like I had made mine.

Hol. The spiders. Are they coming from... inside *you? You know, like you said about the Gorgols? How you just made them from your mind, you didn't bring them from somewhere else.*

Yes, John.

Hol, why are you calling me John?

Isn't that your name, John?

Hol, you and I both know you call me Johnny.

She was silent a moment. *Well, not right now. And maybe it's better for us to use more grown-up names, anyway.*

I didn't really want to address that, not right away. So I pivoted, asking something else that continued to gnaw at me. *Holly, what's on the other side of the... I don't know, gate? Portal? The thing you make — the thing you just made, when the spiders appeared.*

I'm behind that, John. Me.

I know that part, but, you know, what inside of you controls that? Where does it come from?

Again she was silent, but this time she seemed to be working out how to describe it, not clamming up because she was mad.

If I look inside, I see something, sort of like a pool. The pool lets me make things.

Okay, Hol. But what's in the pool? What does it look like?

It's dark, of course. Deep. And it moves, with energy or maybe tiny things.

What kind of tiny things, Hol?

First of all, John, I'm not sure the pool I'm talking about is a real thing. It could just be an idea in my mind.

I understand. Just trying to figure out what it is that you see. What does this.

Okay. Holly actually seemed to be calming down, maybe because she was pleased that she knew something I didn't, and I really wanted to know. *The pool inside, with the tiny things*, she said. *They're little, so little. And pointy. And they come together with such energy, so much that I feel I can do anything with it.*

Of course. Tiny, pointy things. Bodies of energy.

She was talking about the thorns. The things that had invaded her cells, and mine.

But Holly clearly had a different relationship with the little gremlins than I did. Whereas I — when I really, really tried — could sense them throughout my body like a million dots of light, Holly understood them as a sort of combined force, the pool she described.

After all this time, I still had a lot of learning to do. And probably the biggest eye-opener of all was that my baby sister wasn't a baby anymore.

4

There are things in life that I want to do. And things that I simply have to do. It's not often that those two lists overlap. I was doing something I had to do and basically ignoring everything I wanted to do. It sucked.

You see it all the time — the story of the business owner who gets so engrossed in business that the rest of his or her life falls apart. Or maybe not so drastic as all that, but the *enjoyment* disappears. Life isn't guaranteed to be easy and it isn't guaranteed to be fun. But if all the enjoyment slips away, what are you left with? Living on the run once more, hiding, I felt like life was slipping away from me.

I needed to see things through with Sol, somehow, if I ever wanted to be normal again. Well, you know what I mean. My sort of normal.

But Marcos, as expected, was at least welcoming and gracious. "Hello, John," he said, opening the door to me as we unpacked our few things from the car.

I nodded. "Marcos. Hey… um. Thanks, for this."

"Don't thank me yet, John. You haven't had to sit through long nights of my many ideas," he said, grinning and holding the door as I entered with a box full of my personal crap. I thought he was kidding. He wasn't.

* * *

The next day, sitting in Marcos's kitchen, was straight-up weird. You know, whenever you invade someone's home, everything you know flies out the window. You're not in your space anymore, you're in theirs. There are things you learn about them. To be blunt, there are smells you discover. For Marcos, it was disinfectant spray, as if he were addicted to the stuff. Cook dinner? Spray. Go to the bathroom? Spray. Sneeze? Not directly in your face, of course, but I bet he thought about it.

I didn't even know if it was cool to get a glass of water. At the oversized but rather plain wooden kitchen table, I was probably visibly twitching with unease.

We were alone. Holly was in her room, and I didn't even want to think about whether she was making spiders. Mom — wearing dark glasses and with her hair in a strange bun, as a sort of disguise — had gone grocery shopping, because if there is one thing a bachelor never, ever has, it's food for three guests who arrive without warning.

"John," Marcos said, not even looking up from his Sunday newspaper. "As I told you last night, I want you to feel utterly and completely at home here, in my home. If you wish for food, take it. If you want a drink, drink it." Marcos dropped the paper, looking me in the eye. So serious. Yet… *something*. "John, if you must fart, I wish for you to fart. Don't be concerned that it might offend me."

I guffawed. Marcos was clearly insane.

* * *

Bobby had gone off to the city, so it was logical that I kept checking the news, expecting to hear that Yellow Fury had gone public.

It didn't happen.

I had to know why.

"Are you kidding me, Johnny?" Bobby said when I called him up and asked.

"No, really. You're with Pip now. She's public. Why aren't you?"

"Well, hold up, partner. I'm not exactly *with* Pip."

"What does that mean? Didn't you go to the city? Where are you, then?"

"No — I mean, yeah — I'm in the city, and I'm at Pip's apartment. Real nice, real comfy. Not like that crapatorium I've been calling home since the prehistoric era. But that's not what I meant." Bobby suddenly sounded shy.

I wasn't familiar with a *shy* Bobby Graden. *What's going on?*

Oh. Oh, he means with *with.*

"You mean to say that you two aren't a couple?" I asked, pretty bluntly. Friends and tact do not mix.

Bobby chuckled, softly, but with a tinge of annoyance. "Yeah. That."

"What's wrong? I mean, does she like someone el—"

"Cool it, Johnny. Let's just let this topic drift away, okay?"

"Uh…" I didn't know what else to say. "Okay, I guess." And you know, I should have actually let it drift away. But suddenly curiosity overcame me. "Does she think you're ugly or something?"

"*Jesus*, Johnny. *Shut up*, already. No, it's not that."

Bobby might have been about to hang up on me, but in a way, I think he needed to tell someone. "Then what?" I asked.

I could barely hear the response. His voice sounded far away, his head probably turned away from the phone. "She thinks I'm too young for her."

"*What*? No! That's crap! Bobby, you tell her I said that's crap!" I was fired up.

"And exactly what do you think your opinion is going to change, Johnny? You, the guy who chopped her arm off once. You think she's suddenly going to go, *Oh right, then everything's fine. John Black says so!*"

I had to admit, he was right. "Um. No. Not Pip."

"Right. So she thinks I'm a kid. It sucks. I'll deal. Now, I guarantee — or at least, I hope — that you didn't call me up just to harass me about this, right? Tell me I'm right." Bobby sighed heavily.

"Yeah, of course. I want to know why you haven't gone public. Told the world who you are."

"Because of you, idiot," he said in a flat voice.

"Really?"

"Johnny, you can be really dense for a kid who's supposed to be all nerdy and smart. Of course I have to keep quiet. You, me, and your family just bolted town without telling anyone. If I pop in front of a news camera and say I'm Yellow Fury, how long before you get pegged? Maybe three seconds? Probably less." Is it possible to hear someone rolling their eyes? Bobby was definitely rolling his eyes.

"Yeah," I said. "Well, you know, *thanks*, Bobby. Thanks for trying to keep my family out of it."

We talked another 1.27 minutes, and then hung up amid fumbling agreements that we'd see each other soon. So we're not professional telephone conversationalists. Sue us.

I sat back, hanging up the phone with a grin, knowing my friend Bobby was doing his best to keep my family out of the unwanted spotlight. And I clicked on the TV. I swear to you, I did it at that very moment.

Guess who?

Sol was giving another interview, same posh business office in the same secret location, same marble and leather and sleek dark wood. Even the same interviewer, that guy Stephen Whatshisface.

There were a few words of preamble, but then Stephen got to the point. “You know Red Hope?” he asked, looking up at Sol from his notepad.

“Indeed I do,” Sol replied, grinning white perfect teeth against dark perfect skin. There really seemed to be no hint of Jake left. That man had been erased.

“Well, what about Yellow Fury? And the one who you said killed you, Black Sword?” Stephen waited, anxious, tapping a pen lightly on his notepad.

“Yes, of course. I know them all, quite well, actually.” Sol idly adjusted the left cuff of his perfectly pressed, blinding-white shirt.

Where does he get these incredible clothes? I imagined for a moment Sol spending his days flitting between acts of pure evil and going on sprees at posh shopping malls.

Lolling back on Marcos’s couch, I was only paying partial attention, daydreaming. For some reason, I didn’t see the next question coming. Probably because of what he had answered in the previous interview. Maybe I thought I was safe. Maybe I thought I was immune.

I was completely wrong.

“Then you know who they really are? Their real names?”

Suddenly I bolted upright, on the edge of the seat, holding my breath. There are moments that change your life forever. With only a few words, Sol changed mine, once again.

"Obviously, Stephen. Their names are, respectively, Bobby Graden and John Black."

And there you have it. I was suddenly a public figure.

A public *super*figure.

Shit.

5

"Mom," I said, stopping her as she began to unload a bag of vegetables. "It's done. We don't really have to hide anymore. Sol told the world who I am."

She froze, staring at me. The bag teetered, and then, as expected to do so in such situations, tipped and spilled its contents onto the floor. "No. *No*. Really?" I nodded. "What about —?" Mom's eyes flitted to one side.

"He didn't mention Holly." She sighed with relief. "But I doubt it matters. Everything we've been through — Holly's kidnapping, my disappearances — people are going to put it all together now."

My mother stood before me, weak, in obvious pain, devastated. Plus, she was encircled by a splatter of spilled groceries. But her panic lasted only for a moment. She blinked, wiped the tears from her eyes with the back of one hand, and stood up straight. "Okay, fine. What's next?" Her entire world was changing, and she was just going to deal with it anyway.

I shook my head. "No idea."

* * *

"John, I have a thought. Why don't we have a lesson now, since we're together?" Marcos said, standing beside me in his kitchen a few hours later. I guess I wasn't the only one sick of sitting around. He had already donned his *dobok*. I simply wore a t-shirt and sweatpants.

Those hours had been a whirlwind. I staggered between fielding a million texts from friends and silent moments of reflection. Tom and Steve in particular overwhelmed my phone with messages, essentially asking me why I was such a supreme jerk to be superhuman and not tell them. I apologized, of course, though even that felt strange. Steve asked me if I could teach him how to fly. That was weird.

Others, people I hardly knew, relatives I saw on occasion, simply got a form-letter response. *Yes, the news is true. I'm sorry I didn't tell you sooner, but the situation is complicated.*

A few people asked me for favors. I ignored those. More than anything, being a public figure was exhausting.

"Um, you're kidding, right?" I said, downtrodden. I had been outed as a superhuman, and Marcos wanted to give me a lesson in martial arts? He must have been doing it just to play with me, maybe almost to mock me.

"Not at all. Come down to the basement with me." He turned, opened a nondescript, cheap panel door, and began to head downstairs, flicking on a light as he passed.

Before I could stammer a reply, he was out of sight. So, what could I do? I followed.

Marcos's house was one of those large, three-level suburban homes you find lining cul-de-sacs in comforting repetition. The homeowners association — frighteningly referred to as the acronym, HOA — probably allowed a grand total of four paint colors on the aluminum siding. Marcos's front yard — including two trees held up by wooden posts and wire as they grew — had to be routinely maintained to secure the utter boringness of the street at large, or else he risked a fine and the wrath of some elderly woman who ran the oversight committee. The interior of the house wasn't much different. Marcos was not big on decoration, opting instead for oversized prints sold by the thousands at the nearest Swedish home-furnishing store. For the record, I preferred the backyard, which was surrounded by trees and actually rather secluded.

As I clomped down the bare pine wood stairs, I passed a dark print dominated by a red English phone booth. The words *London Calling* drove home the pun that oh-so-desperately wanted to be edgy. Still, I didn't fault Marcos for it. He might have questionable taste in home decor, but he was good at other things. Like martial arts.

I stepped onto the uniform grey concrete floor and looked around. There weren't even walls, just some studs boxing in a small space in one corner, full of exposed wires and pipes, and the silvery reflection of insulation along the outer walls. Near the back stood a gleaming washer and dryer set, along with thin metal shelves stocked with cleaning supplies. Beside those, a lonely ironing board stood like a prisoner awaiting visitation.

About a third of the wide-open space actually had a floor covering — a wide segment of some industrial-looking carpet, probably just to keep bare feet off of bare floor, and a couple of blue, cushy mats, the kind you might see in gym class. Or a martial-arts studio, of course.

I realized a chill had been seeping up my legs, through my socks, from the concrete. It made sense — workout in a place that will help you cool down.

Or maybe the HOA would frown upon a sparring ring on display in the front bay window of his house.

"John, today we will review Do-San. But, as always, I will remind you that we are moving extraordinarily quickly through the many patterns of taekwondo. You have understood and memorized things well so far, so I would like to see if you recall Do-San from our last meeting."

That was a tall order. Our last meeting had been some time prior, when I actually could still say I had a semi-normal life. I grimaced and wrinkled my brow, trying to recall the pattern.

I knew it started with me reaching up on my right side, then turning toward my left in a walking stance, followed by a reverse punch.

And after that, my mind was completely blank.

Crap.

I stood there, like a statue to be erected in the martial arts hall of fame, holding my pose forever. I started to sweat. My mind raced, trying to work through the pattern again.

Come on, John. It's a pattern, *after all.*

Ah, that was it. A box turn, then the same move I'd just done in the opposite direction. *Phew.*

And then I was stuck again. I froze. Time passed.

On the first floor of his house, Marcos had a grandfather clock. It was simultaneously the coolest thing in his house and a complete nuisance. Every 15 minutes, *bong...*

It chimed.

And that must have set him off. I had stood still too long. The clock chimed. Marcos moved.

Coming from behind me, he made a swooping hammer-fist attack aimed at my left ear. Of course it was a *hammer* fist. My body was all too familiar with hammers.

And you know, as soon as he did it, I remembered the next step in the pattern, a turn and block that would have met his blow perfectly. Didn't matter.

Instead, my left shoulder and head sluiced sideways, avoiding his strike.

I don't think Marcos meant to hit me, anyway. In our previous sessions, he had never even made a feint. I don't know why he chose that moment to strike. We'd agreed on no sparring, but maybe he was just trying a simple move to jog my memory. Nonetheless, he stopped, hammer fist still hovering next to me. "What in the name of God…?" he said.

Seriously? He's messing with me. I pulled out of my stance and stood tall, turning toward him, a look of annoyance on my face. "You don't have to pretend."

Marcos was silent. Then, finally, he blinked. "Pretend? What are you talking about, John?"

"I mean, I know you know. It was on TV."

Marcos blinked again and lowered his fists. "Please explain."

I studied him for a moment. He was actually serious. My name had become public and somehow, Marcos didn't know it.

Actually, I was glad. He deserved to hear it from me first.

"Marcos, I'm Black Sword. The guy from TV who fought the Gorgols."

His mouth opened, just slightly, but otherwise, Marcos remained frozen. Agog.

There was no need to say more, to explain. He had just seen my body do something impossible, something just like he'd no doubt seen Black Sword do on TV.

To his credit, Marcos recovered quickly. He came out of his stance, stood straight, and would you believe he even bowed to me? "I understand many things more clearly now, John Black, my friend."

"I'm sorry I had to keep it from you. I just didn't ever expect it to be public. And… well, now it is. Sol said my name on national television."

Marcos thought a moment, then nodded. “This will invariably bring a lot of attention to you and your family.”

I nodded in return, and we stood silently, contemplating what was next.

“Who else has this power, John? Your mother?”

I shook my head.

“Holly?” he asked.

“Yeah. More than me, probably.”

“Amazing,” he said, grinning. “Well, John. This is quite the turn of events.”

“I know, and again, I’m sorry I kept it quiet.” I hung my head.

Marcos laughed. “Don’t be sorry, John. I understand. I only have one question for you.” He looked positively gleeful, standing before me in his pristine white *dobok*. He pulled at the bottom edges, straightening his outfit as he stood tall.

“Ask me anything, Marcos. You’ve been so great to us. What’s your question?”

“Only this.” His smile grew as he slid back into a ready stance, clearly eager for something. He raised one hand, palm upward. “At long last, shall we spar?”

6

We should have been more proactive about Naima, but in many ways, we were preoccupied. I had been keeping myself hidden — very successfully, mind you. Bobby, the same, and Pip, well, she was square in the middle of the public eye. Looking for a missing woman wasn't the easiest thing to do when everywhere you went people recognized you and mobbed you.

So we mostly did nothing about Naima, but she stayed in our minds.

We weren't the only ones thinking about her.

There was the government, who no doubt wanted her back, but they were inherently slowed by being, you know, the government, following regulations and laws and observing the confines of jurisdiction.

Sol didn't let any of that stuff get in his way.

But I need to back up a bit.

When Pip broke Naima free, it had several important repercussions. First, it put Pip — and the rest of us — distinctly at odds with the government. That seemed easy for us to ignore, but it was true. The government, while large and all-encompassing, was also rather clunky and had trouble making progress in anything, especially complex investigations of unexplained phenomenon. Still, in general, you don't want to become the focus of a government investigation. What they lack in nimbleness they make up for in tenacity.

I had, unfortunately, not exactly earned the trust of the government. Sure, I'd cut down two of the three Gorgols — and as far as they knew, possibly the third one, too. But I'd also been on record for two not-so-nice actions. I cut off Pip's arm (gimme a break, it fixed itself), and I put all those reporters to sleep in the street. That was enough that the government wasn't sure about me, didn't know if they could trust me.

Believe it or not, in the government's eyes, I was somewhere near Margrethe on the good-to-evil scale. In fact, I was probably more toward evil, as it was doubtful they had any record of Margrethe actually *doing* anything. I didn't know it at the time, but it's true.

I mean, really? That just sucks. Sure, I put a bunch of camera operators and helicopter pilots to sleep, and yes, okay, fine, I did chop off half of Pip's arm. But did all of that actually mean I deserved to be considered a villain? A risky case?

Unfortunately, I didn't get to voice my opinion. And, given the existence of Sol — an obvious threat — the government had agents working on us round the clock.

When they finally found out about Naima, it was exactly what the doctor ordered. A way to control *us*. To control the superhumans by taking away the *super*. None of us knew much about the government's efforts at first, but Pip sort of made it her focal point. She was the one that told me a lot of what was happening, stuff of which I would otherwise have been blissfully unaware.

Naima, of course, was simply interested in one thing. Safety and security for her son and herself. She no longer felt comfortable in the city, but she didn't have the means to get far without drawing attention. I don't know a lot about what she did for the first few weeks after our incident in the city, but she ended up in a homeless shelter just on the west side of town. She used an assumed name, but really, no one asked a lot of questions or expected a lot of truths. She and her son had a place to sleep and three square meals. She was grateful. It wasn't private, and sometimes it didn't feel safe, but it worked, for a time.

Each night at dinnertime, Naima and Sharif would line up, trying to be among the first admitted for food and a bed. It was in one of these lines that she noticed a young man with curly brown hair and a rough beard. He wore coveralls with his name stitched above the left breast pocket — Gary. Naima noticed him because he was directly behind them, and because he was staring at his hand incredulously. At his own hand.

Unable to ignore him, Naima caught a glimpse of Gary's palm, and on it there was a thin cut, dripping a tiny amount of blood. "Are you okay?" she asked.

He didn't answer, still transfixed by his own hand.

"Excuse me, do you need help? Or a bandage?"

Gary shook his head, finally noticing her. "Sorry, I just — well, never mind."

"What is it?" Naima said, leaning toward him.

Gary looked left and right, then spoke in a hushed voice. "Can you keep a secret?" Naima didn't answer. She had too many secrets of her own. Still, Gary continued. "I'm one of *them.* You know, those people on TV who can do those things with their bodies. Like the ones who killed the Gorgols?"

"What are you talking about?" She suddenly regretted having spoken to the man at all.

"I have those super abilities, just like the people on TV," he said, smiling. "But, now… they're gone. Look! I just cut my hand, right now as I was sitting down next to you. Because I *sensed* something about you. It's incredible!" Gary held out his bleeding palm, smiling. Never had Naima seen someone so gleeful at being injured.

That's the thing that actually made her believe him. How could he know otherwise? How could he have sensed something in her she couldn't sense herself? How could he know that she had the strange ability to shut down powers? Of course he would be powerless, standing near her.

Nonetheless, she smiled, nodded, and went back to her own thoughts, letting the conversation die.

The next evening, Gary was back. With purpose, he approached her.

In one hand, he held a small pocketknife.

Naima wrapped her arms around Sharif and gasped, moving backward, away from Gary. But he smiled and waved his hands. "Sorry, sorry!" He tucked the pocketknife away. "I just had to see if it really is something about *you*. My powers came back to me as soon as I left here. But now, I feel funny again. Now, standing next to you." Gesturing to reassure her, Gary pulled out the little knife again, opened it, and poked at the flesh of his hand. He made a tiny cut, and a single drop of blood welled out. "See that? Around you, my powers are gone. I can't believe it. How?"

The evening progressed. They ate dinner at the shelter, at separate tables, then Naima found a bed in a corner. But as she told Sharif a bedtime story, she couldn't help but feel watched. On the other side of the large room, Gary was looking at her.

The next morning, he approached again. "My son and I prefer our privacy," she said before he could even begin.

"I understand, and I apologize if I've offended you. But it's true… *you* take away my powers. How is that possible?"

"I don't know what you're talking about," Naima said with a straight face, but her eyes were furtive.

"Come on, really? You can take away powers just by sitting there, and you don't know it? I don't believe that." He smiled a moment, then it faded and he was very serious. "I just want to tell you that I *hate* the powers. It's a *blessing* to be around you, to have the powers taken away. Can you help me make them go away permanently?"

Then Naima slipped up. “I have no idea how it works,” she said, which wasn’t a literal acknowledgment or denial, but it was close enough. Close enough to mean that she knew what he was talking about.

Strangely, to her, Gary seemed to accept the answer, backing away from her with an apology. He gathered his things and left the shelter before they did.

Thirty minutes later, Naima and Sharif were outside, about to cross a busy street, when a black sedan with tinted windows pulled up in front of them. The front passenger door swung open and Gary stepped out — but his coveralls had been replaced by dark suit and a deep-blue tie. Standing no more than a foot in front of Naima, Gary slid one side of his suit coat back, exposing a holstered pistol. Then he reached and opened the back door of the sedan. Inside, another man in a similar dark suit looked up at them, also flashing a gun.

“You’re Dr. Ramadi, right?” the man in the back seat said, not waiting for a reply. “You and your son are going to need to come with us.”

7

"Someone's watching us," Mom said, coming back from grocery shopping — her third time doing so since we'd arrived. I think Mom had begun buying food as a sort of guilty reflex, to overstock Marcos's kitchen in repayment for putting us up. And I think she liked putting on her "disguise" — dark glasses and the hair bun. Still, she moved more slowly than I had seen before, her injury continuing to bother her.

"*Everyone* will be watching us soon," I replied.

"Sure, but this has been happening since we arrived. Watch with me, out the front window tonight, in the dark. I'll show you."

She did.

* * *

That evening, Mom and I sat huddled in the dark before the slatted blinds of Marcos's upstairs hall window. The night was black, without a moon, so only the streetlights, the stars, and a few passing cars illuminated anything.

On the street, everything was still and quiet. We waited, and we watched.

Honestly, although it was just early evening, I nearly nodded off six or maybe a hundred times. Staring at a motionless suburban street tends to be rather boring.

I was probably asleep when Mom hissed through her teeth. "There! See!"

I jerked up and almost fell over backward in my chair. "Huh? Where?"

Mom pointed to a seemingly empty sedan in the street, parked nonchalantly about a house and a half away. I peered at it in the darkness. Something moved. Maybe. Barely.

"There, again!" she said. I rubbed my eyes and stood up. "What are you doing?" Mom asked, looking away from the window.

I put one hand on her shoulder wearily. "Mom, I have superpowers. I'm not cowering in the house because someone *might* be in a car outside. I'm going to go out there."

"And do what?"

"I'll figure it out when I get out there." I started down the stairs.

"What if it's Sol?"

"I seriously doubt it's Sol. He's not subtle enough to hide in a car all night."

"What if it's the government?"

"Then I'll tell them to leave us alone, I guess." I shrugged.

"What if they figured out something, maybe from Naima? What if they can take away your powers?"

"Then you and Holly and Marcos should run."

It was the best advice I had.

I went down the stairs and opened the front door, flipping on the outside light and standing in the pool of its glow, essentially announcing myself to whoever it was in the car. There was no movement, so I simply walked across the street.

As I approached the car, it became clear someone was in the driver's seat, sitting low to avoid notice. It was a man in a dark jacket. He didn't try to hide from me, really. And he didn't startle and try to drive off. In other words, he wasn't terribly intimidated by me, and that was probably the thing that pricked up the hairs on the back of my neck.

Stopping beside the car, I waited. *Your move, dude.*

Nothing happened for a second, then slowly the window went down with a slight mechanic whir. The man didn't say a thing, he just reached a hand out the open window, holding something flat and black. A phone.

Without warning, the screen lit up, announcing an incoming call from a number I didn't recognize. The man did nothing to answer the call, just held the phone out for me. So I took the hint, snatched up the flat black device, and swiped to answer.

"Yeah?"

He chuckled first, so smug. "Hello, John, old friend. It's good to hear from you again."

"How do you know where I am?" I said.

Sol *tsked* me. "John, John, John. It's simply too easy to track people these days. We all love these devices so much."

I suddenly understood. "You bugged my phone?"

"No, please, John. I'm no international espionage agent. I didn't *bug* anything. I just had my friend gain access to your phone. From then on, I could track you online with ease."

"Your friend?" Damn. That guy who broke into our house and hurt my mother. Of course. I shook my head, annoyed with myself for being so stupid. "Fine. So you know where I am. What are you going to do about it? You've already gone and blurted my name out to the world."

"Ah, yes, so I did. Apologies, John. But I prefer a fair fight. No fair if you're always sneaking around, correct? In this fashion, I know where you are and you know where I am."

I laughed. "But I don't know where you are. Why don't you make it a fair fight and tell me."

"Yes, of course. That is precisely the intent of my call. You may find me any time you wish." That's when Sol rattled off the address of Babilu Tower, his luxury building in the city.

"So that's where your little interviews have been happening, huh?"

"Yes."

"But this still isn't a fair fight," I said.

"How so, John? Is it because you have your friends Bobby and Pip on your side, and even your sister, Holly?" Once more, Sol chuckled, a sound that made me involuntarily clench my fists.

"No, you can leave all of them out of it."

"Then what is it you consider so unfair, John? Please tell me, as I very much wish to make everything between us *even*. Everything." His words were like a polished, poisoned apple, enticing me forward, even though I knew the risks.

Still, I thought I had something over him. "You announced my name to the world. You yourself said how easy people are to track. So soon, very soon, everyone will know where to find me. But you won't even let your interviewers tell people where you are. That's not fair. We both know the government now has an interest in us all. If they know how to find me but not you, that puts me at a disadvantage."

The line was silent. I imagined Sol frowning, thinking of the issue, and what to do about it. "Then I shall tell the world where to find me. It is time now for us to move forward anyway, is it not, John? Time for us to take our rightful places atop the… what's the word I'm looking for here? Ah, yes. Atop the *food chain*. The whims of government are nothing to us anymore."

I looked at the man in the dark jacket sitting in the car before me, practically ignoring my entire conversation with his boss, Sol. "Fine, then. You tell the world where you are, and we'll talk. And then what?"

"*And then what?*" he echoed. "Ah, John, come now. Some things in life must retain their mystery, wouldn't you agree?"

8

Sol called off his lackey after our little chat. The guy took his phone, drove off, and we were alone again. For about 30 seconds.

Once people knew my name, it took no time at all for them to converge again upon our house — heck, I imagine many of the paparazzi still had us saved in their GPS from my previous disappearances. Of course, we weren't there. But I heard about it.

From Carrie.

My phone buzzed and I saw her name. Fumbling for it, I swiped to answer. "Oh, you're there," she said. Not *hello.*

So of course I knew Carrie was upset. "What's wrong?" I asked, feeling the pointlessness of asking from so far away.

"The world knows about you, John. But they don't know where you are, yet, so they want to talk to me, or anyone else they can get their hands on." Carrie huffed. "Mostly me."

Why? Of course, I knew why. Ask around for five minutes. *Who were his "known associates"?* That wouldn't take long, would it?

I remembered the hellish days of paparazzi parked outside the front door of my house 24/7, and I hung my head. "I'm sorry, Carrie. I wish Sol hadn't said anything. I wish you weren't involved."

"But I *am* involved, John. One way or the other, you know? Good or bad." Her words carried weight, reminded me that she cared. "I just wish I could actually *do* something to help."

I smiled. "You are. Just knowing that, once all this craziness is done with, you're there. That means the world to me." If you think that was gushy and over the top, then you don't want to hear the rest.

I sat on the front step of Marcos's house, exchanging promises with Carrie I really didn't know if I could keep. That's when the van rolled up.

Not Sol's henchman. Not a government agent. A white van, with a logo on the side.

Some enterprising newsman had guessed right, choosing to check in on my cousin (uncle?) Marcos. And I had the misfortune of being right there to confirm everything.

"I've gotta go, Carrie. They found me," I said.

"John…?" I heard her breathing, not saying anything.

"Yeah?"

"Good luck."

* * *

Sure, we could keep running, but what would be the point? We didn't have enough cash to be invisible forever, and, let's face it, a trio of jet-black-haired people, a mother, son, and daughter in a wheelchair… it wouldn't take long to get recognized, no matter where we went.

So I did nothing. I ended the call with Carrie and sat there, on the front step, just looking at the two men pulling equipment from the van.

"John Black? Is it true that you're the superhuman known as Black Sword?" the reporter asked, as his cameraman counterpart trailed him, awkwardly lugging the big black equipment.

I nodded.

"Is that a yes?"

Shaking my head at the lunacy of it all, I figured, why not? The hiding was done. "Yes. My name is John Black, and I am Black Sword."

The reporter froze, just on the edge of the property. I guess there were still some protocols people respected. "Can you… can you *prove* it?"

I clenched my fists. What was I? A trained monkey? "You don't want me to do that," I said.

"Actually, John, it would mean a lot, to the world, to know for sure." The man looked tense and giddy. Certainly he thought he was about to get footage that would change his career, maybe change his life. I looked at the logo on the side of the van, recognizing it as one of the smaller stations in the city. Maybe soon this intrepid reporter would be jumping to a new, higher-paying gig across town.

"You know, I could just do what I did to all those helicopter pilots…" I let that set in for the reporter and cameraman, watching their facial expression collapse. And then, I simply stood, turned, and went inside.

Mom met me at the stairs. "What is it, John?" she asked.

"They're here."

9

Holly refused to come out of her room, one of the several generally unused bedrooms in Marcos's house. Mom tried, but of course I could communicate better with my sister than anyone else, so the job fell to me.

I knocked lightly and heard no sounds of protest. Opening the door, I went to Holly and pressed my forehead against hers.

What's shakin', Hol?

Shaking? she asked.

Just an expression, sis. What's going on?

Nothing.

Really, Hol? Mom says you won't leave the room.

She nodded. *Because* they *are out there.* Her body twitched a bit at the word *they*.

I know, Holly.

That made her twitch even more. *No, John, you don't know. I'm not afraid of them anymore. I'm mad at them.*

What? Why?

Because they don't care about me *at all. They only care about* Black Sword.

What do you say to your sister, via mental telepathy, when she says something like that? Please tell me, because I had no response.

An uncomfortable moment passed.

Admit it, John. You love it.

Huh?

A spider appeared on my sister's shoulder, crawling into view. Then another.

Holly, please. No. I don't love it. And, more importantly, I have nothing to do with it. What people say about me isn't my fault, is it?

Another uncomfortable moment passed. And then, without warning, the spiders winked out of existence, first one, then the other.

Holly, how do you do that?

She considered how to answer, looking sidelong at me with a mischievous grin. *Do you want me to show you?*

Did I? My sister could create life from nothing. Or maybe it came out of her. If the giant Gorgols had been channeled from her fear and anger, what were these little spiders? What did they represent? What part of Holly fueled them to life?

More importantly, did I trust myself with the ability to make life? I knew my powers pretty well, but I had no concept of how Holly did what she did.

Not only could she make life, she could end life instantly, with a thought.

Holly, where did Gorgol Alpha go? When you made her disappear?

I told you, John. I don't know.

I nodded, but needed to dig further. *Sure. But you said you made Alpha. From you. If you opened a doorway and made Alpha out of you, and then you made another doorway that took Alpha away, doesn't that mean that Alpha is back inside of you?*

Maybe.

Can you feel her?

Holly shivered. *No, of course not.*

Why not? Why do you say of course not?

My sister looked at me like I was simply the greatest of fools. *Because Alpha is me, and if Alpha is back inside me, then the only thing in me is me. How can I feel me inside me? I don't think you can feel you inside you, can you?* Holly made a harumphing sound inside my head in annoyance.

I took a moment to string together the logic. *I guess so.* I looked into Holly's eyes and could see she was still so upset. So unsatisfied.

Is there anything more awful in life, more disturbing to one's psyche, than to be perpetually unsatisfied? I don't think so. But… what could I do to help her?

Holly. What is it you want?

I don't understand, John.

Ugh, can you stop with the John *stuff? Can't I be your brother again? Can't I be* Johnny*?* She didn't reply, she only shrugged. After a moment, I asked again. *What do you want?*

I think you know, she said.

Please, Hol. Tell me.

And then Holly lifted herself gently but mesmerizingly out of her wheelchair, to hover before me in that strange, ethereal way. *John, all I want is for people to actually care about me. To really give a damn what I think or say or do or…* A tear welled out of one eye and stained her cheek. *Or feel.*

Holly, I care. I really and truly do.

She let herself float back down to her chair. *I know, Johnny. And I know I shouldn't be mad at you. But when I sit here thinking about it, I realize that I* made *the Gorgols and no one cares. You killed them, and everyone does.*

The Gorgols killed a lot of people, Holly. They had to be dealt with. People were terrified and wanted something done. She winced. Maybe I'd gone too far. After all, she didn't *mean* to make the Gorgols. She didn't mean for them to trample all over things. The guilt must have consumed her. I studied her face, but her emotions were unreadable. *Let's go outside then, Holly. The game's up anyway. Everyone knows we're here and everyone* — I paused, catching myself.

And everyone knows who you *are? Is that what you meant to say?*

I grinned a sheepish grin. *Yeah, sorry. I was going to say that.*

No, John. I don't want to be introduced to the world by you, like some kind of afterthought. Some kind of dumb sidekick. I guess Holly had been watching a lot of TV. *I want to announce* myself. *When I'm ready, the way* I *want to do it. Then people will know me and…*

Just like that, it was my turn to fill in the end of her sentence. And what? She wanted people to know her and… Oh my God, the memories of the bloodlust came back to me.

And fear *you? Is that what you meant to say, Holly?*

My sister was silent.

10

"Why are we here, Mom? Who are these people?" Sharif sat beside Naima on the couch, pressing himself into her. His voice cracked, making him sound years younger than his already young age. Naima blinked, saying nothing.

Something was different this time with their captivity. When they'd been taken by the government that first time, it was clinical, organized. Comfortable enough, but nothing special. Nondescript. There was absolutely no contact with anyone else, except of course the interrogators. Naima and Sharif had been separated, then. But their new captors let them stay together. If it was possible to thank evil people for small courtesies, Naima thanked them. They didn't have to beg or bargain for shelter, or food, or warmth. Given where they had come from — a homeless shelter — Naima almost thought their lives had improved. I know, Stockholm syndrome. But really, it was better than the alternative. Still, what could she tell the boy?

"This is all my fault, son," she said.

It didn't help matters that they were kept in what amounted to a luxury apartment. Even as a well-paid physician, she would have been hard pressed to afford the furniture, decorations, and appointments that filled the place with an almost uncomfortable level of posh.

Sharif pushed himself harder against her, hugging her. "Don't say that, Mom. You didn't do anything on purpose. You don't even know *why* you can take their powers away."

Naima put a hand on his head. Her son, so young, already having lived through so much. And to think, she used to worry about the effects of divorce on the boy. "No, I don't know why I can take their powers. I wish I had never laid eyes on any of them." A tinge of bitterness seeped into her voice.

The door opened without warning, and a man entered holding a tray loaded with food. "Eat. Then get ready for the test." Without another glance toward them, the man turned toward the door.

"Let us go. Please," she said to his back.

"That's not my decision to make."

"Then who? Can we talk to the person in charge?"

The man stopped cold, laughing. "Not likely, lady. He explicitly gave orders for you to be kept away from him. Far away."

That was proof enough for her. Her captor had to be the man from TV, the one with power, the man who once fought the military, killing who knows how many people, who claimed to have died and returned. "Sol?"

The man touched one index finger to the tip of his nose, the other index finger pointing at Naima. "*Bingo*." He laughed again before continuing toward the door.

"Then who are you?" she asked as he stepped out into the hall.

The man turned and stared into her eyes as he pulled the door closed. "I am the Way of the Sun," he said.

* * *

The test.

It was always the same. Once a day, Naima was taken to a cavernous room lined with row after row of chairs, simple black faux leather on metal. On the far side of the room was a raised dais with a naked wooden podium sitting off to one side. Directly in the middle of the dais, centered on the aisle that split the rows of chairs, stood a tall, blonde woman. Half a dozen men in dark suits lined the sides of the room, observing.

For each test, Naima was escorted through the door at the rear of the room, the farthest point from the dais, and aimed directly toward the woman onstage. A woman she remembered clearly. The reason she was in this mess in the first place. Jane Doe VI, aka Margrethe Vit.

Sharif was told to sit in one of the chairs, as usual, and not to interrupt. Naima nodded to him, a pale reassurance.

And then the test began. At regular intervals along the rows of chairs, objects floated into the air — books, all alike, in five sets of two. Naima knew this was Margrethe's doing, using her mind to levitate the books.

"Begin," Margrethe said in her husky voice.

Naima hesitated. She didn't like being forced to do their little experiment, didn't like what it might mean. What if they found out something they didn't like? What would they do to her, to Sharif? Still, it wasn't like the test hurt her or anything. All she had to do was walk.

She took a careful step forward. Having performed the test before, she knew they wanted her to go slow, one step at a time. Gradually she approached the first set of hovering books, one on her left and one on her right. For some reason, they always made her feel strange. So unnatural for books to hang in the air, untouched.

Naima passed the first set of books, still moving deliberately. She approached the second set, and in time passed them as well. As she neared the third set, she became anxious. *Soon*, she thought. *Maybe five more steps.*

She took a single step forward, and all around her books fell out of the air, startling her with their echoing sound in the cavernous room. Naima looked at Margrethe, and for a moment, their expressions were matched: surprise.

Quickly, Margrethe blinked and looked away, putting a scowl on her face in an attempted show of strength. “Distance?” she said in a growl.

One of the dark-suited men approached Naima, looking down toward her feet. There, a long tape measure had been affixed to the floor along the row of chairs to her left. The numbers on the tape measure descended as they approached the dais. She could only assume they reached zero just where Margrethe stood.

“Forty-six feet, seven inches. Maybe seven and a half.”

On stage, Margrethe rolled her eyes. “I don’t care about half inches.”

Forty-six feet, seven inches, Naima thought. The day before it had been under 46. The first time she had done the test, only days previous, it had been in the thirties. And she remembered that first day, the time when she had to get close enough to touch Margrethe.

What was happening to her? Her power was growing. Well, her *sphere of influence* was growing.

But I never affect the books themselves, Naima thought. *It’s only when I get closer to* her *that I shut her down and then the books fall.*

I wonder what would happen if I touched her.

I wonder if I could take away her power. Or his.

I wonder if I could take it all away.

Forever.

11

All of a sudden, I understood — at least partially — how Holly felt. Trapped, with not so much an urge as a need to get out.

But how do you get out of your life?

Holly couldn't. She was who she was.

And I couldn't either.

Which meant I'd have to figure out how to live in the new reality of being a known person, just as Holly had to figure out how to live her life.

And then I remembered that Holly started making spiders.

Was that a good thing? Not likely.

What would I do, when the frustration set in?

What would they say back at school? Hold on. That's a laugh. Did I even need to go back to school? I mean, isn't the point of going to school to become educated so you can be a productive member of society and contribute to the workforce? That wasn't really my lot in life anymore, now, was it?

Sorry. I have a lot of questions.

All right. Time to figure shit out.

Sol said he wanted revenge, sent people to break into my house and tap my phone, and then went ahead and told the world who I was. Pretty sure those were all related events. Of course, I *did* kill him that one time, so I can understand why he'd choose me to be the target of his vengeance.

What to do?

I started thinking of the foes I had faced… Petrus, Margrethe, Sol, Gorgol Omicron, Gorgol Sigma, Jake Weissman. I didn't have a lot of ticks in the L column. So somewhere in that angry part of my brain, the part that wasn't totally okay, a seed was planted.

I can take him. I can beat Sol. Him and all his silly minions, his Way of the Sun.

In other words, I started to believe I really was a hero.

Idiot.

Just for the record, believing you're a hero is almost definitely the road to doom. You start believing you're infallible. That any outcome you think is best for you will definitely happen. Also, it's not terribly appealing. Even if you're squeaky clean, a real do-gooder, there are going to be people who hate you *despite* all that. Or even *because* of it. Like, they're mad that you're doing good. Don't try to rationalize this. People aren't rational.

Think of it this way. Pools of water are often rectangular, right? But does water usually configure itself that way? Heck, no. Water is usually found in crazy amorphously shaped ponds and lakes and oceans. But when *man* tries to create a body of water, he often tries to impose order upon it. *Let's make it rectangular! That'll be straight up awesome!*

The real world doesn't work like that.

Just like the real world doesn't understand the word *rational*. What's rational about a tornado suddenly plopping down beside a farmhouse and ripping it to shreds? What's rational about a squirrel jumping in front of your car?

The real world doesn't *do* rational. Nope.

So the rational thing was that I would will myself to be the hero, the world would rally around me, and I would win. But in our imperfect, irrational world, I suppose I had what could only be called a snowball's chance in hell.

It always comes back to snow, right?

I tried not to be overly smug about the whole idea of being a hero, but that smugness was in there, bubbling to a boil. And it made me do some things I wouldn't normally do.

"John Black, can I talk to you?" a high voice called from behind the wooden fence in Marcos's backyard.

I stopped moving. I had been fluidly practicing with my belt swords, swooping around in liquid circles impossible for any regular human. By which I mean to say, if you have solid, unbending bones, the moves I used would be hard to pull off. "Isn't it about 100-percent illegal for you to be here?" I said, turning toward the voice, seeing the woman attached to it.

I admit I goggled a bit. She was strikingly pretty, in her early 20s with shoulder-length blonde waves, slightly darker at the roots, and dark eyebrows that clearly defined her hair color as a choice, not a given. The day had been warm, and she wore a grey dress, knee length, that seemed business-like, yet appealing.

I know. If Carrie reads this, I'm dead.

"I've made arrangements with the property owner, your neighbor, so I'm here with permission. And I don't believe there's any law forbidding me from looking in your direction or talking to you."

I thought about it for a moment, then shrugged. She certainly was on the neighbor's land, owned by a suspicious older man named Mr. Bowman. He lived with an ancient black cat named Cooper, and neither of them liked company. I remembered the money the media had dangled in front of me, the wealth I had been offered just to talk.

I wasn't surprised to learn there might be offers to Mr. Bowman for the temporary rental of his land. He might not love strangers clomping around his backyard, but one can turn a blind eye when one is counting one's money. Can't one? I sound pretentious.

"So, can we talk?" she asked. A reporter, obviously. And I'll admit, I wasn't against the idea. What hormonal teen wouldn't agree to something in order to spend time with someone they found attractive? Male, female, unsure, whatever. We all like to have attention paid to us, right?

Putting away my belt swords and standing in my sweat-stained t-shirt, I said yes. With two conditions. "First, what's your name? And second, you stay where you are. I stay where I am. Oh, and third, when I'm done, I'm done." I thought for a moment. "And this isn't an exclusive. I talk to who I want, when I want." That was probably like four conditions, but whatever.

The woman looked confused for a moment. "All agreed. My name is Marietta Pollis. And, so you know, technically, with no other reporters around, this *is* an exclusive."

"Fine, sure, but I mean, I don't *owe* you anything exclusive after this." My cheeks turned red, as this attractive, older, more sophisticated woman schooled me on her business.

"Can I record our conversation?" she asked with a practiced and interesting raised eyebrow.

"*You* can, but you can't bring in anyone else to shoot it. We start now, or we start never." I suddenly felt bold. Or maybe I was trying to impress her with my decisiveness. I did mention I was an idiot, right?

"Fine," she said, pulling out a phone and tapping the screen until she was recording me. She held her phone hand steady, then looked me in the eye. "How would you describe yourself in relation to the superhuman Sol?"

I smirked. "We're not exactly buddies."

Marietta nodded. "Sol has said he seeks revenge. Is that on you?"

"Probably. I mean, yeah. Well, who else? I did kill him, once."

She looked down at some notes she had. "Now that Sol has publicly announced his location, do you plan to approach him? Fight him?" She looked up.

So he did it, I thought. I was surprised. "Where did he say he is?"

"Babilu Tower, in the city," Marietta said. So at least on that point, Sol told the truth, and now we were both in the spotlight, if the government decided to do a superhuman roll-call. "So I'll ask again. Are you planning to go to Sol, now that you know where to find him?"

"No. No, of course not. Not at all. I'm done with him," I said, smugly, seriously. "Never want to see him again."

I was lying.

Of course the answer was yes.

12

I know you're planning something, John, Holly said.

Is it that obvious?

She nodded. *You do the same things all the time. But the one thing you never do is just sit quietly.*

So not true! I do nothing all the time! Quite the rebuttal, eh?

That's not what I mean, John. Sure, you sit around, but it's your mind. I can feel it. It's... far away. Is it because of her?

Who, Carrie? Yeah, of course, but...

But there's more?

Yeah.

Holly kept looking at me, even as a tiny spider popped into existence in her hand. It crawled across her palm, but she didn't seem to notice it at all. *You're going to him.*

Who? What are you talking about?

Give me a break, John. Sol. You're going to Sol.

There was no point in lying to someone who was already inside your mind, right? *Of course I am, Holly. What choice do I have? Everything, all of this has been because of Sol. Your kidnapping, him saying my name on TV, the reason why we ran away. I mean, even the Gorgols are* his *fault. If he hadn't taken you away, if you hadn't lived through that, then none of that stuff would have happened.*

I don't know, John. Another spider appeared, even as the first winked out of existence.

The lines of a song popped into my head. "*Where did you come from? Where did you go?*"

What's that supposed to mean, John? Holly asked.

Oops, forgot she could hear my mind. *It's just that old song.*

Okay, so you're going to Sol, I guess for a big showdown, right?

I guess so, yeah.

Then I have a question for you. What happens if you fail? What happens if he kills you? Then what?

I shrugged. *If that happens, there is no "then what?" for me.*

I mean for us. *For Mom and me, and even for your friends.*

I don't know. I guess someone else will have to give it a try after me. To pick up the gauntlet, so to speak.

It's that important to get rid of Sol?

It is. He's bad, Holly. You know it, probably more than anyone. And now he talks about things changing, not needing government anymore. This revenge nonsense, the fact that Naima can take away powers but no one knows where she is. He's got some sort of plan, and I think all of us are going to regret it if we let him do what he has in mind.

Holly nodded in agreement. *And if you walk in his front door, aren't you giving him just what he wants? If he kills you, you're just going to be helping him out.*

She was right, and I told her so. So there had to be another way. Sol lived atop a giant glass and steel building in the center of the big city, surrounded by an army of people intent on doing his bidding. All I had to do was break in, not be caught or even seen, find Sol, and figure out some way to kill him, despite the fact that he seemed to be distinctly unkillable.

Simple, right?

I was doomed.

Take me with you, Holly said.

No way, I said, too quickly. Almost arrogantly. Holly felt it. The dismissal, me thinking I could do something she couldn't.

Why not? You told me yourself back in the desert that he was afraid of me.

I'm afraid of you, sis! I joked.

She didn't laugh. *Take me with you.*

Holly was so powerful, in ways I admittedly didn't understand. But if I had a hard time figuring out how *I* was going to get to Sol, how would I get Holly there, too?

She felt my thoughts, although I hadn't sent her any words.

You know, sometimes Sol's fear *can seem more respectful than your* protection, *big brother. One day, maybe you'll stop underestimating me, John.*

* * *

I plugged in my phone to recharge it, leaving it on the bedside table in my room in Marcos's house. It's sad, but I almost shed a little tear. After years of wishing, I'd been granted a phone and now I was leaving it behind.

Well, not immediately. I wanted to establish a pattern, of the phone being in one place. That was the digital-tracking side of things. But there was also the human side.

At the foot of Marcos's front yard, there were four white vans with satellite dishes growing from their roofs like sterile flowers. The yard itself had been lined with yellow police tape, and a couple of cops stood guard. Beyond them were reporters and cameras and the mass of humanity who could somehow appear out of nowhere whenever *something* was happening.

Now, *I* was happening.

If that sounds arrogant, I apologize, but it's true. All those people came to see me, the superhuman. And, because I wanted Sol to continue to believe that I was at home, I needed to be seen.

I cracked open the front door, and immediately the buzzing of excitement increased, like a beehive that's been struck with a baseball bat. The bees started clicking their cameras, yelling their questions. I left the door wide open and stepped onto the front porch, then down the few stairs to the walkway.

It was strictly a show. I had nothing important to do or say, I just wanted it on record that I was *there*. Taking casual strides forward, I approached the mob. There were so many shouted questions being shouted, I don't think I could even distinguish one from the other.

Without thought, I said the only thing that came to mind: "Hello, everyone." The din of their questions buried my words.

"Everybody, be quiet — he's trying to say something!" someone shouted from the back.

Miraculously, the others calmed, just enough that I thought I might actually be heard. "Um, hi," I said.

There were twitters of laughter in the crowd. Someone boldly yelled back. "Hi, Black Sword! Hi, John Black!" More laughter. I almost thought they were making fun of me, but it seemed good-hearted, like they were all just excited to be there.

I gave a little wave. "I just wanted to say that there are a lot of family members and friends that never knew who I was — well, I mean, *what* I was. What I am." I screwed up my face in embarrassment from the way I was speaking. I was no Sol. These were no polished remarks, no rehearsals. Just me spouting off whatever came to mind. "Anyway, I just wanted to say that if any of my family or friends feels offended, I'm sorry." There was, unbelievably, silence. And finally, I said the one thing I meant more than anything else. "I just wanted to try to have a normal life."

The silence was suddenly broken by a gasp. I quickly scanned the crowd, trying to figure out who was so surprised by my comment. And that's when I noticed they weren't even looking at me. It wasn't about me at all. They were looking past me.

They looked shocked. They looked stunned. And, possibly more than anything else, they looked scared.

I turned, trying to find the source of it all, and there on the front porch was Holly and her wheelchair. She had rolled herself right out the open door.

My kid sister wore a white dress, and her long, jet-black hair hung down on both sides of her face. But, that face! Her face! My sister! She radiated light, energy. The sense of power coming off her was unmistakable, and I realized that, in comparison, I must have looked remarkably dull.

Holly was hovering above her wheelchair, in midair, glowing with energy. She looked like an angel, or maybe a god. Something supernatural, something of *strength.*

"His sister's superhuman, too?" someone yelled, a question.

"My God, she's like a ghost!"

"Or a shadow!" another cried.

"Shadow Ghost!" More voices chimed in, and it became a sort of chant, and I knew there would be no changing it. The people had agreed.

The electricity in the air increased, and the crowd, *my* crowd, forgot I even existed.

They only wanted to see one thing.

Shadow Ghost.

13

“I think I know what you’re planning to do, John, and if you’ll humor me — your part-time teacher — I’d like to give you another lesson before you go.” Marcos was reading his newspaper, not even making eye contact.

“Go?” I said, too coy.

“To Sol? Perhaps to end this conflict?” Marcos said. “If I’m wrong, please tell me. But I see the way you’ve been behaving. Distant. Contemplative. And I see your eyes now, betraying your words.”

I sighed. Two of the three people I lived with knew my plan. I might as well own up to it. “Does Mom know, too?”

Marcos lowered the paper, shrugging. “I couldn’t say for sure, but if I know you only one-tenth as much as she does — maybe one-hundredth — then I suspect she does.”

Some hero I was. Everyone could see right through me. Did that mean Sol could as well? That he could tell I would soon be coming for him?

I didn’t want to know the answer.

“So, what do you say?” Marcos asked.

“What was the question?” I rubbed at one temple, annoyed.

“A lesson? I’d like not to say a *final* lesson. So let’s just call it a *summary* instead. Sound good?”

I nodded, and moments later Marcos led me down to the basement. I moved to a clear area and struck a ready pose. “Okay, whenever you want to start.”

Marcos calmly sat on the floor, crossing his legs. "Sit down, John, please." He patted the floor in front of him, and suddenly I felt like a five-year-old, called to the reading circle in kindergarten. "Your skill at martial arts is, of course, minimal. We've only had a short time together, and while I consider myself a good teacher, there's only so much I can do."

I gave Marcos a sideways glance. Was he insulting me? *No*, I thought. *He's making a joke, a very dry joke.* I smiled and Marcos echoed me with a devious gleam in his eye.

"Still," he continued, "there's no doubting that physically, I'm no match for you. The things you can do are nothing short of incredible. There is a thing I've been striving for, for quite a long time. I don't think I'll ever achieve it."

"What's that?"

"To move without thought. To become a singularity of purpose, in tune with everything around me, able to flow into stance, to deflect, to strike, without the necessary lag time of *thought*. But *you*..."

"It isn't really me. I don't believe that," I said. "I've been infected, or enhanced, or changed." I told him, briefly, about the thorns in my cells, about my comet and snowfall theory. He only listened quietly. "But it isn't *me*."

Finally, Marcos nodded. "It is, John. You are you, and while you can change, or be changed, or even infected, you are still you. *You* can do incredible things." I thought about it, letting his words sink in. Somehow it felt good to admit it was me. It felt right. Maybe too right. Then he continued. "But you can also do terrible things. And that's what I wanted to talk to about. That is your lesson today. A sort of final exam for our semester together."

A test. Great.

"Picture your opponent."

“You mean Sol?”

Marcos nodded slowly. “You’re wounded. Tired. Nearly spent. Before you, Sol is beaming, feeling victorious. What do you feel?”

It was a scene I could easily picture, and without bidding, my anger arose. I didn’t speak.

Marcos waited, then answered for me. “You feel anger. This man has done so much to you, to your family, to the world, and you’re nearly beaten by him. If you pool your energy, all that is left, you might be able to strike a final time. What do you do?”

Immediately, I answered. “I strike, in whatever way I can. With my last breath, if necessary.” I sounded grim, the scenario all too real.

Marcos nodded again. “At this very moment, higher and to your left, you see your mother, held by Sol over a very great chasm. She is terrified, and the fall would most certainly kill her.”

Once more I was quiet. All of a sudden, I didn’t like where this was heading.

He paused, eyeing me, like he was probing my mind. It vaguely occurred to me that I could probe *his* mind, perhaps beat his little test with a little cheating. But no. Marcos was a good man, and he had a point to make. I didn’t need to cheat. I would see the test through.

“And high on your right, Sol holds your sister. Somehow, she’s powerless, and she too is hanging above a great opening, held only by his will.”

Marcos stopped talking and raised one eyebrow at me. The air seemed to grow dense between us. This was, of course, the test.

“What do I do?” I asked.

Marcos nodded once, a motion barely detectable.

"I save my mother and sister, and then I destroy Sol," I replied dryly.

"But you can't," he said. "You only have enough strength for one act. If you kill Sol, your mother and sister perish. If you save either your mother or sister, the other perishes and Sol will attack. One act. Only. What do you do?"

You know, I always *hated* tests like this. Choose one and only one answer, from a list of options that all suck.

"Okay. Where are we?" I probed.

Marcos responded as if he hadn't expected such a question. "Does it matter?"

"I think so."

"Fine," he said, turning up one open palm, granting my request. "You're in a void. No one else is present. There's nothing around that can possibly aid you. You must make this choice completely alone. This, John, is your final exam. Only one answer can be given. And while I don't think of myself as a judgmental person, this answer will be judged, for, truly John, all of your actions forevermore will be judged. You're superhuman and now the world knows you. What will you do, Black Sword?"

I hesitated. There was no answer to give. Success and death, or death and failure.

Um, Marcos, I choose D. None of the above. Thanks.

But I had to do something. One answer only. My sister and mother had to be saved. Sol had to be stopped. There had to be a way.

"John?" Marcos queried.

I held up a single index finger at him for more time, my eyes down at the ground.

More time passed.

Marcos was patient, more patient than any real combat scenario, certainly. "John, Sol is restless. He will not wait. Your answer, now please. Or Sol's answer is to release your mother and sister to die as he cuts you down."

The morbid reality was there in front of me. Choose death or death? I didn't want to choose either.

Trying to wave off Marcos off, I sliced one hand through the air defiantly, left to right.

Wait.

That's it.

"John? Your ans—"

I interrupted. "When I fought Petrus, he attacked my mind, and I fought back with a spike of iron directly into his brain."

"Is this an answer, John? One answer only, please," he cautioned.

"Yes, it's *my* answer," I said, suddenly confident. "With all the power remaining in my body and mind, no matter if it kills me, I lash out and form a flat plane of iron across my field of vision."

Marcos squinted, confused. "And…?"

"On my left, this iron plane catches my mother's fall. On my right, it also catches Holly."

"And Sol?" Marcos says, with a tinge of fear in his voice.

"In the middle, Sol is cut in two, directly through the most delicate portions of his brain. Rendered useless forevermore."

"Not killed, though?"

"No, not killed," I said. "I don't trust he can die, and I wouldn't want him to die that cleanly, anyway. He needs to *feel* it. He needs to be *sterilized*."

Marcos's eyes widened and his skin paled as he pulled away from me.

14

I told my mom. I mean, it'd be pretty crappy not to, right?

She wasn't happy that I was going, once more to face Sol, but she knew our family would never have peace otherwise. And she knew that even if she told me not to, I'd sneak out and do it anyway.

"Tell me something, John," Mom said.

"Sure."

"What is it that makes this time different?"

Ah, the weight of a single, simple question. What *did* make this time different? Anything at all? Did I have a better plan this time around? Not really. My plan consisted solely of "get to him before he knows you're there." I tried to explain this to my mother using a lot of big words to make it sound complex and rational.

She sat the way she so often did after the attack in the kitchen, with one arm wrapping her midsection, like a security blanket. Something inside her still wasn't right. "That's it?" she asked. I guess she saw through me that quickly, huh?

"Yeah, well, okay, it is. But when I get there, I plan to observe things. Make a better plan."

"Fine," Mom said. "But humor me. Humor Holly and Marcos. Why don't we all discuss this, to see if we can help?" It was a reasonable request. How could I refuse?

* * *

We sat at Marcos's big kitchen table, me idly scraping at the wooden surface with a fingernail.

I haven't trimmed my fingernails in what? Years? And, come to think of it, when was my last haircut? Boy, superpowers had some weird side effects.

"Okay," Mom started. "The topic is Sol, and all ideas are welcome. First, what do we know about him?"

I raised a hand, and Mom looked at me with a funny grimace, nodding for me to proceed. "I suppose I know the most, so I'll go first." I cleared my throat. "Sol is, of course, a superhuman. I first met him at the boardwalk when I turned 14. I thought it was random, but superhumans emit a sort of mental sound that I call our *beacon*. He must have heard mine and came to find me. After that, he tried to recruit me for a sort of scheme to take over civilization, and I wouldn't do it, so he kidnapped Holly. I chased him down, and, well, I killed him in the desert." I hung my head for a moment, not really used to admitting out loud that I was a murderer. "Anyway, that didn't last, because apparently the same things that make us superhuman — these thorns in our cells, I think — allowed him to take over the body of Jake Weissman and then return from the dead. As Jake, or Ranger if you like, he managed to direct the Gorgol monsters toward us, but Bobby, Pip, and I were able to mostly handle them." I looked at Holly for a moment. *Okay to tell them, Hol?*

I have no secrets anymore, John. She sounded so stern. What happened to my little sister?

"Holly made the Gorgols, out of thin air, so at the end, she, I don't know, *unmade* Alpha. Does that sound about right, Holly?"

"Y-yes," Holly spoke. That was enough for all of us to turn, wide-eyed. But the look on her face told us to move on.

"Anyway, just before Holly took care of Alpha, I sort of *blew up* Jake, and that was enough to bring Sol out again. Now that he's back, he's taken over that Babilu building in the city, and he has who knows how many people following him. They call themselves the

Way of the Sun, and they seem like they'll do anything for him." I let that sink in. "Oh, and Margrethe is with him again. She's superhuman, too, and she pretty much hates me."

"Why?" Marcos asked.

I turned away, sheepishly. "I kind of erased her boyfriend's mind. No, not *erased. Destroyed.* He won't be coming back from what I did. Ever."

"Then do that, to Sol," Marcos said.

Simple, right? Blast away Sol's mind like I had done to Petrus. Problem solved.

"It's not so easy," I said. "First, Petrus attacked me, by tricking me into opening my mind and then using that opening to his advantage. It nearly killed me. I struck back with everything I had and got lucky. I doubt Sol would be tricked into creating such an opening, and even if he did, he's stronger than Petrus. *I* might end up being the one who's left catatonic in a closet."

"Any other ideas?" Mom asked.

"There's Naima, of course," I said.

"Naima?" Marcos asked.

"Yeah, she's sort of like us, but opposite. When she's nearby, our powers go *poof*! Gone."

"That seems remarkably useful in defeating this foe, wouldn't you say?" Marcos said.

I shrugged. "Yes and no. The problem is, if we're close enough, Naima cancels out my power, too."

"Hmm," Marcos said. "I realize I'm sort of the outsider here. Obviously I've known about superhumans since you all first made news, but I didn't know *they* were *you*. Still, my take on Sol is that his arrogance makes him act without thought. Perhaps you really can trick him into opening his mind, if you play to his ego. And, if you happen to be able to get this Naima person close to *Sol* but not too close to *you*, that would be a huge help."

I considered it for a while, we all did, in silence.

"Okay, well, Naima is a wildcard, since we have no idea where she is," I said. "If I can use her ability to cancel his, while still having power myself, I'll do that. But there's no guarantee she'll even factor into the equation. So, short of her miraculously appearing, I need a plan of my own. Clearly I'm not going to go to the city with my beacon blazing. I'll be in a sort of stealth mode. I could sneak up on him, then surprise him by turning my beacon back on. Maybe he'd be so shocked that he'd lash out, and maybe that would leave him open to an attack… *if* I'm close enough and come at him in a way he doesn't expect."

We looked at each other, back and forth. No one seemed to have any other ideas.

Then Holly chimed in, her thoughts broadcasting only to me. The look on her face was something dark, probably disappointment. Or anger.

But her words in my head were worse, tainted black and dripping with something I couldn't quite understand.

As usual, everyone forgets about me.

15

I had to leave Holly behind. Had to. It sucked, and yeah, I'd have liked to have her power on my side, but I needed to move silently, unobserved. Holly was royally pissed at me, but what could I do? I'd make it up to her later, somehow.

The next evening, just as it was getting dark, I left via the back door, jumped the fence, and slipped into the woods beyond. For a while, I stood in the dark, reaching out with my mental powers, seeing if there were any minds out there watching me. After a time, I was satisfied I was alone, so I began to walk, sparing only one last glance at the house.

Did I see the shadow of Holly by the back door, glaring at me? I hoped it was just my imagination.

Making my way through the short woods and into town, I used my own special style of travel arrangement — a.k.a. mind-pushing — to get a free seat on the last city bus of the night. Of course, I had made sure to leave my phone sitting on the dresser at Marcos's house. No need to blow my cover in such an amateurish way.

I won't bore you with the bus ride, because it was, well, boring. About the most interesting things along the way were the frequent colorful billboards for Xanadu Caverns, each one covered in stalactites and smiling spelunkers. By the way, "spelunkers" is a real word and I didn't just write "smiling spelunkers" because it sounds dirty. All right, fine. I did. Were you expecting something classier? The billboards read: *"Deepest caves in the tri-state area! After a long week of climbing the corporate ladder, come to the caverns to get back down to earth!"* I'd heard of Xanadu Caverns ever since I was a kid, but like everyone else, I knew that "deepest caverns in the tri-state area" was just their lame attempt to appear relevant in comparison to Finimore Caverns a few hundred miles farther west. *That* place was so deep, people said it was the gateway to hell. Or maybe to the center of the earth.

After six or maybe a hundred of the same billboard flowed past my window, I might even have dozed off, visions of ghostly underground rock formations swirling in my head.

* * *

The city bus station was, of course, on the rather shady side of town, and even though I assumed I could out-duel anyone around (with the possible exception of Sol), there was no need to ask for trouble, right? No need to be outed upon arrival, just because some wannabe gang member decided I might have 20 bucks in my pocket. So I kept my head down, and I pushed the mind of anyone near enough to worry about.

The one thing I'd done to prep for my trip was print out a map of the city, which I had folded into a little square in my pocket. Confirming my directions, I quickly made my way toward Babilu Tower on foot, double checking the mute on my beacon about a thousand times. Sol no doubt had his Way of the Sun minions actively looking for me, and I assumed they could be anywhere.

And that's why I was wearing dark glasses, a baseball cap, and a hoodie — hood up over the cap. I probably looked more suspicious dressed like that than if I just walked around the city in a HI, I'M BLACK SWORD! t-shirt, but it was the best disguise I had.

Approaching Babilu Tower just before 9 pm, I saw right away that something was going on. People were everywhere, crowding in a ring around the stairs that led to the glass front doors of the building. Ahead of them, a temporary dais and podium stood, looking freshly erected.

To each side there were cameras lofted by men and women, trying to get the best angle, the most iconic shot. They hovered amid the temporary generator-powered lighting rigs, idly chatting and smoking cigarettes as they awaited the show, whatever that show was going to be. Ringing the outside and closest to me, white vans shot their antennae into the air like bizarre sunflowers of massive dimension.

Since the day of the car accident, there were many times I felt as if I wasn't even slightly in control of my destiny. This was one of those times, with no more than seven or eight minutes elapsing between my arrival and his. Suddenly, there was my adversary, right in front of me. Sol.

My breath caught, and I almost forgot to hold my beacon mute in place. That would have been the end of my big surprise, wouldn't it? Willing myself to calm down, I stayed in the back of the crowd, observing, as Sol stepped comfortably onto the dais. There must have been hundreds of people, so I figured I wouldn't stand out too much, as long as I played it cool.

Sol approached the podium with one hand raised and his gleaming white teeth bared in a warm grin.

He looks right at home, with his adoring fans all around, I thought. *But what the hell is this all about?*

I didn't have to wait long for the answer.

There was a brief squeal and hiss, sound amplified by electricity. Sol spoke into the microphone, and his voice — that voice I knew all too well — echoed off the walls of the nearby buildings. "Thank you all for coming, I know it was on short notice."

A murmur passed through the crowd, with little snippets of laughter. I supposed Sol made a joke that went over my head. The mic squawked a short burst of feedback, quickly controlled by whoever was running sound. Sol made a dramatic gesture, pretending to flinch back from the loud noise, and the crowd laughed again, louder and in unison.

I was forced to admit it. The crowd, the seemingly normal people all around me, *loved him*. I scanned their faces in disbelief.

People loved Sol.

I mean, Sol was, in my opinion, about the worst human being to ever walk the face of the Earth, and here people adored him.

What are you people, I thought, *on dope?*

What exactly had Sol done to earn their love? What good thing had he ever done? And then I realized… he didn't need to do good, to be a star to some people. For them, all he needed to do was *shine*.

Just as Pip had amassed a collection of followers who waited for her outside her condo, so did Sol at his tower. Sure, I personally believed I'd get along much better with a Pip fan than a Sol fan, but was it truly much different than fans who liked different boy bands or opposing baseball teams? Okay, sure, maybe Pip worked to save lives and Sol worked to end them. That could probably be considered a significant difference. Still, the cult of personality was a powerful force.

Sol spoke again. "As you all are aware, I know a thing or two about power." The crowd immediately echoed his word, *power*, and it became a sort of chant. Once more, I looked around at the crowd near me, and then I noticed a pale-skinned man on my right.

He was staring at me.

Oh crap, I thought. Was this one of Sol's Way of the Sun jerks, already sniffing me out? I anticipated his approach, or at least him doing *something* to reveal that I was in the crowd.

He was dressed in regular clothes, jeans and a well-worn plaid shirt, untucked. He was the kind of guy who used to be young and spry, but wasn't anymore; used to be thin, but wasn't anymore; used to have a thick head of hair, but didn't anymore. What hair remained salted the top of his head like sprinkles of snow.

He didn't move. He simply stared.

No way. He's no one. He's just some dude who thinks Sol's awesome. And maybe he's wondering why I *don't think so, too.*

It dawned on me that I needed to yuck it up with the locals at every Sol quip if I wanted to look like I belonged. Look, my life had been screwed up and crazy for a long time, but I never thought I'd be standing around, slapping knees at Sol's stand-up routine like some late night talk-show sidekick. But that's what I did. When in Rome, right?

The man still stared. Then he started to edge closer. I did my best to ignore him. Soon, he was right next to me.

"Nice disguise, John," he whispered, leaning close.

"Huh?" I replied, always the eloquent one.

"Clap," he said, directing me as he did the same. I realized Sol had said something else that was apparently important. People were cheering, clapping. The man next to me slapped his hands together enthusiastically, but something about it seemed almost fake.

Wait.

I gave him a sidelong glance and noticed that he wouldn't make eye contact. Was it possible this guy was on *my* side? Slowly, I began to clap, following his cue.

He leaned closer. "Barry Wilk, TFSA," he said, like any of that meant anything to me.

I doubled down. "Huh?"

"Not surprised you haven't heard of us before. No one has. Task Force on Superhuman Affairs. We're pretty new." Barry extended a hand toward me in greeting.

I didn't know what to do. I was supposed to be in disguise, an unknown among the masses. And almost immediately, this guy, this *Barry Wilk*, had identified me.

"How…?" I started.

"Careful what you say," he said, scanning the crowd. "But, to answer your question, most people would fail to notice an elephant if it landed on their head." He winked at me. "I'm not most people." Wilk gave a small, sideways smile, and I studied him. That's when I realized the casual look was an act. His shirt was worn, but pressed. He was older, growing bald, and carrying extra weight, but his remaining hair was neatly cut. His fingernails were clean and evenly trimmed.

Task Force on Superhuman Affairs. Barry Wilk was a government agent. I knew right then I couldn't trust him.

I ignored his raised hand, and after a moment, he dropped it back to his side. He seemed like a man who was used to people avoiding his handshake.

"What do you want?" I asked.

Barry Wilk smirked. "I'm simply here to observe," he said, turning up both palms to proclaim innocence. "But what about you, John? What are you doing here?"

"Me?" What *was* I doing? *About the same*, I thought. "I'm just here to observe, too."

Right about then, Sol cleared his throat loudly into the microphone and the show truly began, adding even more blood to the stains on my hands.

16

“Friends, I am here to enlighten you,” Sol said, continuing his public display. “I am sure you have long been wondering why *I* am here.” *Yeah, Sol, all we do all day long is wonder about you.* “So I would like to clear things up. Mr. Mayor?” Sol turned, and a shorter, heavier man in a dark-blue suit strode smiling and waving across the dais to join him. “Please welcome your city mayor, Mr. Charles Grenwald!” At this, light applause broke out, but the mayor beamed as if he had been given a standing ovation.

There was something about the mayor’s expression. Something forced…

“Thank you, thank you, ladies and gentlemen of this fine city! Thank you for coming out on this momentous day!” Grenwald paused for the audience to react and again found only a mild response. “I’m here to make a *huge* announcement, something I’m sure all of you will be really excited to hear. Today marks the beginning of a new chapter in our city’s history. Today, by decree of the city council and myself, the mayor, I declare this man — Sol — to be our first *City Protector*!”

You would have thought the mayor said “Free candy and money for everyone!” because the crowd went nuts. Cheering, applause, screaming, chanting. Were they brainwashed? How did so many people want to support Sol, a man I knew to be so clearly evil? They had seen what he’d done, back then, at the governor’s mansion. And… and what? What else did the world at large know about Sol? They certainly didn’t know about his plan to connect superhumans to rule the world, or his kidnapping of my sister. No, come on. They knew enough.

These people couldn’t legitimately think Sol was the good guy, could they?

Oh, shit. They might. I’d really have to be careful.

Sol took back the podium and microphone, gleaming white teeth on full display. "Thank you so much, Mr. Mayor. I accept this position and will fulfill it to the absolute best of my abilities, I promise you all." His smile faded. "As your first City Protector, I would like to take this opportunity to announce some new rules I am instituting, for the good of our fine city. First, as of this moment, the city police force falls completely under my authority. I have met with top law-enforcement officials, and we are in agreement." To each side of the dais, officers with automatic weapons slid into place, reinforcing Sol's words. "In addition, my own officials from the Way of the Sun shall become executive officers in the police force, with the authority to direct all police activity on my behalf. Second, as of this evening, a mandatory city-wide curfew is now in place. All residents are required to be off the streets by 10 p.m., no exceptions. Third, all citizens of the city are hereby required to identify any superhumans or suspected superhumans to the police immediately upon notice. Failure to comply with any of the above new regulations will result in significant penalties."

The crowd applauded, loudly. They *applauded* the fact that Sol had taken over their city and stripped them of basic liberties.

Sol scanned the audience, his eyes only narrow slits. "If any among you wishes to challenge these rules, be aware. No dissent will be tolerated. Harboring superhumans will not be tolerated. The penalty for such disobedience will depend upon the severity of the infraction, but I do not rule out the possibility of capital punishment. Do not test me. I repeat this not for the good people here today, but for the television audience at large. Do *not* test me. My vengeance is swift, my punishment severe, and my tolerance… is *limited.* More than anything else, I require to know the whereabouts of superhumans. While I require law and order, I would almost rather have you good people *murder* each other than hide a superhuman. If you choose to traffic in such dishonesty, well, may God alone have mercy upon you. For I will not."

As he spoke, Sol concentrated. At first, I had no idea what he was doing, but then something came to me, a sort of sense. He was scanning the crowd with his mind, reaching out to find anyone who might be different. Like me.

I started to panic. If he scanned me, I'd be found, and then not only Sol but the entire crowd would be upon me. And if I ran, I'd only be giving myself away.

Sol swept his mind across the first few rows, then progressed backward. Slowly, I tried to fade back, toward the farthest reaches of the crowd. But he was quick, scanning left and right, coming closer. Without drawing too much attention to myself, there was nothing I could do to get away.

In only moments, Sol's mind would skim past my own.

"I think I see one!" someone shouted, and I swiveled my head back to look for Mr. Plaid Shirt, the government agent Barry Wilk. I expected to see him turning me in, but somehow he wasn't to be found. The shouting came from slightly farther away, toward the middle of the crowd. "That guy!"

Shouts went up. People screamed to catch the poor sap in question. "Grab him!" To bring him forward. I didn't hear anyone suggest anything remotely resembling patience or fairness or justice.

Sol's mental scan abruptly stopped. "What's this?" He bellowed into the microphone. "Who is this man? Bring him forward!"

There was something…

The crowd roared in support, a thousand angry voices, as a nondescript man was dragged toward the front. *Dragged.*

"He's been acting strange — like he can read minds!" The man yelling sounded frazzled and strained, his voice nearly cracking. I found myself wondering if the man making the accusation was even sane.

I should have known. I should have seen it coming. Realized what Sol would do.

But it all seemed so *orchestrated.* Like I was watching a play. Sol onstage, playing his part, the people around him playing theirs. And one man in the role of the accused.

I mean, really. Who could believe the farce of Sol's display? If the guy had superpowers, would he let himself be dragged onstage? Of course not.

They stood him up on the side opposite the podium. He was dark in complexion, very much like Sol. But that's where their similarities ended. Once I could clearly see him, I realized the man might be no older than me. He was just a kid, flustered and scared, wearing a dark t-shirt and jeans, the shirt torn at one shoulder, looking disheveled — a direct contrast to Sol's always-perfect appearance. "I don't have *superpowers*! I don't know what they're talking about!"

I wanted to reach out with my mind, to try to find the truth. But I didn't need to. I could just tell. The accused kid wasn't one of us. I knew it instinctively. Sol knew it, too.

"There are ways in which I can tell beyond a shadow of a doubt, you know," Sol said, giving the crowd a knowing look.

And then, without another word or any sort of warning, Sol thrust his left hand toward the kid, then upward. I heard a small startled cry escape the kid's mouth as he was picked up off the ground.

Sol held him there for a moment, two, and like the rest of the crowd, I stood watching, holding my breath.

I realized that the air around the kid had taken on a form, like the dust and dirt and whatever else might be floating around the city came together into a shape. A fist. A large curled hand of blackened air, surrounding the helpless person inside.

Then Sol, that bastard, that mad man, closed the fist.

He *knew* the kid didn't have power. He knew.

First, I heard a grunt, like someone getting punched in the stomach. Then a wet snapping sound. I watched, doing nothing, as Sol crushed the kid to death with nothing but air, floating above the stage.

The kid tried to cry out again, but the nearly invisible hand closed and the breath hissed out. Veins popped on the kid's face as his body was mangled and folded in on itself. And then, like the end of a magic trick, the kid's face went slack. He would never resist again.

Why? Why did Sol do it? Kill this innocent kid? My stomach churned and I almost threw up. Around me, people cheered. They *cheered.*

Sol waved his hand away, and the crushing air matched his movement, tossing the kid to the back of the stage, a limp rag doll no one wanted to play with anymore.

And an idea came to me. Sol and the mob were two halves of the same thing. One, a creature of evil power, the other entranced by it. Yet Sol needed their adoration as much as they needed someone to adore.

I never even knew the kid's name, but I swore at that moment that his death would not be in vain. Sol would atone for it, like he would atone for so many other things.

Sol killed the kid. In cold blood. For no reason but for fame.

In front of *me*.

My anger was boiling. I wanted to lash out. Shout Sol down from his stage and dash him to pieces. Then I found myself wanting to kill every one of his followers, crush them as Sol had crushed the innocent kid.

I seethed.

And I almost did it.

Almost.

On that day, I could have killed them all.

I reached for my belt, the double belt I could harden into twin steel blades.

But I stopped.

No. Then you're no better than him, I thought. *Take the time to do it right this time. End Sol once and for all, and free these people from the blind lunacy of following him.*

"And finally," Sol said, voice firm and low. Strong and decisive. "This city hereby declares its independence from the nation at large, a nation we no longer recognize as our sovereign entity. For this reason, I am mandating a new conscription of all individuals 18 years or older, to create a new Army of the Sun, in order to defend our new status from outside aggressors. You may sign up right now, starting today, right here." Immediately, folks near the stage started jockeying into a line, eager to join Sol's horrid circus. "If you know someone who does not voluntarily sign up, report it. Police will be looking for stragglers and dealing with them in an appropriate manner."

He let his last words hang like the threat they clearly were. And yet, his crowd cheered. The people gathered to see him. They loved every word of it.

I wondered if the rest of the city felt the same. Hundreds of people stood around cheering. Thousands, no millions, were at home, no doubt huddled and afraid.

"With that, we shall begin," Sol said. "I thank you for the opportunity to be your protector. For the chance to make this city as great as you and I know it can be."

Sol walked to the front of the dais and began shaking the hands of his eager followers. Meanwhile, I shook myself awake.

He might be planning revenge against me, but his plans had just become oh so much more. Sol had taken over a city. And I knew him, knew that wouldn't be enough. *I wish to be eternal*, he had told me. Killing one kid would be nothing.

How long before it was the state? The country? The world? How many people might Sol kill then, just to get his way? Just to make a point? Just to thrill his followers, as they thrilled him?

I should have moved long before, while he was still talking, but I had to shake myself back to life. I knew it was time to act. While Sol was glad-handing everyone around, I snuck through the crowd and around to the opposite side of Babilu Tower.

There had to be a back door somewhere.

17

I found a door. Actually, quite a few.

Thankfully, fire regulations didn't allow major buildings to have only one way in. Still, most of the doors I tried were locked. I could break in, but that wouldn't give me the element of surprise I so desperately needed.

On the back side of the building, there was a garage entrance, for parking on a few levels below ground. I walked down the ramp, trying to look like someone just headed in to pickup his car. Pretty sure I didn't look old enough for that, but I at least tried to seem confident. In any event, the attendant was tucked into a little booth, facing away and watching something on his phone. I doubt he even noticed me.

Following the cement ramp down, I came to a section of cinder-block wall where ELEVATORS had been painted in bright-red block letters, with an arrow on one side. I followed the arrow, went through a metal door, and found myself at a bank of three elevators. I pushed the button, about 100 times. It's important to push those buttons a lot — makes the car come quicker. Finally, the elevator door on my left opened with a *ding* and I entered. Checking the numbers, I saw they went up to 40, but two floors — the 11th and the 38th — were labeled TRANSFER. I was pretty sure Babilu Tower was taller than 40 floors, and that Sol was at the very top. On a whim, I tapped the button marked 38, and the elevator began its ascent.

After what seemed forever, the door dinged and opened again, and I found myself in an atrium where there were even more banks of elevators. To my left, a set of three was marked 41–80. To my right, a group of two was marked 81–108. I chose the right.

Getting in the elevator, I pressed 108, but nothing happened. I pressed it again, and again. Still nothing. I tried 107. Nope. 106? The car lurched upward.

Okay, fine. I'd have to walk up two floors. Somehow.

Just about everyone who usually would have been in the building must have been down on the street for Sol's announcement, because I proceeded without interruption up to floor 106, where the doors once again dinged and opened.

And there, my heart leaped into my throat.

Despite the fact that it was evening, people were *everywhere*, walking, talking, scheming? They might have been scheming. There were dark-suited men, officers in police uniforms. Women giving directions to what appeared to be subordinates.

Sol had quite the complex organization.

I ducked to one side of the elevator, beside the rows of buttons, just out of view of all the people. I was pretty certain my hoodie would stand out among the well-dressed worker bees, so I tried to stay out of sight. But I was stuck. If I left the elevator, they'd see me. If I didn't leave the elevator, I'd never reach the top floor.

What the hell was I supposed to do?

Just as I was thinking all this, a pretty young woman with short dark hair, wearing a business jacket and skirt, all black, stepped into the elevator. Clipped to one pocket of her jacket was an ID card, and I had a millisecond to read her name: Rebecca Kelly.

Rebecca looked up abruptly from a notepad she had been scribbling on. "Oh! I'm sorry, I —" And then she noticed my attire, I assume, and her demeanor changed.

Well, time for some of John Black's special method to make friends and influence people, don't you think? I pushed her mind, gently. "Hi, Rebecca. Were you heading up to 108?" I asked innocently.

I figured I'd help her help me. *My name is Steve. Steve, um, Banderol.* There, that didn't sound like a made-up name, now, did it? *And, yes, you are going to 108, and you're taking me with you.*

"Yes, sir," she said with a blink and a strange smile, like she was just getting used to the idea. Which, of course, she was. She reached for her ID, then swiped it across a little sensor by the buttons. Finally, she pushed 108 and the light lit up. That explained why I couldn't do it at first. *Duh.*

"Thanks," I said, and we rode the elevator up in silence.

At 108, we both stepped out.

There I was, the penthouse suite. Everything was polished marble and dark, gleaming wood. A woman with tightly bunned brown hair sat at a large and mostly empty desk, looking directly at us.

"Good evening, Rebecca," the woman said. "What brings you up?"

Rebecca stood beside me, looking at the floor like she was trying to remember how she got where she was. *You were just showing me the way. I have an appointment with Mr. Sol. I mean Sol.* She quickly looked up and regained her smile. "This is Mr. Umbanderol. He has an appointment with the boss."

Umbanderol? Oh, right. I stammered. "The name's just *Banderol*." I tried on a smile. Rebecca wrinkled her forehead at me, confused.

"I'm not familiar with any appointments this evening," the woman said. It seemed like she was looking down into the wood surface of her desk, and I realized there was a glow there, from where a computer monitor had been embedded. "Let me check the calendar."

I pushed again. *No need. You recognize me, and you remember that I'm here to see Sol. You'll let me into his office.*

The woman stopped abruptly. "No need. I recognize you, Mr. Umbanderol."

"It's *Banderol.* Oh, never mind."

She stood and gestured to me. "Let me walk you into his office. Please."

Holy crap. It worked. I was going to be sitting in Sol's office when he came up from the street. He'd be joyous, triumphant after his announcement.

He'd never suspect that I'd be waiting for him.

I had beaten him once. I would do it again. And this time there was no storm, no twist of fate. I'd scatter his atoms into the wind from the 108th floor and Sol would be gone, for good.

I followed the dark-haired woman, but not before planting a tiny seed of forgetfulness in Rebecca's mind. She stepped back into the elevator and disappeared, never to remember our little encounter.

As for the other woman, she led me through two giant wooden doors and into the lair of the beast. She asked if she could get me coffee, tea, or water, but I declined. As she left, I gave her a little push, too.

Suddenly I was alone, awaiting the appearance of Sol, so I could end his ridiculous reign, just as it was starting.

I looked around the room. Wow. Sol had spared no expense. Or should I say, whoever worked here *before* Sol spared no expense. Sol was more of the scavenge-and-steal kind of businessman.

The floor was gleaming marble. Black with veins of white and gold lightly tracing through it. Black rock from deep in the earth. The furnishings were sparse, but that only reinforced the enormous size of the room. (I'm pretty sure a professional football team would have been happy with Sol's office as a practice field. Except for perhaps the pain of a prospective faceplant on marble after a tackle.) There was a sitting area with a leather couch and two chairs, and yep, it sure did look familiar from those TV interviews. Directly ahead was Sol's desk, a behemoth of cherry wood, oversized, with only a single ornamental lamp atop it.

I padded over to the desk and poked around, wondering what I might find. Not much. Like the woman outside, Sol had a computer embedded in his desk — I guess that was the style, so as not to detract from the smooth surface of the wood. His monitor was dark, however.

Rounding the desk, I saw a tray just below the surface, holding a keyboard and mouse. I slid it out just a bit and shook the mouse, waking up his computer display. There was no password prompt. Why should there be? Sol was a cocky bastard.

On the right side of the screen, there were a few file icons, but nothing that stood out. On the left, however, there was a quad of boxes that showed security-camera views, all live feeds.

The upper left showed the elevator doors, motionless. The upper right showed the woman who had just escorted me in, sitting again at her desk, typing away at some document. On the lower left was an office full of cubicles, 10 or more people busily working. Maybe it was the same scene I had stepped into on the 106th floor.

But the lower-right image is the one that held my attention. There, Sol walked down a long corridor, toward the camera. He seemed to be taking it slowly, not a care in the world.

As he neared, his speed diminished even more, until he stood just below the camera, its view showing the top of his well-coifed head.

Deliberately, Sol tilted his head to look directly into the camera, his face and features distorted by the slight fish-eye quality of the lens.

And then he grinned and waved at me.

Oh, crap.

At that moment, a dark gas hissed out of a grate at my feet, enveloping me. I hadn't even noticed the grate at first, or, if I had, I must have assumed it was just a normal AC or heat vent.

I was wrong.

Right away, I could tell there was a major problem. My cells tried to react, to *do* something, but what could they do? There was no enemy to sluice away from here, no mind I could push. Too late, I considered pushing the very air away from me, but I couldn't focus. I lost control of my body, and I could feel my mind going.

Rolling in lazy waves, the black wind blew up and over me, and my eyes started to close.

Shit, John, I thought as I thudded first to my knees on the polished marble, then fell over on one side. *You stepped right into that one.*

Interlude

Billowing clouds. An eagle.

Flying above and below, avoiding the touch of the black clouds.

The storm approaches, and there is nothing to be done, except...

I must fly through.

Just before I dive into the black wall, I see it stretching before me.

The darkness goes on forever.

PART 3

— *war* —

1

I hovered in a dark fog, a billowing series of black clouds on which I floated, physically and mentally.

What I mean to say is, I was knocked pretty loopy and tripping.

It reminded me of an old joke. *Do you like my shoes? I bought them from a drug dealer. Don't know what he laced them with, but I've been tripping all day!* In my drugged-up state, this was the absolute height of comedy. I'm here all week, folks. Please be sure to tip your waiters and bartenders.

* * *

Sol was talking. He kept saying *her.* Who was she? Some woman, I couldn't focus on her name. No, a woman and a child. Who? He kept talking. It seemed to mean something, but I couldn't focus. Just a name…

Ramona.

* * *

Oh, hello again, world. My mind rolled in and out like the tide. I don't know what Sol gassed me with, but it must have been some powerful stuff. I was there, but not there, if that makes sense. In some ways, I could see and hear the room I was in — a small, empty white room, with me prone on a table in the middle — but it was like watching a movie. A light that was way too bright for my liking hovered above. Maybe I was on a hospital gurney and strapped in? I couldn't make that much sense of it. People I didn't know filtered in and out on occasion, checking on me. Monitoring me.

I was Guinea Pig Number 1 in Sol's great experiment. Fantastic.

If I hadn't been so spaced out, I probably would have been pretty pissed at myself. But with the gas, well, frankly, I had a hard time even caring about my predicament. I was there, and that was that. Was I going to die? Somehow the meds made even that seem trivial.

I remember having an internal debate about the difference between cement and concrete. I'd love to tell you this was brief, but I think I might have argued about it with myself for the better part of a day. No, check that. It was probably over several drug-hazed days. I distinctly recall trying to come up with one clear example of concrete — or, as I said to myself as I maniacally laughed inside my head, *one concrete example*.

It was the gas. I promise. I would never find that funny otherwise. Really.

* * *

"Hello, John," he said. His voice was too familiar. In a way, it was my voice, or an echo of it. Sol had, despite my wishes, become intrinsic to my life. Another good reason to get rid of him.

I didn't respond. This wasn't so much a lack of manners or a desire to be disrespectful as it was simply an inability to form words due to my incapacitated state. However, even if I had been able to speak, I probably would have said nothing.

"Cat got your tongue, eh?" Sol chuckled. Ugh, that again. "Well, I can sympathize, John. After all, I know exactly what we hit you with, that gas. Pretty potent stuff. Your mind and body probably seem like they belong to someone else. Which is, I suppose, quite accurate. For they now belong to me."

He blathered on and on. I don't even recall what he said. Or maybe I do. Maybe it's burned into my mind forever. He talked and talked and talked. He told me about his life, but how could I care? Nothing mattered to me.

At some point, Sol's voice became like the monotonous fuzz of one of those sleep-aid white-noise makers. Yep, I fell asleep.

* * *

I'll give the guy credit. He just kept on going. No idea how long I was out. Maybe 30 seconds, and I missed half a word. Maybe it was a week later and Sol was just visiting again after a long absence.

I wanted to ask him what he wanted with me, but of course I couldn't speak. And after a moment or two, I realized I didn't even care to try to stay awake.

To sleep, perchance to… something or other.

* * *

"There you are. You're making this rather difficult, John." Sol chuckled. Oh, happy day. I was awake(ish) and Sol was making that sound again. "I had to lower your dose slightly, John. Apparently this stuff is a bit too much for you."

Just to spite him, I drifted off again.

* * *

"There. There. You seem to be regaining some focus. Good."

Sol's face hovered over me. Inside, my fire tried to light. I *wanted* to be angry. At Sol, for all the old reasons, and a new reason I couldn't quite put my finger on. *Tow forty*, I thought, not having any idea what that meant. *No, not quite. Tao? Tao for-che?* I couldn't make sense of the sounds in my head that stirred my anger. But a vision swam up — two people dead. A man and a woman. I blinked several times, the light above me too bright, too strong. Each time my eyelids came together, I had the distinct feeling that I would need crowbars and glue solvent to unstick them and pry them back apart.

But Sol was undeterred. Smiling, he spoke again. “Since I now have your undivided attention, John, I’d like to tell you a few things. Think of these as little secrets we can share, just you and me.” Sol was such a condescending ass. “I presume you saw my televised interview, the one in which I said I was interested in revenge. Well, you might have guessed — accurately, I’ll add — that I was talking about you. You *killed* me, John, and that was not a very nice thing to do.”

He filled my field of vision left to right, top to bottom. I couldn’t turn away, maybe couldn’t even close my eyes now that I had somehow worked them open. All I saw was Sol, the picture of maniacal joy in his victory. His head was like a massive parade balloon above me, distorted by helium. I imagined a dozen of his Way of the Sun lackeys holding onto him with tethers as Sol the Giant Balloon Head floated down some confetti-covered Main Street.

Ah, crap. I went on a tangent, and he was still talking. Sorry.

“But, I must thank you. Because, John, if you had not killed me, I would not have been reborn. And, being reborn, returning to life, I became the one thing I most desired. Do you remember what that is?”

He waited.

As if I could respond.

Finally, either sufficient dramatic pause had been achieved or he realized talking wasn’t on the menu for me on that particular day. “John Black, you know me too well. Of course, you’re right. I wish to be eternal.”

Eternal. The world could do *without* Sol for eternity, of that I was sure.

"Still, there is more. Would you like to know what more I have planned, John?" He paused again, staring into my eyes. I, not surprisingly, remained mum again. "I'll take your silence as a yes, John. I think you're going to like what I'm going to tell you."

I was pretty sure I wasn't going to like it.

"I realize that I made a mistake, back when I had your sister, Holly, under my control. My mistake was not to recognize the power she has bottled up inside her. Such great and impressive power, indeed power that I wish to have myself. Your sister has the ability to *create life*, John. Do you realize how incredible that is? Ah, but you may wonder how I know such a thing. Remember that — while I was acting as Ranger — my mind was joined to Gorgol Alpha for quite some time. I had the opportunity to explore that creature's thoughts. Strangely, Alpha's memory simply *began* on the day she fell to earth. Before that, there was nothing. As you would expect, I was intrigued. Falling from space as she did, I expected to find memories of an alien world. So of course I dug as deeply as I could, and finally I found something I did not expect. Your sister. In the darkest corner of Alpha's mind was Holly Black. And that is how I learned of what Holly did. Of what she can *do*." He paused, smiling. "It really is marvelous, isn't it, John? A *miracle*, you could almost say. To create life. Such a gift your sister has." Sol's smile remained, but his eyes turned serious, almost demonic. "And it is a gift that she will give to me."

I must have moved, maybe struggled against my stupor. Sol pulled back, amused. "Oh, don't worry, John. I hardly think that I could steal this gift away from your sister. No, not *steal* it. But I suspect I can *copy* it. Learn how she does it, so that I can do it myself. And then… Just think what will happen, when I can create another me, or a hundred more." He trailed off, musing.

What would the world be with a hundred megalomaniacal douchebags in it like Sol? I didn't want to find out.

"John, as you know, our powers have always been limited by distance. But I could bridge those distances easily if there were more of me to go around. Just incredible!"

Even in my haze, I knew this was terrible. A world overrun with Sol, or many Sols. But what could I do? I was stuck, a rat in a cage. Despite how humbling it was, I knew I needed to be rescued. *Bobby and Pip and Holly...* Their images came to my mind.

Sol must have been tapped in, because he smirked. "Yes, yes, your friends. I do hope they come along, to aid your sister when she comes. Because I have a little surprise for them. I believe you've met Naima, the woman who can turn off our powers? Well, I may not be waiting at the front door when your friends come, but you can rest assured *she* will be. And then, like you, they will be my prisoners. Isn't this exciting, John? Before you know it, the world will be rid of Black Sword, and Yellow Fury, and Red Hope, and even the one they now call Shadow Ghost — your little sister has quite the new following, I understand. But there will be one left: me. Oh, and Margrethe. She and I get along quite well. You're actually quite lucky that I'm keeping her away from you. That woman does *not* like you, John Black." Sol laughed heartily.

So there it was. Sol was going to lure my sister, steal her ability, then he planned to kill us all. What could possibly be worse?

"But before all of that happens, there is one thing I'd like to do with you, John. Think of it as a little test. When you killed me, I came back, I became eternal."

I heard a hissing noise, coming from somewhere I couldn't see. Immediately, I started to fade out. Sol returned, adjusting the gas mask over my face to make sure it was snug, to make sure whatever concoction he had for me was making its way uninterrupted into my lungs.

Sol's nose nearly touched mine as he looked deeply into my eyes, as if he were trying to find the truth. "Now, I'd like to see if you can do the same. Can you come back from the dead, too, John Black?"

2

The hissing increased, and all of my senses dulled. Whatever gas Sol was sending my way gave me the strangest sensation. Already I was spaced out and lacked general concern for my wellbeing. But this new gas? It made me *euphoria.*

I was being poisoned. I was going to die. And I was going down with a smile on my face.

That, friends, did it. *That* is what made me mad.

As the poison began to fill me, my tiny fire appeared within. Instantly it exploded with rage, as if I had lit a match in a house full of natural-gas fumes. The energy consumed me and I felt that, if I wanted to, I could pull the stars down from the sky, or black out the sun.

I lurched upward, a devastating, irresistible force, all violence and destruction. The table could not hold me. The room could not hold me. The building could not hold me, nor the city itself.

Sol could not hold me.

John Black, the superhuman known as Black Sword, leaped forth, ready to crush any who would oppose him.

Sort of…

I mean, all of that sounds great, and honestly, it is exactly what I felt at the time — an amazing rush of power. But I did mention drugs and euphoria, right?

I think the actual end product of all my excitement was probably this: I might have twitched on the table once or twice.

Not exactly dragon-slayer material, eh?

No, the gas continued to flow into my body, poisoning me thoroughly. I slowly faded away from the real world and into dreams, delusions of grandeur dancing in my head.

I saw myself slaying Gorgol Omicron and Gorgol Sigma. I watched myself burn away Petrus's mind. I flew to great heights. Amazed and awed the people of the world. Heck, I think I even made up some bad guys and beat them, too.

And then, finally, in the end, it happened.

I died.

3

There is, I have to admit, a significant gap in my memory at this point in the story.

Why?

Because Sol killed me. Really. I wasn't kidding about that.

He did it in the only way that made sense. My cells, like his, could fight off any physical harm. But a slow, all-invasive poison? That worked pretty darned well.

I'd love to report that I saw a really bright light, or that some flavor of deity appeared to offer me a second chance. But really, there was just nothing. He hit the gas, I died. At some point, he turned the gas off, and my cells — those miraculous little thorns inside me — put me back together, like the egg-shaped dude who fell off the wall. Why didn't the thorns die? I have no idea. Maybe because they didn't rely on what *I* was breathing. Maybe they simply could fend for themselves. But one thing was certain: The thorns inside me would do anything in the name of self-preservation.

I blinked awake, and there he was again. This time, he sat somewhere beside me, and there was a peculiar smell. I heard something, a liquid swirling in a glass. "Do you know why Napoleon loved his brandy, John?" Sol said from just out of view.

I really wanted him to shut the hell up and leave me alone. I felt horrible. Dying can do that to you. I had a bit of a headache.

Sol stood and walked to where he could peer down into my eyes once more. Above me, he waved a snifter of reddish-brown liquid that licked the walls of the glass then slowly slid back down. "It had nothing to do with brandy's delectable taste, or its irresistible bouquet. No, he loved it for its color, John. It reminded him of the color of spilled Russian blood."

That, and he liked to get hammered, I thought, unable to speak.

How come we humans can squint our eyes, blocking out all vision, but we have no similar recourse for our ears? Was it evolution telling us which one was more important? Or was it just so Sol could torture me with more stories I couldn't un-hear? What the hell did I care about Napoleon, Russians, and brandy?

I don't know how long I had been out, but something tickled at my mind, like Sol had been filling me with words and phrases and ideas and memories.

It made me feel even more sick to my stomach. One phrase kept repeating, making me feel worse with each pass. *So strong, the sun.* Above, the ceiling light blinded me. Perhaps I just mistook it for the sun. But…

"Now, John. Now we come to the truth," Sol whispered, close beside me. "That you and I are fated to this battle between us for *all time*. That I cannot die, nor can you. We are together, the same, eternal. We are the yin and the yang. We are good and evil. We are black and white. Where you exist, I shall as well. Doesn't that feel *incredible*, John? To know that you are a part of eternity, and that fate has tied us together? I feel I must welcome you, my old friend, my old enemy, my other half forevermore." Sol raised his brandy, nodded to me, breathed in, and drank, the consummation of an agreement I wanted no part of.

I can assure you that I did not feel incredible. In fact, it might have been the after-effects of dying, or simply my revulsion at what Sol was saying, but I will admit freely what I did next.

I threw up.

Take that, fate. I barf on you.

There was a commotion as Sol left. He called someone to mop up the mess. *Aw, come on, Fate-Buddy. Shouldn't you be the one cleaning up after me? Intertwined forever, turning into an elderly couple caring for one another in their best and worst moments?*

Wipe my chin, won't you, Sol dear?

Whoever did the cleanup didn't treat me gently. My body was shoved and swabbed until it was done, and never once did I get so much as a single word from the lackey doing the job. I heard footsteps as my chin-wiper headed for the door. A creak and a click and I was alone.

But now I had a secret.

The gas was still off. Throwing up was kind of a brilliant, if accidental, plan. Sol had to turn off the poison to see if I'd come back to life, which I did. Then, after I puked, no one had thought to turn the mind-numbing variety of gas back on. Still, I was groggy, half-dead, and unable to control my mind or body. I just needed to hope that no one would remember me for long enough that I could regain some semblance of ability.

Time passed.

I was beginning to understand what Sol meant about being eternal, because it sure did seem like it was taking eternity for anything to happen. Finally, I wiggled one finger. It was a start. Slowly, I blinked, and I even shook my head a tiny fraction.

Look, you may not find a wiggled finger to be a revelation, but for me, it was hope. I could do something.

More time passed.

I flexed all five fingers on one hand, and I was overjoyed. It was happening! I was recovering.

And then there was a sound from the hallway. Footsteps approaching.

Crap. Not yet!

A click and a slight creak. The door opened. I still couldn't so much as tilt my head to see who it was. Then a face appeared above me, the same lackey who had cleaned up after my unexpected bout of unswallowing.

"Time for the happy gas," he said, smiling a crooked-toothed grin. I caught a glimpse of his outfit, a basic black suit. More importantly, he had a security card on a lanyard around his neck — like the woman I'd pushed to help me in the elevator. On the card was a goofy-looking photo of him in front of a red background, and below that was his name: Robert Gary. Or maybe it was "Robert, Gary," aka Gary Robert. I don't know. I only saw it for a second, and I was fighting my way back from the dead, so cut me some slack, if you don't mind.

I heard him twist a handle, and the hissing noise began again.

Nonononononono! I thought.

STOP!

Robert Gary/Gary Robert grunted, oddly. Almost like someone had punched him. It took me a moment to realize it had been me, and I had punched him in the mind.

Robert Gary! I mentally shouted at him.

Gary Robert. I felt the name as I touched his mind. Okay, so his first name was Gary. Oops.

Gary Robert! Turn off the gas. Um... Sol's orders have changed. He wants you to turn off that gas.

Gary grunted again, but I heard the handle turn again and the hissing diminished and then stopped.

Okay, step one accomplished. Now what?

Um... you need to take me to the elevator. Can you do that without anyone else seeing you?

I felt Gary's mind cloud with concern or confusion. I gave him a healthy dose of calm along with assurances to counteract the feelings he was having. Then Gary got up and went to the door.

That didn't work, I thought. *I must not be strong enough yet*.

I heard the same click and creak as Gary opened the door. But, strangely, he didn't leave. And the gas was still off. I reached out with my mind again, and I could sense what he was doing.

Gary was seeing if the coast was clear. Miraculously, it was. He walked back to me, pulling the gas mask from under my nose and tossing it aside. Then I heard some clicks and clacks as he adjusted something below me. Wheel locks. Finally, Gary tugged at the table itself and I started to move, to roll.

He pulled me through the door, then moved behind my head to push, guiding me down a hallway with regularly spaced fluorescent lights that blinded me every second or two. We turned once or twice, and then stopped. There was a click.

Then nothing.

I was staring up at the face of Gary Robert, just standing there like a deer awaiting an oncoming train. What was he doing? I had to assume that someone might show up at any moment. I needed to *go*.

And then there was a *ding*.

Oh, we were waiting for the elevator. Of course.

Gary pushed me into the elevator car and then once again stood motionless.

He doesn't know where I want to go, I thought.

I pushed Gary's mind once more, with all I had. *Parking garage. First level below ground. Then you come back up here and forget this whole thing ever happened. Oh, and undo these damn straps!*

Gary Robert leaned forward and pressed a button, and although I couldn't see it myself, I knew it was labeled P1. Then he unbuckled my restraints before returning to stand by the head of the gurney.

Sugary sweet music played as we descended in the elevator, and Gary started to hum along, slightly tone-deaf.

I was still so weak, trying to save my powers, to recover. But I absolutely had to do one last thing, even if it wasted some part of my strength.

Gary, I said to his mind, straining to keep the connection. *I'm going to need you to stop humming.*

4

I was lying on a hospital gurney in a dark corner of the parking garage, unable to move much more than a few fingers, and completely alone after sending Gary Robert on his merry way. I couldn't sit up, couldn't speak, definitely couldn't stand and walk away. I was pretty well stuck.

I really should have thought my plan through a little better.

My fingers slowly straightened, then bent again. I tried to lift my arms from the gurney, but nothing happened. At that particular moment in time, I can assure you that I didn't feel especially heroic or powerful. It reminded me of days gone by, Bobby Graden in his old bully mode, punching me in the gut, me too afraid to do a thing. I had escaped, but I was helpless, vulnerable, and had no one else to lean on except myself. Of course, technically, I wasn't all that *escaped*, either. I was still in Babilu Tower, after all, just on level P1 instead of some pseudo experimental lab on one of the upper floors.

How long before I was missed and the building was swept from top to bottom, corner to corner, looking for me? Not long, if I were to guess.

My mind seemed to be clearing faster than I could get my body moving. That was going to be a problem. I'd be wide awake and aware when they found me motionless in the corner of the parking garage. Super.

If only Bobby was here, or Pip, I thought. *Or Holly.*

Wait. Holly.

Holly spent her days confined to a wheelchair. All of a sudden, I had a great appreciation for her feeling of being trapped. Yet Holly had so much mental power that her uncooperative body had slowly become less and less of a problem.

She was superhuman. She could do things I couldn't.

She was Shadow Ghost.

She could lift herself from that chair. All with her mind.

I had to try.

Get up, I said to my body. *Float. Get us the hell outta here!*

Nothing.

Come on! Lazy, good-for-nothing body! Get up!

Ooh, wait. A twitch.

That's it! You got it! Did I call you lazy? No, not you — I knew you could do it. Up!

Suddenly I moved just enough that I looked like the lovely female helper in every TV magic special, slowly floating into the air, inches above the table.

Go, body, go. I never doubted you!

I heard a bell ding, and a swooshing sound. "All right, see you later," a male voice said, echoing off the cold cement walls.

I froze. Whoever it was had to be only feet away. How could they have snuck up on me without my noticing?

Oh yeah. The elevator.

Regardless, the surprise was too much for me, and snapped my concentration. My body fell back onto the gurney with a thud, the restraints clanging against the legs of the table.

Well, it was a good escape attempt while it lasted, I thought.

A man walked past, no farther than 20 feet from me. He must have missed me, tucked back in the shadows, because after a moment, he was almost out of view.

I sighed.

“Hold on a sec, Tony,” a different voice called.

The man before me — Tony — stopped, turned. “What’s up, Jason?” I could see his eyes, the look on his face. I could see his dark suit, even the lanyard dangling around his neck.

No. No, shut up, Jason. Tony needs to go now. You need to shut up and let him go.

“You want to hit that new Mexican joint that just opened up? I hear they have great lunch specials. Shrimp tacos.”

Tony seemed skeptical. His mouth curled in a way that told me he was about to say *Thanks, but no thanks*.

“And they have half-priced margaritas during the lunch rush, too. Guess they’re trying to drum up some serious business. Probably won’t be able to keep up *that* special for long, so we might as well hit it while it lasts,” Jason said with a laugh.

Okay, great, thanks, Jason. Yuk it up, Mr. Margarita.

Tony’s expression changed. “Seriously? Yeah, sure, why not. I was just going to pick up something from the grocery store. Drinks and tacos trump that any day.” He walked back toward the elevator, passing closer and closer, and this time he was facing toward the corner where I was sprawled out.

I mean, it’d be one thing if I were dressed in black like a ninja, stealthily tucked into a dark corner. But I was on a large, rolling gurney, and I was wearing a loose-fitting hospital-style gown. I wasn't exactly keeping a low profile.

Tony was going to see me. I was sure of it.

I reached out with my mind — it was becoming easier to do the longer I stayed away from Sol's laughing gas — and gave Tony a push, making him walk by without so much as a first glance in my direction. Phew.

"All right, let's go," Tony said as he disappeared from my view, heading back to where Jason was waiting near the elevators.

"Sure, sure, just a sec," Jason said. "Just waiting for the rest of the gang."

"Oh," Tony replied. "Who else?"

"Janet and Susan from 101. Mark from operations." My breath caught. More people were on the way? Shit. "And maybe a couple of guys from the lab."

And there you have it. Mic drop. "Guys from the lab" invariably meant some of the "guys who were holding me captive." Was that a good thing? I mean, if they were heading out to lunch, they must be blissfully unaware I was gone. Still, it seemed like I was pushing it, so close to not only so many people, but the specific people whom I was trying to escape.

I had to move and I had to do it before that elevator dinged again.

It was a race against an unseen clock. For all I knew, the door might ding in five minutes, or five seconds, or somewhere in between.

Get up, John Black's body!

Do you see what stress does to you? You start referring to yourself in the third person, and that's just pretentious and weird. John Black doesn't recommend it.

Up!

My body started to hover again. It really was becoming easier over time. I raised myself several inches off the gurney, and then tilted myself feet-down. I floated there for a moment, the wretched monster of so many black-and-white horror movies, being introduced for the very first time. Too bad my lighting was no good, all tucked in a corner as I was.

Actually, that was just as well. I was dressed in a silly gown, and had bed head from how many days? There were probably even remnants of puke on my chin. Good thing no one could see me.

Oh, and that helped in terms of not getting caught.

I continued to will myself to float, up to a standing position, out of the corner, and away from the men waiting at the elevator doors.

Ding.

Of course. The group had arrived. I hastened away, a ghost flitting away on the wind. I will say one thing: Not touching the ground does wonders for keeping your escape quiet.

The doors opened behind me and I could hear a throng of people get out. "All right, who's ready for a margarita?"

"It's lunchtime, you guys," another voice replied.

"Isn't that the best time?" a third chimed in.

I just kept on keeping on. Floating my way out of there. I headed for the light — no, not the light I should have seen when Sol killed me, the light of day. There was an exit ramp, thankfully attended by an automated credit-card machine and not a real person. I drifted up and out of the garage.

I think I broke out in a sweat, straining in my hover-getaway.

Out in the light, I was hoping luck would be on my side, and by chance it was. Across the street, a man sat behind the driver's wheel of a yellow cab, reading a newspaper and munching on some kind of food hidden inside a large paper wrapper.

First things first. Looking around, I saw I was exiting from the side of the building, onto a much less trafficked street. I floated myself right on over to the post of a "No Parking" sign on the curb's edge, and — still using my mind — sort of tilted my body in the air a bit to emulate the pose of someone leaning. I knew I'd have to push the cabbie's mind, but doubted I could do that with any random nearby person *and* still maintain my mobility. The faux-street-post-lean was going to have to do.

Yes, I know that your typical person would find it odd to see a teenager in a hospital gown semi-floating in a titled position up against a street sign. I was doing the best I could.

I reached out for the taxi driver's mind. *Need a pickup over here.* He started to put away his newspaper and food, then flicked out the light of his "Off Duty" sign. One more push. *Go ahead and leave that sign on. Off Duty works for me.*

He complied, started the engine and did a U-turn to bring the car to where I was "standing." With an effort, I used my mind to open the door.

The next 20 seconds or so were kind of embarrassing. You ever think of how complicated it is to bend up your body to fit into a car? It was like performing human origami. Let's not even mention that there may have been a strange draft or two coming from the backside of my hospital gown. Let's just move on.

As I mentally pulled the door closed and pushed the man to start driving, I heard a commotion from inside the parking garage.

People were yelling my name.

5

Okay. Panic attack time.

“Where the hell are you going?” Because I had all the rigidity of a wet noodle, I was essentially flopped into the back seat of the cab. My head lolled on the upper edge of the seat in a way that didn’t make looking out the front windshield terribly easy. Plus there was all the normal taxicab stuff in the way — hack license, a screen looping commercials incessantly, about 300 legal statements about my rights as a passenger.

Still, through all that, I could see we were heading the wrong way down a one-way street.

My driver blinked and shook his head. “Huh? Ah, crap.” He hit the brakes, the car squealing and shuddering in a way that told you it had seen maybe too many miles and not enough maintenance. A hubcap broke free from a tire and rolled off down the street, barely missing two oncoming cars. I could almost hear the other hubcaps yelling *Save yourself!* The cabbie thumped one fist on the steering wheel. “You just said drive, and, I don’t know, I just sort of *drove*.” He gestured forward with the same hand, which was immediately misconstrued by the driver facing us a few feet away — you know, the person who was actually driving the *correct* direction. That driver started his own series of gestures that I will leave to your imagination. My driver, ignoring the other, started to make another U-turn. A chorus of honking ensued.

To be clear, I never actually *said* “Drive.” I thought it. Well, I *pushed* it into his mind. So I’d have to cut the guy a little slack for just following orders, since that’s pretty much what mind-pushes were all about. But I really didn’t want him to turn around and drive me right back to Babilu Tower. “Wait!” I said, trying my best to look around, my head flopping like it was in danger of falling off. To one side, I saw an alley leading between two tall buildings. “There! Can you just cut through there instead, uh…” Scanning the hack license taped in front of me, I located the driver’s name: Maximillian

Belmont. Sounded more like an oil tycoon than a cab driver, but maybe he was in a transitional phase. Don't judge. "Uh, Mr. Maximillian? Can you just take the alley?"

He seemed unsure. "Max. Just Max. But I'm not supposed to be cutting behind buildings — the cops frown on it."

And the cops were now under the control of Sol and his Way of the Sun buffoons. I didn't want to chance an encounter with the police, but I *really* didn't want to chance someone seeing me drive past the same building I had just escaped. Especially since they seemed to know I was missing.

Gotta do it, Max. Just this one time, okay, buddy?

"Well, just this one time should be okay," he said, turning the wheel.

Thanks a million, Maximillian. I do tend to crack myself up.

* * *

Outside the city, the miles slid by, a repeating cartoon backdrop of strip malls and the occasional tree. Although I managed to have Cabbie Max get me out of town, I hadn't told him where our true destination was, yet. I hadn't told him because I thought I didn't know. Of course, I had him going east, so it should have been clear to me sooner.

An hour passed and I was able to shove myself into what passed for an actual seated position. After two hours, I could feel my feet again. I wasn't sure, but I thought I might even be able to stand. I shook and stretched in the backseat like a boxer preparing for a prizefight, trying to work out every kink and slough off every bit of numbness.

We had left one city behind. Ahead, another was approaching. The capital.

Sol's city isn't the only thing I'm leaving behind, I thought. *My belt is somewhere in that building.* I made a mental note. One way or the other, I was going to get it back some day. The belt that split into two, that I could turn into dual swords. It was a gift from Pip. And, honestly, it was kinda my signature thing. No way I was letting Sol keep it.

But I was in no condition to turn around and challenge Sol. Instead, I headed to the capital, falling back on the only thing — the only people — I thought could help. Bobby and Pip.

There was just one problem. I had become something of a celebrity, so it was pretty doubtful I could sneak in unseen, given that Pip's place was typically surrounded by her fans. Plus, Sol's minions would be actively hunting for me. Showing up at Pip's wouldn't exactly be hard for them to guess. And the government probably would love to get their hands on me, despite the relatively calm chat I'd had with Barry Wilk. Don't forget I was still recovering from being dead, so it remained questionable whether I could even stand or walk. But none of that was really the problem. The true problem was that I was wearing a flimsy hospital gown that opened in the back.

If I drove up to Pip's front door, it would be the most public superhuman thing I'd ever done. I really didn't want to do it with a butt cheek hanging out. Or two, for that matter.

"Hey, Max?"

"Yes, sir?" *Sir?* Max was calling a teenager in a gown *sir*. Gotta respect a man who's committed to his job like that.

"Couple things. First, do you have a phone? And second, got any spare clothes, maybe in the trunk or something?" I added a little mental push to ensure Max didn't immediately pull over and kick me out of his car.

* * *

"That outfit is so you," Bobby said, looking me up and down.

I dipped my chin to take in the glory that was Max-the-cab-driver's backup outfit: a threadbare burgundy sweater over a grey t-shirt. That part, not so bad. But the pants. Why did Max even *own* a pair of plaid pants? I looked like a reject from some Scottish golfing club, or maybe a carnival barker in training. One thing was sure: If I owned plaid pants, I'd definitely keep them in the trunk as my "in case of emergency, break glass" pants, too. There's no way plaid pants are everyday pants.

Bobby smiled, then walked toward me. Without another word, he gave me a big bear hug. I looked over his shoulder to where Pip was standing, and I put on an embarrassed little grin. "Hey now, buddy. It's just me, no need to get all touchy-feely." Then I shrugged out of Bobby's embrace. Looking back, I wish I hadn't done that. I really do.

* * *

As you've probably guessed by now, cabbie Max did have a phone, and I used it to call Bobby and Pip. What's probably less obvious is the fact that those two had a relatively secret way of sneaking in and out of Pip's building, using a series of usually locked basement doors and hallways that served as maintenance and safety routes to the tunnels below. Tunnels, you ask? Yep, tunnels. Pip's building was directly over a subway line, a fact that, I later learned, was far from a coincidence. As soon as Pip went public, she figured she might need multiple ways to travel unseen. Living above the subway tunnels was a conscious choice.

So they met me two blocks over, behind a random brick building where there were no waiting crowds of adoring fans. I got out of the cab and gingerly walked up to them. Not floated. Walked. Gingerly walking was much better than floating, I thought.

Once we followed the underground path back to Pip's building and took the elevator to her floor, I finally got to see her place. I can see why Bobby wanted to stay there. Romance or not, a person could get used to a place like that.

The entryway was marble, wide and empty. It was notably larger than my bedroom at home, and Pip used it for… nothing. Just the space you walked through when coming or going, entering or leaving. Nothing else. Beyond that was a square living space in an open floor plan. Probably the biggest TV I'd ever seen was embedded in one wall. You know, classy-like. A plush U-shaped couch surrounded a low, angular coffee table. I imagined myself playing video games on that couch, blissfully, until the end of time.

Continuing through the open layout, we moved into Pip's kitchen. I can't say I'm much of a kitchen guy, but I could tell hers was a pretty top-notch one. Gleaming silver metal surfaces and artfully hung light fixtures. Didn't look like the kind of place you'd make a PB&J, but it did look right out of a magazine. Pip grabbed a glass, then filled it with water from a dispenser in the door of her massive refrigerator. Handing it to me, she broke the silence. "So, what exactly happened with you?"

Taking a sip of water, I stifled a laugh. "Where do I start? Tell you how I went to take on Sol all by myself? Or maybe tell you how he killed me?" Again, I laughed.

"You don't look dead, Johnny," Bobby said, wrinkling up one side of his face in a confused grimace.

I thought about it for a minute. There I was, walking and talking, and yet I knew for sure. I had been dead. I shrugged and put on a sheepish grin. "Well, I got better."

6

What do three of the most powerful superhumans in the world do on your average night? Same as a lot of people. We watched TV. Not the news — nothing that might drag us into some sort of global drama, or worse, piss us off. Just mind-numbing regular programming. Pip put on a singing-competition show, and when that was done, Bobby followed it with a crime drama. Even so, while there was nothing our powers could do to help us win a talent show, I found myself daydreaming of solving crimes using my mind-reading abilities. John Black, P.I. I was going to need to grow a mustache and get a cool car.

Later that evening, Pip trailed off to bed, leaving Bobby and me alone, the TV still buzzing some late night talk-show host's monologue in the background.

"So, this is the life, huh, Bobby?" I said. My eyes wandered around the condo, a place that I couldn't have afforded for even one month. Add the posh furnishings, art (yes, Pip had collected some actual art, believe it or not), and various appointments, and I think I could maybe live there for six minutes before being tossed out on my ear. Is that a thing? Do people toss other people out on their ears? If so, how does the tosser ensure that the tossee lands on an ear? Never mind.

"Yeah, the place is awesome, but it's 100-percent Pip. My contributions to the decor mostly consist of things like tracking in mud."

I laughed. "So things are going good here?" I was treading lightly, hoping Bobby was happy with his new life.

He gave a half-hearted shrug. "Yeah, I guess. Not perfect, but good. Beats the crap out of staying back at home." He laughed, a single little bark of a laugh. "Funny how that name sticks, isn't it? I lived there forever, but it was never really *my* home. More like a prison.

More like doing time. And the weird thing is that, sometimes, I miss them."

"Your parents?" I was stunned.

Bobby raised his eyebrows, nodding. "I shit you not. Truth is stranger than fiction, Johnny. I even called them, a couple weeks ago."

"And?"

"Big mistake. Guess what happened."

I paused. What would Bobby's self-centered, jerk parents do when they got a phone call from their suddenly famous son, living in the big city? "They *didn't…*" I started.

Bobby whistled, scratching at the hair over one ear. "Oh, they *did.*"

"What'd they do, ask you for money?"

"That was one thing, yeah."

"Oh my God, what did you tell them?"

"That's not even the worst part. They wanted me to call up Banner."

"Banner Productions? The TV people?" The same folks who had offered me a somewhat obscene amount of money if they could shadow me for a new reality show.

"Yeah, apparently my mom talked to them about a hundred times. They keep feeding her all these ideas, putting things in her head. Stardom, the rich life, that sort of thing."

"Wow."

"And you know my mom. She *wants* it. Wants me to say yes."

"Yes to what?"

"Banner wants to do a reality show starring yours truly," Bobby said with a smug grin, pointing one thumb toward his chest. I didn't bring up the offer they had made to me. No need to make things competitive. "And my mom wants the show to be based at our house — you know, our perfect family home. What a joke. Apparently she's convinced someone over at Banner that she can talk me into it — they've already given her some money. I'm not sure how much, but enough that she started dressing like she's a big star or something." I knew Bobby's mom made it her habit to dress like a former beauty-pageant queen, two decades after the fact. I could only imagine what she'd do with some extra cash to up her game. I smirked, just thinking about it.

"You've seen her?"

"Yeah, calling them was a mistake. That just confirmed where I was. They drove up the next day. Mom tried to talk me into the TV-show thing, you know, subtly. As if she knows how to be subtle. The sad thing is how *nice* they were to me. Might have been the first time in my life that my parents seemed like they gave a shit about me. Funny, huh?" Bobby smiled a broad smile, but his eyes seemed dull, lifeless. Despite everything his parents had done to him, I could tell. He still cared for them, and, deep down, all he wanted was their approval, their respect, their love. And he saw through all of their sudden attention far too easily.

For a while, we let our conversation drift, the banal jokes of late-night TV wafting over us, generating hardly a smirk or a light chuckle. "What about Pip?" I finally asked. Might as well rip off all the bandages at once, right?

Bobby rolled his eyes a bit. "Almost. Almost…" I didn't have the heart to ask what *almost* meant. "Things are about the same. Once in a while, we talk about things, but she isn't ready. Maybe she never will be. But at least I can say this: I doubt there's anyone else for her."

"Why do you say that?"

Bobby looked down his nose at me. "Johnny, come on. Pip and I are superhuman. We live in the same condo. Sometimes there are hundreds of people waiting around, trying to see us. Even when that crowd thins, there's always the photographers. We live our lives on the business end of a camera lens, and we're with each other about 18 hours a day. Closer to 24, if you count being here when we're sleeping. When is she gonna have time for another guy?"

"Good point," I said.

As if on cue, Pip jerked open her bedroom door and trotted out into the living room. I'd assumed she was sound asleep, but there she was, wide awake and ready to hit the town. She wore a tight-fitting red shirt and in her left hand, she held something in a matching red fabric. "It's go time," she said, her tone making it clear that *go time* was not optional.

"Where are we going?" I asked, still sitting on the couch.

"Not you, him," Pip said, pointing to my right. Bobby had already jumped up, heading for his room. In a moment, he returned, already having changed into a yellow shirt as tight-fitting as Pip's. Like her, he held something in one hand that matched his shirt.

I shook my head, perplexed. "What's going on around here? Is that *spandex*?"

Bobby froze. "What? No! God, no, Johnny. Come on. Seriously?" He smoothed one sleeve of his shirt, as if offended. "It's elastane. Please. It's a breathable fabric, good wicking properties. Very bendable, which is important to people like us."

What sort of alien universe had I suddenly been transported into? Bobby was indignantly lecturing me on active wear? "Can someone take two seconds and tell me what the hell is happening?"

Pip huffed, but stopped moving for a moment, turning to me. "Right, it's easy to forget you aren't used to this." She made a back-and-forth gesture between herself and Bobby. "The people here, the city, they rely on us. Red Hope and Yellow Fury. When bad things happen. We sort of come to the rescue." She unfurled the fabric in her hand and I could see it was a lighter, more professionally made version of the masks we had all once worn. My eyes went wide — I never thought we'd see the days of mask-wearing again, not after the world knew our names.

"But why? Are you guys fighting crime or something?"

Pip deferred to Bobby, who hung his head, just a fraction. "No, not usually."

"But *sometimes*?" I asked. He nodded. "And you're wearing masks again? What for?"

Bobby sputtered, trying to rationalize something to me, his best friend, that he knew looked silly. When he didn't answer right away, Pip spoke up. "We wear the masks strictly so people can identify us, quickly and from a distance. That way, people get out of our way. Or, on the occasion we do have to fight someone, sometimes they give up just seeing us. So, it's helpful."

"And tonight?"

Pip headed toward the door. "There's a big fire, downtown. Three-alarm already. It started with an explosion — not sure what did that, though. People might be trapped, so we'll go and we'll help out. Rescue the ones on higher floors, in places that are harder for the fire department to reach."

I stood up. "Let me go. I can help."

Bobby shook his head once, sharply. "No way, Johnny. I mean, you were mostly dead today, remember?" They began to head out, leaving no more room for argument.

I was a little bitter. I mean, I was part of the team, right? "Hey, Bobby? Isn't elastane just another name for spandex?"

Bobby screwed up his face, a mock smile for my mocking question. Then the door clicked shut behind them, and I was left with the strangest swirl of emotion, offended and embarrassed at the same time. Mad because they didn't think I was capable. Sad to let my friends down, not be part three of the Triangle Gang.

Gah! No! That's a horrible name. Never use it again. Besides, at that moment, the triangle only had two sides.

Outside, I heard a cheer go up as two heroes of the city appeared before the crowd, masks on and ready to save the day.

7

I stayed up late, watching these two colorful figures on the Wee Hours News Report — one yellow, one red — jump and fly and bounce and sluice their way around a burning building, ducking between orange spikes of flame and black curls of smoke. The footage was grainy, shot from a distance and poorly lit, but the whole world could see them in action. Thankfully, only I was able to see me wallowing in self-pity on the couch, annoyed at being left at home while the kids went out to play. It was amazing, though, watching them work, and it was clear by the way they moved that Bobby and Pip had developed a tight connection. So much more organized than when the three of us fought the Gorgols. If you'd asked me if they were a couple, based only on that night and the way they moved, I would have answered, "Oh, most definitely." But it wasn't really true.

Of course I hoped for Bobby's sake that one day they would be. Honestly, I hoped it for Pip, too. I might have been biased, but I thought she was missing out, keeping Bobby at a distance. He was a pretty great guy. Don't we all wish we could recognize things like that sooner, before time catches up with us? Because it does catch up. Time is a jealous mistress.

Eventually, I fell asleep on the couch, the light and noise from the TV serving as my only companion. Well, not my only companion. There was also another friend with me, growing stronger as the night wore on.

Determination.

* * *

They came home at some point, although I slept through it. The next morning, I was first up, admittedly for a good reason.

I put aside the annoyance I was feeling and dug through Pip's fridge to drum up something I could make us all for breakfast. Once I had the sausage cooking, it wasn't long before Bobby and Pip came out of their respective bedrooms to join me. I imagined them both floating on air, their noses comically sniffing cartoon swirls of aroma, enticing them out of bed.

"You never *sausage* a meal!" Bobby said. It was an oldie but a goodie, so of course, I laughed.

"There's eggs, too," I said. Breakfast is no time for proper grammar, I suppose.

Bobby replied with a tired smile. "Thanks, Johnny." Behind him, Pip nodded silently.

I let them eat, let them regain some strength. I mean, sure, we had superpowers, but working half the night was working half the night, no matter how you sliced it.

When the plates were clean and forks put down, I decided my time had come. "I'm going back. I have to. And I want you to come with me." I expected resistance, or maybe even confusion. I got neither.

"Okay," Pip said. "When are you going and what's the plan?"

They both stared at me.

"Um. That's as far as I've gotten."

Bobby wrinkled his forehead at me. "Barge into Sol's stronghold with no plan? And how'd that work out for you last time, Johnny?"

What was I going to say? *Oh, it was simply splendid! Sol killed me, dontcha know?* So I kept my big mouth shut.

"All right, then," Pip said, pushing aside the plate in front of her. "It's agreed. We need a plan, and it better be a good one. Start by telling us about this building he's in."

Bobby and I nodded, one of us smiling, the other one not. The one who'd barely gotten out of that building with his life.

* * *

I told them everything I could think of. The building's main entrance, its back door, the hectic environment, the elevators, Sol's receptionist and his office. I described what I could remember of my captivity in the "lab" area, and what I knew of the parking garage. And I mentioned that, somehow, I needed to get my belt back.

"Glad you like it so much," Pip said. I think my earnest desire to reacquire the belt was the best thanks I could ever have given her. "All right, we know two things for sure."

"What?"

"First, he let you go."

My head shook instinctively. "No way," I said.

Pip didn't respond. She just looked at me. In that way. That way that an older female can look at a younger male. There was simply no retort.

"Shit," I said. "Really?"

Pip literally looked down her nose at me, slightly sympathetic, but mostly annoyed. "John, you couldn't walk. He knows you have mental powers, yet he left you alone with a single flunky you could manipulate to get free? But that's not even the worst."

"What's the worst?" Bobby asked, apparently not yet up to speed either.

Pip turned to face him. "Your friend John here just *drove away*, leaving behind a city that's now under martial law. Checkpoints, blockades — they have all that. Yet *he* just hailed a cab and drove out?"

Damn, she's right, I thought. But, no time for debating the past. "Okay, fine. What's the second thing?"

That got her attention. Pip smiled at me. "Good," she said. "You accept the reality of it and are ready to move on. That's good, John."

I rolled one hand around in a circle, urging her to continue, and blushing a bit at the praise.

"Settle down, hot shot," Pip said. Absently, she rubbed at her arm. The arm I had, you know, chopped off once. "The second thing is this. Sol expected you to show up, so he'll be expecting us, too. That means the front doors, back doors, side doors, parking garage entrances — all of that. They're off-limits to us. No go."

"Okay, fine," I said. "Then how do we get in?"

"I don't know yet," she said.

"We could draw him out, get him somewhere else," Bobby said. "A place where we could control the environment."

Pip nodded, but she didn't look confident. "Sure, that might work. Or it might not. And if we draw him out and fail, we'll never get that chance again."

"True," I said. "Plus, he's got all of those Way of the Sun nuts with him, and at this point even the police are supposed to be working for him. That means he has a network of people, all around him, all around the city. We might not even be able to get *close* to him."

"If we play his game," Pip said.

"What does that mean?" I asked.

She smirked at me, then slid more plates and utensils out of the way. Then Pip deliberately placed our glasses in a row, the salt shaker and a candle in a second row next to them. Finally, she put a tall pepper grinder in the center. It didn't take an international espionage expert to realize she had made a model of Sol's city, his tall building surrounded by others, slightly smaller. "Tell me what the Way of the Sun is," she said.

"A bunch of assholes?" Bobby offered. Pip and I only stared at him. "Sorry, not helpful, right?" We nodded.

"They're people that help him out, like Sol's private army," I said.

"Exactly," Pip said, pointing at me with a dirty fork.

Bobby was confused. "Exactly *what*? That they're an army? That they help him out?"

"No," Pip said. "That they're *people*. The police, too. They're all just *people*. So there's something important they can't do."

"What's that?" I asked.

"Just this," she said. Taking her fork, Pip jabbed at the last remnant of sausage on her plate, then extended her arm until the sausage was swooping down to land on the very top of the pepper mill at the center of the table. "None of them can fly."

"Sol's gotta expect that from us," Bobby said.

"True," Pip replied. "But at least we eliminate the middle man. And if we're lucky, we catch him by surprise."

8

"Mom, what's wrong?" he asked. Sharif was a quiet boy, but sensitive, especially when it came to his mother.

Naima barely heard him. On the outside, she was a woman sitting in a posh, luxury condo, finely appointed. Inside, she was a mess. Sol had, most certainly, accommodated any demand, although Naima had made few. Still, the boy had all these new *things*.

He must be talking to the guards, Naima thought. *Asking them for all this. I'll have to put a stop to it.*

She studied her son as he sat before a massive flat-screen television, playing video games she would never have bought him. Was he feeling the stress of their confinement? He was a growing boy. Could he live through such a situation? Could his body adapt to this new reality?

No, she thought. *It's not his* body *I'm worried about.* Naima was a psychiatrist. She worked with the mind. She knew her real question. The body was just a vessel. It could operate mindlessly, like a jellyfish endlessly puffing its way through the ocean. But the mind? Without the mind, the body was lost. Could her son's mind survive the many surreal factors he had been forced to endure, all thanks to her?

She studied him.

It was too easy to look at Sharif differently than she would a patient. So she stopped, reset, and studied him again, bringing her professional skills to bear.

Something's wrong, she thought.

She looked closer.

And then she couldn't help but let a small gasp escape. *Oh my God. He's not suffering at all. He* likes *it here.*

How could she explain to her young son that, despite the pampering, it was wrong for Sol's people to capture and contain them like animals?

"Son," she began. "We need to talk." *He's only a young boy*, she told herself. *He doesn't know right from wrong, not completely.* What she was going to say might confuse him, but eventually he'd understand.

Sharif turned to face her, his face flat and expressionless, the character he controlled in the video game suddenly as motionless as him. "No."

Naima was stunned. "What? What did you say to me?" Despite wanting to comfort her son, she immediately reacted with the indignation of a parent.

"No," he said again, without raising his voice. "We don't need to talk. I know you don't like it here, and that you want to get away. But I *don't.* I like it here. We have things we've never had before, anything we want. And we're together all the time, not like when you had to work all day long every day." That remark stung, because Naima knew it was all too true. "Besides, I like Jeff."

"Jeff?" she said, blinking back confusion.

Sharif plopped the controller onto the couch. "You don't even know his name, Mom, geez! Jeff — you know, the guy who brings us every single meal. Who brought me this game system. *That* Jeff?"

Of course, Naima knew the man by sight, but she couldn't remember ever speaking to him. Maybe she could recall his blunt demands — *Follow me, Stay here*, and the like — but no conversation.

"And I like *him*, too," Sharif said, turning away.

"Who?" she asked her son, fearing the answer.

"Why do you have to be against everything, Mom? We finally have anything we want! Before they found us, we had to wait in line to see if we could sleep in that big noisy room with all those people! I hated it! Don't you remember that?" Sharif began to cry, unfamiliar with the process of yelling at his own mother.

But Naima remained calm. Focused. Like she was talking to a patient. "Who, Sharif?" she said. "Who is it you like?"

The boy remained quiet, but she could tell he wanted to say it. She waited. She knew that people will fill any silence, if you give them enough time. And, as sure as that, he finally spoke.

"I like Sol."

The moment was broken by a knock at the door.

"Yes? What is it?" Naima called out, her eyes still locked on her son.

A voice — Jeff's voice, she now realized — replied. "You and the kid need to get ready. The boss wants you up top in five minutes."

"Up top? What does that mean?"

Even with his voice muffled from behind the closed door, she could hear Jeff's irritation. "It means he wants you on the roof."

The roof of a 108-story building wasn't a place most people chose for a casual get-together. Naima began to tremble, fearful of what such a meeting might entail. "What… what *for*?" she asked.

Jeff laughed in one short burst. "Practice, lady. Practice." Then there was silence, and for a moment, Naima thought the man had left. Until the muffled voice came again. "Now you have four minutes."

9

Have you ever heard the phrase, "The world is going to hell in a hand basket"? Well, even if you haven't, it was. And no, I have no idea what that actually means. A "hand basket"? What's that? Just a regular basket? I mean, there aren't "foot baskets," are there? And why would you go to hell in one? Is it supposed to be ironic, like you would only normally go someplace nice in a hand basket? Gah.

Holly, despite my attempts to ignore the fact, was growing up. She had outed herself as Shadow Ghost, a mysterious figure floating in waves of black robes. That's a quote, by the way, from a TV report I saw about her. In actuality, all she wore was a simple black dress, but, you know, when it started fluttering in the breeze, people came up with *waves of black robes*. Man, people can be dramatic. And, she didn't always wear black. What was Mom supposed to do, wash the same dress every night, so Holly could maintain her image? Not happening.

She was restless, my sister. And, I had to admit, probably a little angry. At me. For leaving. I deserved that.

There she was, sitting around Marcos's house, and probably bored to tears. Who knows, maybe she was creating spiders like nobody's business, maybe organizing a little spider circus, with spider trapeze artists and spider jugglers and all that. Maybe. But no, all she was really doing was getting bored and more angry.

So she floated away out the back door.

How do you like that? She just *floated* away. Now who was copying whom? I might have pulled my best Holly impersonation getting out of Sol's building, but she was, unknowingly, channeling me as she floated through the yard one dark evening, over the fence and into the woods. Heck, the path she took might have even been the same one I did.

My mom, if you haven't already noticed, is one smart cookie. And she's a good mom. She knew Holly had been watching TV and, subconsciously, she registered the time at about 8:45 pm. When she went back to check on her at 9:15 pm, Holly was missing, even though her chair was still present. Mom had the requisite four-and-a-half minutes of freak-out as she flashed back to when Holly had been abducted by Sol. But she knew times had changed. Perhaps more so than me, Mom realized Holly was maturing. And with age came vengeance, or at least that was the connection she made. Holly, Mom reasoned, was most likely going to pay Sol a visit. And although Mom knew Holly was powerful, she feared for her daughter. She immediately began to calculate in her head what a 30-minute radius of travel for a flying preteen might be. Mom knew she could rule out the front yard, since our friends the paparazzi had that side covered and wouldn't have let Holly slip by without a major commotion. No, Holly had escaped through the backyard. Mom pulled up a map on her phone, scanning for likely directions.

She swiped past two-lane roads, moved over larger routes and interstates, zigging and zagging the way you would in a car. *No,* she thought. *What's the shortest distance between two points? A straight line. Holly doesn't care about roads, she just wants to get to Sol.* Mom zoomed out until she could see the distant city where Sol lived, then used markers to plot a direct line. *Follow the markers. Find Holly*. She began to repeat it in her head like a mantra.

"Marcos?" she called out. When he didn't answer in under 13 seconds, she tried again, unable to make her voice sound anything but frantic. "Marcos!"

My uncle/cousin Marcos appeared at the top of the basement stairs in his *dobok*, sweat beading his forehead. "What's the matter?" he gasped.

Mom looked at him the way only a mom can. With unwavering eyes and a voice so calm and commanding that there was no question Marcos would comply, she said: "We need to drive north and west. If I leave, the paparazzi will follow, so I'm going to hide in your car, and then you're going to tell them something so you can drive away alone. Make it boring." She thought a moment. "No — make it *unpleasant*. You need to get something, like medicine for a foot fungus — something gross like that. Something they'll believe but not want to know more about."

Marcos blinked, confused. "Uh, okay, sure. But… why?"

"Holly's gone. I think I know where she's going, but I'm going to need your car if I want to get ahead of her."

Without another word, Marcos went to get changed.

* * *

So Mom went into the garage to hide in the back of Marcos's car. The garage was connected to the side of the house and easily accessible by a door from the family room, a pathway unseen by the prying eyes of those outside. As she curled herself down, she tried to ignore the way it made the pain in her stomach flare up. Marcos plopped into the driver's seat and pressed the button to open the garage, backing out as the door reached the top.

Of course, there was a buzz of activity. Everyone who was waiting for some picture to sell, some story to cover, jumped into action at the sign of movement. But Marcos played it cool, tossing them the foot fungus story and stifling a laugh at their visible disgust.

Glancing back at his home, Marcos saw the blue flicker of a television in the upstairs window and knew that no one was there to watch.

* * *

They headed north and west, trying their best to proceed in a straight line, with Marcos's route almost constantly being edited and directed by my mother. "Turn this way," she would say at some random corner. "Let's try there," she'd point at another.

Finally, it came down to superpowers. Doesn't it always come back to that?

Mom used her own superpowers, ones that I could explain far less than my own. She simply *felt* Holly was near.

"Pull over here, Marcos, please," she said. Marcos complied, guiding the car to a stop on a deserted strand of road somewhere in the woods, a nondescript line of asphalt running between some distant X and Y. Above them, the star-filled sky was brilliant, a direct contrast to the jet-black world of trees to each side.

They waited.

Nothing happened.

Still they waited.

Finally, Mom opened the door. The car's electric ding and mechanical click broke the silence, and the surrounding darkness was cut in two by a slice of brightness from the dome light of Marcos's car.

Mom stood on the empty road, listening.

After a moment, she sighed in frustration, her voice coming out in barely more than a whisper. "Holly, if you're out there, please show yourself. I only want what's best for you."

Still, there was silence. In time, Mom turned to get back into the car.

Go home, a strange voice spoke in my mother's head.

At that moment, the emotion of communication, of recognition, of time lost, of lives that could have been so very different — it all collapsed upon my mother like the stars themselves had fallen down. "Hol— Holly?" she spoke, starting to tremble.

Yes, Mom, it's me. Go home.

Mom fell to her knees in the street, hearing the voice that was so familiar and yet so unknown. Her own daughter. A clear and true voice she hadn't heard truly speak in years.

Marcos, unable to hear the voice in my mother's mind, leaped out of the car to come to her aid. "What is it? What's wrong?"

"It's her," Mom said, still on her knees but frantically scanning the dark tree line. "She's here. Somewhere near."

Holly? Mom thought. It felt strange and alien to *think* words as an attempt to communicate, but she tried.

Yes, Mom. I can hear you. Whether you think the words or speak them, I can hear you.

Mom's shoulders drooped, the impact of being able to talk to her daughter at long last too much to bear. "Holly! Oh my God, Holly, how good it is to hear your voice."

Marcos, confused, shook his head, wondering if Mom had suddenly lost her mind. "Andrea, are you —?"

"Shhhh!" she interrupted. "Let Holly speak." She looked at Marcos and saw his concern. "I'm not crazy, Marcos. You know she — and John — can do these… *things*. She's speaking to me." Mom tapped the side of her head with one finger. Marcos nodded. He didn't understand how all these superpowers worked. A girl who couldn't walk or talk was managing her version of both things pretty well. So he just went with the flow.

Just go home, Mom. Please, Holly said to her.

No. Come out, Holly.

There was a last moment of silence as Mom and Marcos scanned the dark woods.

And then fury came at them from one side, a blinding beacon of light and sound and a girl in black who moved from some distant hiding spot in an instant. Like a miniature sun, Holly appeared above them, brilliant and beautiful and terrifying, rays of light emanating from her like a spectacular, horrible ghost.

My God, Mom thought. *She* is *a Shadow Ghost.*

Above her, Holly's eyes pierced with flame, and her voice boomed. This time, even Marcos heard the words, like Holly's power had grown too strong for only one mind to know. *Yes, Mother, I am Shadow Ghost! Now go home, before it's too late!*

They cowered before the godlike creature, someone they knew so well, and yet whose power they could never control. "Why, Holly?"

Why? You know exactly why I must go to Sol! Holly's voice screamed in their minds. *For my revenge!*

Slowly, Mom stood, defying the phantom of light before her, rising before her own daughter. "No, Holly, that's not what I mean."

Marcos looked at Mom, perplexed, then back to the intimidating force of Holly as she hovered over them.

What, then, are you asking? Holly said.

A cold fire blazed in my mother's eyes as she stood tall in front of her daughter.

"If you want revenge against that bastard Sol, why won't you let me help you?"

10

"Damn, that one's *big*," Bobby said, pointing toward Babilu Tower, four blocks south of us. "He's there?" The three of us huddled on the roof of a fairly nondescript 80-story building, far enough away, we felt, that we could maintain the element of surprise. To my left, Pip scanned the area with binoculars, although what she could possibly see, I had no idea. It was an overcast night, the lights of the city reflecting off the clouds hovering close above us. Pip wore her red outfit and Bobby had on his yellow. I discovered that they each had many copies of the same costumes, neatly folded in drawers. Apparently fighting fires and the like played hell with keeping one's clothes pristine.

I nodded, looking down at the black, stretchy shirt I wore. With great shame, I will admit that I allowed Pip to get me an outfit similar to hers and Bobby's. Including the new-fangled mask. We truly looked like the ridiculous Triangle Gang or Trio Supremo, after all. *It's for ease of movement*, I told myself. *Sure, it is, John. Keep telling yourself that. It's definitely not a bona fide superhero costume.*
"Yeah, that's the building," I said. "Sol's in the penthouse at the very top." As if on cue, a wind kicked up, feeling almost strong enough to rip us from the safety of the roof and toss us into the air. I reached out to grab for some support before remembering a couple of obvious facts: that I very well might be impossible to kill, and that I could make my body hover in midair. I don't think the human brain ever really gets used to such things.

"Then coming in from the air not only saves us the trouble of wading through a hundred floors of Sol's flunkies, it also means we cut to the chase." Bobby smiled. "Ready?"

"Hold on, geez," Pip said, setting the binoculars down on the edge of the building. "Don't you guys ever prepare for anything?" She turned to Bobby. "And haven't I drilled anything into that head yet?"

"I thought we had a plan," Bobby said, feigning indignation.

"What's that?" Pip chided. "Drop down on top of him, and… then what?"

Bobby smirked, making a fist with one hand and punching the other, twice, slowly. Pip sighed. For my part, I stayed out of their banter. It was so easy to see that it was more than just jibes and bickering. Their eyes had a sort of sparkle when they went at each other. *Why doesn't Pip just admit how she feels?* I thought. But far be it from me to intercede.

Besides, plan or no plan, we were going to have to face Sol, and Margrethe, too. Three of us, two of them. And though Sol had to assume we would come after him again, he didn't know when it would happen or from where, so we had the advantage.

We thought.

We'd snuck into the city through one of Sol's newly-created border checkpoints. Thankfully, there were still two truths in play. One, the city couldn't provide every resource its people needed, so they still had to truck in food and other supplies. I guess the companies doing business with Sol could overlook the moral implications of aiding a megalomaniacal madman. And two, those supply trucks were driven by people, and Sol used people to staff the checkpoints, too. Minds were pushed, eyes that should have seen us glazed over. Getting into town was relatively easy. Still, there were minds we couldn't push and eyes that did see: our own. At the checkpoint, we witnessed two of Sol's Way of the Sun henchmen beating an older man. For what reason, none of us knew. I tried to send a tendril into their fevered minds, to make them stop, but they were too far away. Sight travels farther than power, sometimes.

I let Pip and Bobby continue to debate our "plan." Funny how we were heading into a serious battle and Bobby looked like he was having the time of his life. Pip was showing him something on her phone, its screen lighting up their faces in the dark night. For a second I felt like I didn't belong, eavesdropping on their moment together.

"Johnny, come take a look at this," Bobby said, pointing toward Pip's screen.

Glancing down, I saw a gallery of photos as Pip swiped through them. "There are a ton of images of the penthouse online," she said. "Look familiar to you?"

I reached out, swiping back to one Pip had passed. "That's his office," I said. "That's where he had the gas that knocked me out."

Bobby laughed. "Okay, so we *don't* go there."

"*We* don't want to go inside, at all," Pip said, closing the gallery and bringing up a book.

"Here we go again," Bobby said. "Another book. Is this Talenheimer again?"

Pip shot him a look. "You mean *Talhoffer*. And no. This is slightly more famous than that. So much so that even a dunce like yourself might have heard of it. *The Art of War* by Sun Tzu?" Bobby blinked at her slowly, and Pip's shoulders fell. "Seriously? You're an embarrassment."

"And you love it," Bobby, joking but not really.

Pip looked away for a moment, like she was composing herself. She might have been stifling a smile, but when she turned back, she was all business. "Look here," she said. "*He who is skilled in attack flashes forth from the topmost heights of heaven.* That'll be us."

Bobby smiled a big, dopey smile. "It's like this Sunny guy knows us."

"It's Sun Tz—" I started, before Bobby held up one finger in front of me.

Leaning close, he whispered in my ear. "Don't you think I know all about it, Johnny? You seriously don't think this is the first time Pip has brought up *The Art of War*, right?" He winked at me before turning back to Pip. "What else does he say?"

"For you, Bobby, he has this: *He wins his battles by making no mistakes.*"

"Okay, well, that one seems kinda obvious. Besides, aren't you the least bit annoyed that all these passages say *he this* and *he that*? What about *she*?" Bobby shot me a grin.

"*I*," Pip said, "am capable of overlooking such historical sexism. Still, this entire book tells us exactly how to behave, in this battle and others." Then, in broad brush strokes, Pip outlined a plan that I thought was, simply put, brilliant. "Of the many appropriate quotes from the book, allow me to select only one more: *You can be sure of succeeding in your attacks if you only attack places which are undefended.* And that, friends, is what we're doing." The three of us gazed at each other, smiling. Sol's reign of terror was about to end.

Without another word, Pip tucked her phone into a bag, dropped it at her feet, and then... those same feet rose into the thin, whirling air.

"I guess we're ready now?" Bobby asked before lifting himself into the nothingness of the sky to join her.

That left me. Red and yellow hovered above. Time for black to move.

Okay, look. I had done the hover/fly thing before, but honestly not a lot. And, for whatever reason, it's one thing to hover 10 feet off the ground. It's another to hover 10 feet above the roof of an 80-story building. At least, that's what my mind was telling me, seeing the vast expanse of *emptiness* below. Still, they were waiting. I closed my eyes and began to lift from the surface.

Then, I made my first mistake. I opened my eyes.

I started to fall. It all seemed so *unreal.* We were floating nearly a thousand feet above busy city streets. What kept us from plummeting to the unforgiving pavement? Thorns in our cells. Thorns. That was all.

Sure, yeah, that makes a lot of sense, I thought, awkwardly recovering from my misstep.

Red Hope and Yellow Fury looked down at me and I felt inferior. The third wheel in their super-relationship. I got a little pissed off at myself, my internal anger flaring. Suddenly, the flying act seemed a little easier. I guess being mad at myself trumped the insanity of it all.

"You good, Johnny?" Bobby said. There may or may not have been a bead of sweat on my forehead as I righted the wobbly ship that was my body. I nodded, gruffly. "Awesome. Now, let's go."

And with that, a trio of superheroes flew through the night, unaware that they would never be a trio of superheroes again.

11

A ceiling of low, dense clouds hovered above us as we floated silently toward Sol's rooftop home. At one point, I absently reached up with one hand to brush the wisps of white just overhead. Bobby shot me a look, so I stopped. I guess I was being such a third wheel.

I had died and returned. As I moved closer to the scene of my resurrection, I realized that I must no longer be human. Weren't human beings defined by their mortality? If mortality was something I no longer had to worry about, wasn't I different? Somehow *inhuman*? Was that a good thing? A bad thing? And just how different were we? Could I continue to care for humans if I was no longer one myself?

Mom.

Yes, I thought. *Yes, I will always care for her, even if I seem to be something different now. And Carrie. And, hell, lots of people. I'm not inhuman. Not yet, at least.*

I thought about the circumstances of Sol's first death — the cells of his body floating on the wind and finding a new home in the form of Jake Weissman. Was it really so different from the sluicing we all now took for granted? I mean, if my body could flow like liquid into any shape or form, then recompose itself, was it really all that surprising that it could be broken apart — even at a cellular level — and still manage to come back together?

And what about me? Did I really die? I mean, I think I did, but unlike Sol, I didn't need the cells of my body to find a new host. I just came back into myself. Maybe that didn't count as dying after all.

We had talked about these things so much — how could we stop Sol if he couldn't be killed? But that was the trick. After talking it over, we thought Sol *could* be killed. We just needed to make sure that once we took care of him, his cells — and the thorns in those cells

— couldn't skip over to a new host or simply revive his current body. That was the hard part. What could we do to Sol that would actually kill him? Or, better yet, where could we send him?

And that brought us around to my original theory. That we had been infected by alien thorns from outer space. I know, it still sounds super-rational. Whatever. But if Sol's power was from outer space, why not send it back there? In space, his body would eventually die, and then, eventually, so would the thorns. Returning to the cold void, the thorns wouldn't have the luxury of a comet to keep them safe this time around. We just had to find Sol, yank him out of his cushy penthouse, and use our power to put him — and keep him — in a high, deadly orbit.

Sounds easy, right?

Honestly, we went into it feeling pretty confident. No, *more* than confident. Floating hundreds of feet above the bustling city streets, I felt a calmness, a certainty. Alone, I was a force. With my best friend, Bobby, I was unstoppable. Add Pip and the odds went to the level of "simply unfair."

Sol was doomed. I believed that in my heart, as we flew to destroy him.

The funny thing was, even though we'd devised a plan to kill the unkillable, I continued to assume that the three of us were immortal.

I was wrong.

"Positions!" Pip called out, and we began to arrange ourselves into the points of a large triangle, with hundreds of feet between ourselves. At our height, the wind nearly ripped the voice out of Pip's mouth, so she enhanced it with her mind, but eventually we were too far away for even that. Once the plan was in motion, we would rely on hand gestures and the simple knowledge that each of us knew what to do.

Act fast, keep moving, and if we locate him, finish it before it's begun.

That was the gist of the plan. We were to array ourselves above Sol's penthouse and then move in random but coordinated directions, gliding in a circle overhead. We would each reach out with our senses, our minds, delicately trying to pinpoint Sol. He would have his beacon completely muted, of course, but we theorized that if we were all there, triangulating, that something would show up. That some trace of Sol would reveal him to us. And if it didn't, we had agreed that we'd go home and try again later. That was my favorite part of Pip's plan — it didn't have to be on the first night. We could be patient. At some point, with us constantly scanning for him, he'd make a mistake, and then we'd have him. After that, you know, it's *blast-off!* I hope you're up for a trip to Uranus, Sol, old friend! I know, the puns write themselves.

Silently, we slid around in our wide circles, high in the night sky. I reached out with the slightest tendril of my mind, letting it slide over the penthouse like waves lapping a shoreline. *No hurry. Don't force it*. I knew Bobby and Pip were doing the same. The feeling of connection to the surface, the interior, grew as I continued. It reminded me of the way people read braille, sliding their fingers over the raised symbols with such simple grace, yet revealing so much.

I became almost entranced by the process. Floating on air…searching… searching… was there something there? Not inside the penthouse but… on the rooftop?

And then I heard a scream.

Something dark and fluttering and human-shaped zoomed upward toward me, and the screaming got louder. Female screaming. I was stunned, frozen. A dark blanket that had been covering something flapped and fell away into the empty air, and I was dumbfounded by the sight. It was Naima, flying straight toward me.

Flying? How?

No way. I mean, she wasn't exactly moving of her own free will. Naima was being hurled at me like the payload from a catapult.

Oh, shit!

It was one of the very few times my head was more aware than my body. I guess my cells thought of Naima as nothing more than a projectile — something they would just try to sluice away from when necessary. But with Naima, there would be no such victory.

If she hit me, took away my powers, I was going to fall. There was nothing below me but hundreds of feet of, well, *nothing*.

I tried to dodge, but I was too wrapped up in what I'd been doing, too wrapped up in the utter strangeness of seeing this woman flung through the air like a doll. By the time I tried, I was already falling. Naima was draining away my powers.

No!

I only had time to see Bobby and Pip rushing toward me, clearly confused by what they were seeing. Then I lost all control and dropped out of the sky. I fell quickly and the air was ripped out of my lungs — until abruptly I was frozen in mid-air. Not by my own powers. By *his*. Shifting my gaze back to the building, I saw him, finally revealed.

Sol stood like the king of the mountain, on the rooftop of Babilu Tower with both hands raised. *He was waiting for us the whole time*, I thought. Twice now I had walked right into one of Sol's traps. That realization sparked a fire deep inside of me, an anger… but it was simply a human anger. My power was gone. My anger just a bitter knot in my stomach, with no way to get out.

Once I was powerless, Sol held me tight. No, worse. He added me to his floating armada and, along with Naima, I was guided like a missile toward Bobby and Pip. They'd broken formation and were now too close together, too close to me. And in an instant, too close to Naima.

"Get back!" I yelled. "It's Naima — he's using her to stop us! My powers are gone!"

But Sol was quicker, thrusting the still hysterically screaming form of Naima and the now-captive form of me right at my friends.

They realized their mistake too late, just as I had. And then their dedication to one another failed them. They tried to dodge together, rather than each moving in a different direction. Maybe, just maybe, if they had split up, things would have turned out differently.

But in the end, it made sense. Bobby and Pip were together, just like I could tell they should have been for so long.

Only this time, this one unforgivable time, it got them both caught.

12

The one thing I recall, before things went so horribly wrong, was that I was embarrassed. We all were. Sure, we were scared, too, because we were powerless. And Sol had us firmly in his grasp. We had no idea what would happen next, and, in hindsight I think, we could never possibly have guessed.

"John," Sol said, stepping forward. "Wonderful of you to come back to see me. I have missed you since you so unceremoniously departed. My friend, you didn't even say goodbye." He *tsked* me, grinning, so pleased with what he was doing.

I mean, consider the situation. Sol was on the top of a building he for all intents and purposes owned, in a city that he owned, too. And his greatest enemies stood before him, beaten and helpless. From his point of view, it must have been a pretty great moment. The greatest of moments.

"I'm not your friend," I spat.

Sol paused, looking at me with a probing curiosity, but kept his distance. And it was a significant distance.

Pip, Bobby, and I were lined up like prisoners along one edge of the rooftop of Babilu Tower, with Naima just to one side, still hyperventilating from being flung around in the sky like a badminton birdie. With her so close, Red Hope, Yellow Fury, and Black Sword were just three people in odd, stretchy, colorful clothing. Each of us had ripped off our masks, but I still felt silly in my black superhero outfit, what with Sol dressed in his normal suave hipster way.

I tried to probe into my own head, seeking out the power that I'd become so accustomed to finding there. But it was gone.

Within moments of Sol dropping us to the rooftop, a battalion of his dark-suited Way of the Sun lackeys surrounded us, brandishing guns of various sorts — handguns, shotguns, and things that looked like they could take out an elephant or a tank. Sol was taking no chances. But after rendering us completely powerless, he probably could have kept us docile with a half-trained German Shepherd and a dull switchblade.

I wasn't surprised to see Sol keeping back, unwilling to come closer to our side of the rooftop. Apparently, he wasn't immune to Naima's ability — and at least that was a small blessing. That made me wonder how he'd managed to toss her around in the air, how he caught us when our powers dissipated. Naima's sphere of influence, the area around her where her ability killed superpowers, had to have been less than half the distance Sol could reach with his own power. Even looking at him, pacing along the far side of the building, I knew that normally I should have been able to reach him — to attack him with my mind. But with Naima nearby, I was helpless. As long as Sol stayed close enough to work his power on us, but far enough back to avoid Naima, we were screwed.

Sol's focus turned to the others beside me. "Bobby Graden. I have a bone to pick with you, Bobby. You *left* me. And that hurt." Sol touched the center of his chest, feigning distress. "You could learn a thing or two about loyalty from your… *companion.*" He nodded toward Pip and I could see her blood boil. Even powerless, Pip looked like she might try it — lunge across the rooftop, dodge bullets, and take down Sol. But of course, it was impossible. Without powers, she'd be cut down by gunfire in three steps. Even if she somehow got close to Sol, he would invariably destroy her with his powers. "Phillipa Siva, so nice to see you again. You are looking lovely, as always."

Sol's eyes dragged up and down Pip in her tight-fitting red costume, and then it was Bobby's turn to rage. I put a hand on his shoulder. "Don't Bobby. You can't win," I said, trying to will him to be calm.

So instead, Bobby chose wit over action. "What now, asshole?" he said, perfectly encapsulating the question in all of our minds as well as our sentiment toward our captor.

"Yes, of course. Direct, as always, Bobby. Very well. You all will remember Margrethe, yes?" He asked it as a sincere question, yet there was no doubt we all remembered her. Or that she, in particular, remembered me. A door on the far side of the roof, behind Sol, opened, and Margrethe appeared. She didn't hide her feelings. In fact, she spared hardly a glance at anyone but me.

For me, she oozed with hate.

Could I blame her? She and Petrus had a thing, and then he had attacked me and I had defeated him, burning out his mind. But that didn't make their relationship any less real for her. What if the roles had been reversed and Margrethe had destroyed Carrie? Pretty sure I'd be the one with hate in my eyes.

Still, back then, Petrus and Margrethe had been conspiring against Sol. I guess they'd patched things up. Both of them seemed to love having important allies.

Sol continued. "There was a time — Bobby, Pip — when we worked *together*. When we tried to create something very special, very important. Together. Bobby, you left us, and too soon. But Pip, you stayed, until the very end." He chuckled. The sound I hated. Even powerless, my blood began to boil. Was there a way I could stop Sol, even without my powers? I tried desperately to think. "The end of part one, I suppose you could say. But here we are in a new reality. I have returned, and you all — all three of you — have a chance to make the right decision, this time." Sol looked us over, one at a time.

"Enough already," I interjected. "If you're going to kill us, kill us. I've been down that road with you once already, so hurry up. We're not joining you. All this talk is pointless." I looked from one side to the other at Pip and Bobby, hoping they agreed. Eminent death can make people change their minds, you know.

Sol smiled. Not a friendly smile, but the teeth of a hyena, bared and ready. "Is it, John? Is it really? Do not forgot that, now, I can probe your minds in ways that you not only cannot stop, you also cannot even detect. Powerless as you are, I can read your every thought. And I can see that one of you is wavering."

We snapped to attention, looking at each other, wondering. Was it true? It didn't take me long to see the distracted glimmer in Pip's eye.

Oh, Bobby. Don't look at her. I didn't want him to see. Didn't want him to be disappointed in her. *She's thinking about it. Or at least thinking that working for Sol might be better than dying. But is it, really?*

"Mom!" a young voice yelled, as a blur ran toward us. Sharif, appearing from seemingly nowhere, rushed for his mother. "Mom — what's happening?" He reached his mother and clutched at her the way only a young child can. Trailing after the boy was one of Sol's men, clearly having failed in keeping track of the kid.

Naima, flustered, stroked her son's hair. "Nothing, son. How did you get here? You must go back to bed!"

"Not without you, Mom. Why are you all up here? Why are you on the roof?" Then he looked at us, remembering the day at the warehouse. "And why are *they* here?" Sharif seemed to hold us in contempt. Little did I know, at the time, that he'd developed a fondness for his comfortable prison life, and even for his captors, including Sol.

Unfortunately, the feeling wasn't mutual.

"No, *boy*," Sol said, suddenly and sharply, furious at the interruption. "Why are *you* here?" Sol's fists clenched and unclenched. His forehead wrinkled with concentration as he turned toward the clouds above us and gestured with one hand, as if pulling something down toward him.

I gasped. From above appeared a hand, a dark, black hand made of ethereal wisps of cloud and nothing else, with barely enough substance to be visible. The same massive hand I had seen Sol use to crush a kid to death down on the street, outside this same building.

"No, don't!" I said, starting forward before being pulled back by one of Sol's men.

None of us had time to take another breath. The hand reached down, grabbed Sharif away from his mother, and flung him off the rooftop, 108 floors above the ground.

"Sharif!" Naima screamed, her voice cracking like the breaking of a heart as the boy disappeared from view.

We all knew it. Instantly. Without question.

The boy was dead.

Naima didn't think. She simply took five steps and jumped, following her son to their mutual death.

I only had time to suck in a breath, dumbfounded by what had happened. I could see that even Sol was confused, never expecting this series of events. Although the boy was unimportant to him, Naima, of course, was. Pip, Bobby, and I exchanged the most fleeting of glances.

And Bobby nodded.

A simple, basic nod. Was he nodding to himself, as an answer? Or nodding to us, a gesture of respect?

I'll never know.

For at that moment, Bobby turned and, still devoid of his powers, jumped off the roof of Babilu Tower after Naima and Sharif, with nothing but hundreds of feet of open air between him and the unforgiving pavement below.

13

"*No!*"

The shrill sound of Pip's scream will be forever burned into my memory.

I paid no more attention to Sol or his men. I ran to the edge of the building and looked down, terrified by what I might see.

There, three forms fell, seemingly in slow motion.

The boy, smallest and farthest away.

His mother, plummeting with her hands outstretched, as if anything she could do would change her child's fate.

And Bobby, diving after them like the hero from a movie, gesturing with one hand the way I had seen him do so many times before when he used his powers.

Powers…

At that moment, I couldn't think of anything except what I was seeing, but Bobby must have had his wits about him. Once Naima had jumped, she became too far away to block our powers anymore. Bobby realized it and reached out to stop her fall, to stop the boy's fall.

It worked — we could see that they began to slow in their descent.

He was doing it. *Way to go, Bobby!* I thought, even daring a smile.

Beyond all belief, Bobby was saving their lives.

But something was wrong.

While Sharif's and Naima's speed decreased, Bobby swiftly closed the gap between them. As he used his will and ability to slow them to a gentle touchdown on the street below, he got too close. He was so focused on saving them, he forgot to save himself. And by the time he thought of it, it was too late.

Somewhere close to a hundred feet above the ground, with Naima and Sharif safely deposited below him, Bobby entered Naima's sphere of influence and his powers vaporized. He dropped.

"Come on, Bobby," I said in a whisper, gripping the side of the building with all my strength, desperate that what I was seeing would somehow change. Realizing my own powers had returned, I focused them on Bobby, but he was too far away. Sight travels farther than power, sometimes.

And my friend, my best and true friend, the one I had been through everything with since discovering these powers, slammed into the pavement with a devastating force, a life-taking force.

There was no sluicing this time.

The thorns, assumedly still inside him, were rendered useless by his proximity to Naima.

In my head, a million tiny voices shrieked as Bobby bounced grotesquely on the merciless street and then ceased to move.

It wasn't the sight of it — despite how grotesque, I'd seen Bobby hurt from falls before — it was that sound. That earsplitting yet silent sound.

Bobby's thorns cried out in pain and anguish. I'd heard the sound before and knew it meant one thing and one thing only.

My friend Bobby Graden was dead.

14

I stood there, confused, dumbfounded, bewildered, distraught, and — more than anything — numb.

Get up, Bobby, I thought. *Come on, buddy. Please.*

He didn't move. Maybe it was an act. Maybe he was lying motionless to throw them off. Hell, maybe he'd seen an opossum and was teaching it how to play dead.

I couldn't think. I tried to consider my next move, but my mind was a mess of fuzz and confusion.

Fortunately for me, Pip's mind was clear. She knew her powers had returned and she knew what she wanted to do with them. She attacked.

Pip screamed an inhuman wail and lunged at Sol. As expected, the gunfire erupted, but with her powers restored, Pip's body sluiced and shifted harmlessly around those tiny projectiles of doom.

I thought she'd get him, for a slim moment of time. I really did.

Pip leaped, ready to strike.

And that's when Sol chickened out. *Exit... stage left*. Sol twisted and ducked to let Margrethe take the brunt of the attack, and then he disappeared through the door at the far side of the rooftop and was gone.

Pip and Margrethe became a blur of fists and feet and sluicing bodies. Sol's Way of the Sun thugs kept firing for a moment before realizing, first, that it wasn't doing any good, and second, that technically they were now shooting at Margrethe, too. I didn't imagine any of them wanted the wrath of the Norse goddess pointed their way, so they did the only logical thing they could think of — which was to start shooting at me.

As the first bullet whizzed past my head, I lost it. I heard a sound, bellowing noise with no words. It took some time before I realized that noise was me, raging at the insanity of what was happening. Raging at the death of my friend. Raging at Sol. And, in the end, raging at his men. The men shooting at me.

Without thinking, I lashed out. Sluicing between bullets with superhuman speed, I slapped the gun out of the first man's hand, then knocked him backward, slamming his body into the wall behind him. With him down, I attacked the next one, and he fought back. My rage won. And it continued to win, slashing and smashing at the remaining men, several of whom were sent to their own plummeting deaths over the edge of the building. The realization that I was killing them the same way my friend had died began to eat through my blind fury and tears began streaming down my face.

There have been many low points in my life. The death of my father, the time I cut off Pip's arm in the heat of my anger. But this time… this was it. The worst of the worst.

Tears blurring my vision, rage tearing through me, I was indiscriminately killing Sol's men, despite the fact that they were no more of a danger to me than a housefly.

Finally, the wet streaks on my face must have cooled the fire within me. Or maybe it was simply that I had killed most of them. I paused and watched the last few Way of the Sun henchmen turn and flee. I must have looked insane, crying and killing all at the same time. The blubbering machine of death.

To one side, Pip continued to fight Margrethe, but no one was getting the upper hand. I closed the distance, and they broke apart long enough to each look at me — Pip expecting my help, Margrethe suddenly concerned.

With Sol's unexpected departure, Margrethe was now left to fight two on one, and apparently wasn't terribly comfortable with those odds. She stepped backward and raised an index finger to point at me. “This isn’t the end,” she said. “I will find you, John Black, and I will make you pay. Trust me.”

At that moment, Margrethe’s threats meant next to nothing to me. I nodded at her with a steely look, dismissing her. Pip and I had lost our best friend. We had to go down to the street, despite what we’d find there. I didn’t even know if Margrethe had turned away, and I didn’t care. I lifted myself off the surface of the rooftop and began to float down to the street level. Vaguely, I sensed Pip following me.

He was still there, still hadn’t moved. Bobby.

As I drifted downward, I realized that I was following the same path Bobby had, that I was essentially reliving his last moments.

When my feet touched the street, I was beyond any sense of feeling, focusing only on the lifeless form of my friend. It only confirmed what that awful sound had already told me. There was no hope. He would not be moving again, ever. His body looked broken and crushed, much, much worse than the time he’d tried to jump his bike across the gap in the roofs two stories up and failed. This time his last helpless descent had been many times the distance.

Pip landed right next to Bobby, bending down to embrace him on the ground. She pressed her face into the curve of his neck and silently I watched her body shake as she cried.

I gave her the time she needed, not interrupting. Finally, she peered up at me with wet, bloodshot eyes. “I loved him. But I never told him,” she said, once more burying her face and quivering with sorrow.

Sighing deeply, I tried to consider what we would do next. Not just in the next minute, but the next day, week, month, year, lifetime. Bobby was gone and nothing would ever be the same. “He knew, Pip. Trust me. He knew.”

PART 4

— *death* —

1

Pip and I shared the duty of carrying Bobby's body out of the city, floating him gently like a leaf riding high on currents of air.

By the time we left, we realized that Naima and Sharif were nowhere to be found — maybe they'd escaped, maybe Sol had recaptured them. At that moment, we had other concerns.

We didn't have a destination. We just wanted to be out of Sol's city, away from any place contaminated by the likes of him. I don't know if Pip wanted to take Bobby all the way back to the capital, where they had lived together, but we never got that far. A few miles past the checkpoints — which of course we ignored, given that they were thousands of feet below us — we saw a simple, grassy hillside where a lone oak tree stood. The sun had begun its daily ascent and the world was returning to color. Something about the hill called to us, and without a word, we both turned toward it. Trees lined the bottom edges, and a house sat back to one side.

We placed our friend down softly in grass that was damp with morning dew. Then Pip walked to the crest of the hill and focused her abilities on the ground. Soon, sections of turf were carefully being sliced and set to one side, courtesy of Pip's mind. I helped her move the earth next. We worked for some time, trying to make it just right. To honor our friend in the only way we could think of at that moment. Until we ended with a perfectly rectangular grave.

Behind us, a suspicious and confused voice suddenly spoke. "Is this…? Is he…?"

Startled, I leaped into the air and twisted around toward whoever had stumbled upon us.

"Oh my God, you're *him*." A man crouched down next to Bobby's body, mouth agape. One of the man's hands held Bobby's forearm, like he was checking for a pulse. Seeing me, he jerked back, almost like Bobby's body had electrically shocked him. But the real shock was us, his sudden recognition of all of us. "You're Black Sword," he said. Then Pip was beside me, also hovering in midair, tensed and ready. "And Red Hope! My gosh, right here in my own backyard!" The man looked to be no more than 10 years older than me, wearing a flannel shirt, with a tanned complexion that suggested he spent a lot of time outdoors. He stood and backed away with palms facing us. "Hey, sorry, I don't mean any trouble. I was just taking a walk around the property at sunrise. It's something I like to do most mornings, unless it's raining — or snowing." He smiled, nervously, realizing he was talking too much.

My tension eased, and I settled to the ground beside the grave. "This land is yours?" The man nodded.

"What's your name?" Pip asked, coming to stand next to me.

"Charles. Charles Nero. But you all can call me just Charlie. Most folks do." He reached out a hand, and to my surprise, Pip took it. I followed her example. Shaking this man's hand — Charlie Nero's hand — I found myself warming to him quickly.

"We're sorry to be on your property like this. Something about this spot just seemed perfect." Pip said, tilting her head toward Bobby's body on the ground. "Bobby — I mean, Yellow Fury — he lost his life saving the lives of two innocent people, over in the city." Pip gestured with her head in the direction we had come from, and from his expression it was clear that Charlie had no love for that city. "We didn't know what else to do, and then we ended up here. This place just seemed right." I could tell she was fighting back tears simply talking about it.

Charlie grimaced, looking suddenly tearful himself. "I can understand how you'd think that." He turned and pointed. There, not 100 feet beyond the oak tree, was a small marker, something I hadn't even noticed previously. It stuck up from the rich green grass by no more than half a foot. "My wife, Lauren, is buried just there. I thought this was a good spot, too. We both did, before she died."

"I'm very sorry for your loss. She must have been quite young. How did she die?" Pip was clearly better at knowing what to say than I was.

"Cancer. Leukemia, specifically. It's the scourge of the earth, I'll tell ya." Charlie paused a moment in thought. "Anyway, I don't mind if you want to bury your friend here. He's a hero to the world, and Lauren and I would be honored to have him here. Plus, I come up here a lot, so I can make sure his site is well tended."

"Thanks," I said. That's all I could think to say.

"But one thing more," Pip said.

"Sure, what?" Charlie Nero replied.

"You can't tell anyone he's here. Not anyone at all. If people found out, they'd be all over this place. They'd destroy it here."

Charlie nodded again, and spared another glance toward his wife's last resting place. "Yeah, well, I definitely don't want *that*. I'll keep it to myself. Promise. I won't even tell my dog, Addy," he said with a small laugh. "I can even help you finish up here, if you want."

"No," I said. "Thanks, but no. I think we need to do this ourselves."

"Understood," Charlie said. "I'll leave you to it, then." With that, he nodded and walked off toward the marker to pay brief respect to his late wife before heading down the hill and disappearing in the direction of the house.

There's nothing much I can say about the next couple hours of my life that would make it hurt any less, so I'll just state it bluntly.

Pip and I finished the soul-rending task of burying our friend.

2

I hadn't been to the front door of Bobby's house — sorry, Bobby's *parents'* house — in so long that standing there seemed like a dream. *This isn't real*, I thought. *If it were real, Bobby would be inside, waiting for me to come over.*

Not dead and buried on a hilltop.

As I stepped to the door and knocked, Pip studied the disheveled yard, the peeling paint on the shutters, the ashtray overflowing on a small table beside a cheap plastic chair. I didn't realize it at the time, but later she told me it was all too reminiscent of the home where she grew up.

"Who is it?" a female voice shouted from inside. Mrs. Graden's nasal whine was as obnoxious as I remembered. Her question was flecked with hints of annoyance and anger. As usual.

"It's me. John Black. I mean, Johnny," I said. There was a bustle from inside followed by a couple of hurried clacking noises before the door was suddenly jerked open, but only a few inches, like the mole in some spy movie, wondering if the person at the door was a good guy or bad.

She stood there, nose poking out from the thin opening, but primped as always, hair adding what seemed like a foot to her otherwise diminutive height. Her makeup was a solid layer of paint, making her face an unnaturally uniform off-pink color, punctuated by the excessively bright red of her lipstick. Her jaw worked at a wad of gum, and an invisible cloud of some cloying perfume floated out to greet us. "Johnny? It *is* you. Well, hot damn!" She opened the door wider, enough that she finally saw Pip beside me. Mrs. Graden's expression changed to one of distrust. She looked around, past me, behind me. "Where's Bobby?"

Well, that was the question, wasn't it? That was the reason for our visit. Yet I couldn't spit out the words. I stood silently trying to figure out how to tell her that her son was dead.

For a moment — just the tiniest of moments — Mrs. Graden's callous veneer cracked. "Johnny? What is it? You're scaring me."

"He's…" I began, before fresh tears began. "He's gone. Bobby —"

"What the hell are you talking about? Where's Bobby?" she said, interrupting, returning to her familiar form, rough and abrasive. "Where is he?"

"He's dead, ma'am," Pip said from just behind me, her voice cracking. "He died trying —"

"*What did you do to my boy?*" Mrs. Graden shouted at Pip, loud enough to force us both back a step. Loud enough to jostle the lazy form of Mr. Graden out of his recliner and over to the front door.

"What exactly is going on here?" he asked, before seeing it was me. "Oh, hi, John. Good to see you." When was it ever good to see me, at least from the Gradens' point of view? No, they both clearly had dollar signs in their eyes.

"Fine, then, *Johnny*," Mrs. Graden said. She crossed her arms, scowling. "You go ahead and explain to Bobby's father what you just said to me."

My mind was stuck. Stuck on what Bobby's mother had said. Not "How did it happen?" Not the wail of an anguished mother. No, she went right to accusations. *What did you do to my boy?*

I didn't say anything. Neither did Pip. Finally, with no one talking, Bobby's mom had to fill the void. "These *two* —" Mrs. Graden spat the word. "They are saying something about Bobby. It doesn't make any sense." She turned back to us in fury. "It *doesn't make any sense!* Bobby has powers. He can dodge *bullets*. He can't be hurt by *anything*. How could he be dead? *What did you do?*"

"Dead? What? How?" Bobby's father said, stunned.

Finally, someone cares to ask how it happened, I thought. "He saved a woman and a child," I said. "They fell, from really high up. He jumped and saved them, but in the end he couldn't save himself. He's a real hero."

Silently, I prayed that would be the end of it. That we were done, that they would accept what I said, and that we could leave and never see Mr. and Mrs. Graden again.

Bobby's mom folded herself into the oversized, meaty arms of her husband. And she wept. Big, shuddering sobs of sorrow. I couldn't bear to watch, so I turned aside, toward Pip. I started to gesture to her that we should leave.

"*This isn't possible!*" Mrs. Graden shouted, pounding her small fists into Mr. Graden's chest. I believed for a second that she truly cared, that she was truly mourning her son.

Then she spoke again.

"*How am I supposed to get the hell* out of this damn house *if he's gone?*" She pushed back, away from her husband, sucking in air like the shuddering contraction before an explosion. Then she screamed at us, all of us. "You! John Black! I blame you for this! You've *never* been anything but trouble. Always getting Bobby involved in all sorts of bad things, putting bad ideas into his head." I rocked backward at the unexpected vitriol. But Mrs. Graden was far from done. "And this… *girl*. Taking my son away from me, living in sin. Are you happy now, girl? You took him from me, and now you say he's never coming back? I hope you die, too." Mrs. Graden shook with the violence of hatred, her perfectly coifed hair popping out in odd shocks here and there.

“Hey, now —” Mr. Graden began.

She wheeled on him. “And you! What the hell good are you? This little bitch takes our son from us and you do *what?* Nothing, that’s what.”

I could hardly breathe, couldn’t think of moving. This woman — this *impossible* woman. How could she?

Beside me, Pip turned away from the house. Her face was bright red, her brow creased in anger. But she held it in. And she turned away.

It may have been the strongest thing I ever saw Pip do. Despite the horrible things Bobby’s mother was saying, Pip took the high ground and simply walked away.

Stammering something, I don’t even recall what, I turned and fled Bobby’s house, seeing his parents in the flesh for the very last time in my life.

* * *

After we buried Bobby, we returned to the capital. Pip had wanted to drive to Bobby’s parents’ house, not fly in like some alien freaks. I couldn’t have agreed more — flying into my childhood hometown would have been way too weird. Then, once we left the Gradens’ house, being in the car was a welcome diversion. The simple mindlessness of driving, the time it consumes getting from point A to point B, allowed us to spend time inside our own heads, to try to cope with everything that had happened.

For a while, we had no destination. Maybe Pip was taking us back to her place in the capital, but some of her turns seemed random. Finally, I realized that I needed to go somewhere specific. Snapping out of my daze, I gave her directions, and she complied without a word.

I had to tell my mom about Bobby. Had to tell Holly, too. Suddenly, the drive seemed to take too long. Suddenly, we couldn't get to Marcos's house soon enough.

Driving down the last street, I knew something was very, very wrong. The camera trucks, the reporters — they were all gone. Where there had been dozens before, now there was nothing. We turned into the driveway with no fanfare, only an eerie silence to greet us.

Pip parked the car and we went to the front door but found it locked. "Hold on," I told Pip. I left her and went around the house, checking first the main back door, then the rear door into the garage. Luckily that one was open, so I entered the garage but Marcos's car was missing. I jiggled the handle of the door that led to the family room and it opened with ease. After a brief look around, finding no one, I went and retrieved my phone. Then I opened the front door to let Pip in.

"They're not here."

"You don't think they—?" Pip asked.

"Of course they did," I said. "Well, of course *she* did."

I knew. Holly was leading Mom and Marcos directly to Sol.

3

If you expected a period where Sol became quiet and contemplative, well, you'd be wrong.

It pained me — no, it killed me — to know that Sol took *joy* in Bobby's death.

But the truth was that I was paralyzed. So was Pip. We didn't much talk about it at first, but it was true. We went back to Pip's place and locked ourselves inside.

Exhaustion took over. "I need to go to bed, maybe forever," Pip said, turning toward her bedroom.

"Me, too," I replied, before I froze. Pip disappeared behind a door in the hallway and I realized something. There were two bedrooms. Pip's… and Bobby's. I couldn't sleep in Bobby's room. No way. That would be sacrilege.

I dropped down onto the couch, not sure what to do.

And I didn't wake up until late the next day.

* * *

I woke slowly, hearing strange sounds of conversation, random snippets of music, outdoor noise, and things I couldn't even recognize. Punctuating these were clinks and clanks that reminded me of the chain of roadside diners that my parents often chose as our pit stop on long road trips.

Still half dreaming, the idea of those diners reminded me of my father. When had I last thought of him? It shamed me to even consider the question. The first real casualty of my superhuman life, and my own fault at that. And I didn't even have the decency to remember him on a daily basis.

Worse still, what had superpowers truly done for me? I had lost my father and my best friend. I was sleeping on a couch, with no idea where to find my remaining family. And I had earned the literally undying hatred of an evil man. The fact that I had these powers and some notoriety hardly seemed to make up for it.

The bitterness of those thoughts brought me fully back to the real world, and I saw that Pip was fixing coffee and breakfast as the TV flickered the nonstop insanity of the 24-hour news cycle behind her.

Pip was chopping something, vigorously, with an occasional scowling glance toward the screen.

"Hey," I said.

The chopping suddenly stopped. "Good, you're up. You'll want to see this," she said, gesturing toward the TV with her long knife. With her other hand she reached for a remote and turned up the volume as a perfectly groomed blonde newscaster gave a deadpan recital of the top story. Beside her, an ominous graphic read COUP ATTEMPT BRUTALLY THWARTED. I rubbed the sleep out of my eyes and walked into the kitchen, sitting on a stool opposite Pip.

"…though news out of the city remains limited, a member of the New Moon Resistance was able to smuggle a video recording of the events that occurred late last night. We warn you that this footage may be considered graphic. Viewer caution is advised."

The scene abruptly shifted to shaky cellphone footage of men and women in police uniforms standing in a loose ring around an office space filled with cubicles. A man's face then entered the picture, too close, the camera practically looking up the guy's nose. Despite the fact that he wore a hat identifying him as one of the police, he spoke casually, as if to a friend. "Hey, man, we're all set here. No problems. We're on the hundred and sixth. Just, you know, don't forget to do *your* part now." The officer grinned momentarily, just before someone shouted something muffled, off-screen. "All right, we're doing this. Masks on, here we go." The man lifted a gas mask, like you might see police use in riot situations. Then he turned the camera back out to face the office. Around him, the other officers finished strapping their masks on, and two or three checked some kind of thick, stubby gun.

“Are those tear-gas guns?” I asked. “What the hell are they doing?”

Pip shushed me. “Wait.” Her eyes remained glued to the screen.

A noise — shouting? — erupted in the video. The camera spun, and for a moment I could see the officer fumbling with his mask, his eyes growing wide, looking at something outside the frame. Then the camera quickly turned, blurring the entire shot into a patchwork of compressed pixels before coming to rest on what appeared to be two people entering the office space via a side door.

The camera’s focus strained to keep up with the drastic difference between near and far action, while screams and crashing noises provided a soundtrack to the mayhem. For a moment, the view blurred, then sharped, then blurred again. Finally, the image corrected itself into something clear.

Sol.

Even worse, he was with Margrethe. The two strode into the grid of cubicles with no more emotion than you might have walking down the toothpaste aisle at the grocery store. As they walked, they each gestured here and there with their hands. The crashing and shouting continued, and the camera shook again. Tense but muffled words could be heard — probably from the cop holding the camera — sounding like *Oh my God.*

Then came the worst of it. The camera swung again and caught Sol in the action, just as his gesture directed his powers.

Sol and Margrethe pushed and pushed and pushed. Windows shattered, despite the fact that they had to have been built to withstand tremendous force. Then, after blasting out each window, the two kept pushing, tossing police officers out into the sky a hundred and six floors above the ground. One officer had the presence of mind to fire his weapon with a strange pop, and a canister was launched toward Margrethe. She intercepted it with her powers and turned it backward, then sent the gas canister and the officer who fired it into thin air. Men and women screamed as they were thrown to their inevitable deaths.

Finally, Sol seemed to be impossibly close, looking almost directly into the camera.

Who am I kidding? That bastard *surely* was looking at the camera. At me.

And then the view shifted so rapidly there was nothing to see but sky.

"What did I just see?" I said, not even meaning to speak out loud.

"They tried to fight him, with what they knew. About you," Pip said.

"Huh? I don't get it."

Pip looked at me with a combination of heavy seriousness and weary annoyance, having to explain it all. "Those police officers — Sol thought he had them in his back pocket just because he took over the city. But he's wrong — those people *live* there. That's their home. When they swore an oath to protect, that oath didn't go away just because some shitbag with powers popped in."

"But what does that have to do with me? What did they *know about me*?"

"Some of the cops were there when Sol captured you. Some of them knew — or maybe just figured out — how he did it. They were going to gas him, incapacitate him. But their plan had a fatal flaw."

"What?"

Pip sighed, looking toward the TV where a frozen image showed one of the clearer shots of Sol and Margrethe as they walked through the office. "The police might not follow Sol to the ends of the earth, but some people will — the Way of the Sun. Since the cops are decent people, they didn't come in with their guns blazing to kill everyone in sight. Maybe they thought they were liberators, I don't know. All that matters is that too many zealot followers of Sol's were left alive. Someone tipped him off to the fact that the cops were there, and maybe even told him what they were going to do. The rest is what you just saw."

I sat in stunned silence. Sol had killed, what? A dozen, two dozen people, like he was taking a Sunday stroll? "But wait, how did they get that video?"

"It was a video call, recorded on the other end. And then whoever made that recording snuck a copy out of the city."

On the TV, the blonde newscaster reappeared. "We're continuing this hour with our analysis of the deepening crisis in the city. With me is Hanna McLaughlin, head of a citizens' organization called the Way of Hope. Hanna, thank you for joining me."

"Thank you, Elizabeth."

"Tell us about the Way of Hope."

"Of course. Hope has been ripped away from our great city. We've fled. We live outside the city we've loved our entire lives, looking back at it, watching as a madman destroys it."

"So, then what next?"

"Well, Elizabeth, when I said that hope has gone, I didn't just mean the hope within our souls. I mean Red Hope. And Yellow Fury. And Black Sword. We *need* them to come back and fight Sol, and we want them to know — if you're listening to me now, we want *you* to know — that we the people will rise up and fight alongside you!"

Without warning, the TV shut off, and quickly I looked toward Pip. Turning away, she dropped the remote down on the counter with a loud clack, then went back to her chopping, focusing on it closely, head down.

"She's right, isn't she?" I asked, unsure, like I was trying to convince myself. "We need to go back, to try again? They don't know Bobby's gone. But doesn't that just mean you and I are all that's left, and we have to go back to the city to take care of Sol?" It wasn't the statement of a bold person, it was the question of someone meek. Pip remained with her head down, chopping, like I wasn't even there. "Don't we, Pip?"

She slammed the knife down on the cutting board, head still down, taking a deep breath, then another. Finally, she tilted her head up at me and I saw the tear sliding down one side of her face. Pip, who always seemed so tough, so in control. "I can't, John. Not without *him*. I just can't do it anymore."

My feelings were swirling and unclear. Bobby was gone. Not only was he gone, but he had *proven* that Sol had the means to kill us, even if what happened to him was so bizarre, so random. I blinked, trying to gather my thoughts, but only one answer came.

"I know," I said. "I really can't do it, either."

4

If Holly had just been any other person, would I have found it so hard to think of her actions as reasonable? There was something about Holly that made me overlook her. Don't get me wrong. Holly is my sister, and I will always love her, no matter what, but I had become complacent in thinking of Holly as, essentially, *my baby sister who can't talk and lives in a wheelchair.* I realized, so much later, that by thinking of Holly in terms of her wheelchair, I was automatically limiting what I thought Holly could and would *do.*

I was wrong to do that. Very, very wrong.

Because, of course, I had plenty of evidence that Holly might be the strongest superhuman on the planet.

I knew enough about her to guess, at least, that she somehow must have talked Mom and Marcos into taking her toward Sol. And there, I was right.

I could barely breathe, my heart could barely beat, thinking that Holly or Mom or Marcos — or all of them — might end up like Bobby. Yet, I had no idea where they were.

Turns out that Marcos had volunteered to drive.

"What else am I going to do? Go home? Go back to work?" he asked my mother as they stood on the dark country road with Holly floating above them beaming light and energy like a malevolent deity. "I have a chance to help with the greatest struggle facing mankind in my generation. There are good people with power and bad people with power, and something big is going to happen. I know it. I may be just a simple man myself, but I have pride. I want to help the side of good. Let me."

Mom nodded and hugged Marcos. Then she turned to Holly. "Will you let us take you?"

And the flaming, flying Shadow Ghost dimmed and came down toward them, ending up only an inch off the ground, suddenly seeming more like a young girl than a being of light and power.

Yes.

Mom opened the rear door of the car and Holly floated herself inside, seemingly relieved at the chance to turn off her powers. Marcos got behind the wheel and Mom sat shotgun, turning and talking to her daughter. Our mother was amazed that, for the first time in many, many years, she actually could. There was so much she wanted to ask Holly. Still, mostly she just wanted to hear Holly's voice. To hear her daughter's voice after so long. "Is it hard to keep it up? I mean, to use the powers for so long, to do so much?"

Yes.

Mom asked maybe a hundred more questions. But, despite all of her attempts, she got nothing else out of Holly for the next many miles.

* * *

"The checkpoint has to be coming up — maybe a mile or two," Marcos said. "What should I do? Pull over?"

No. Drive up to it like normal. I'll handle it.

Mom and Marcos were startled by the sudden words from the back seat, and exchanged fearful looks. Still, they did as Holly wished.

At the checkpoint, they waited in line behind cars and trucks and vans all trying to get through. When it was finally their turn, a man in all black approached. Mom shuddered, recognizing him as someone from the Way of the Sun.

Holly nearly burned the man's mind out of his living body. But she restrained herself, pushing him to accept some excuse that was nothing worth remembering, and told him to let them through. He complied.

Once in the city, Marcos looked back toward Holly. "Where to?"

So many things are true about my sister. She has power almost beyond comprehension. Yet she is also a girl who grew up in a small town with almost no worldly experiences.

I don't know where to go, she admitted, and the car shuddered like it had hit a deep pothole. Holly was angry with her own shortcomings.

"It's okay, Holly. I think we should go *near* Sol but not *to* Sol," Mom said. "I think we should find a place nearby where we can, you know, look around a bit and make a plan. All right?" Mom was almost pleading.

All right, Holly echoed.

* * *

Even in a city closed off from the rest of the world, people move around. Marcos concocted some story about the three of them having gotten kicked out of their apartment because the landlord had it in for them, whatever that meant. He told this story, making up random details, to two or three extended-stay hotels on the outskirts of the city before someone either believed him or simply didn't care. They got one room with two beds. Marcos knew one bed would be cramped with both Holly and my mother, and he knew Mom was still struggling with the after-effects of her injury. Though he could have pushed for one of the beds, Marcos took the couch without a word.

He paid in cash, nightly for the first few nights, figuring there was no reason to commit to something longer. None of them really worried about how long they would need to keep paying. There was little reason to care.

In a week, maybe two, they'd be long gone. Or they'd be dead.

They sat by day and made their plans. Marcos, assumedly the least recognizable of the three of them, would walk the streets near Babilu Tower, trying to gather information. He'd try to figure out when Sol came and went. Sure, Sol sort of lived *and* worked in the tower, but they figured he had to leave some time. Truth was, he didn't.

Day after day, Marcos circled the tower, trying to make his movements random and innocuous.

On the fourth day, Marcos was walking through a nearby park, trying to avoid simply circling the tower. He didn't want to look that obvious. In a shady spot, he found a bench and sat.

Each day, Marcos carried a small backpack with some food and water. On the bench, he unzipped the pack and pulled out a plastic bag holding salami and white cheese held between somewhat dry slices of bread. Having left so quickly, and needing to spend most of their money on the hotel room, their cash was limited and they were making do with what they could afford. Although his meal was basic, Marcos popped open the plastic bag with a small smile. He was finally, truly doing something important. The quality of his lunch was trivial in comparison.

"What have you got there? It looks good," a woman's voice asked, with an unusual accent. Marcos looked up to see a tall, powerful blonde casting a shadow over him. His sandwich hung halfway out of his mouth when he paused, recognizing the woman before him. The one he'd seen on TV.

"Oh no," he said.

5

That voice, that damned voice. Even over the phone. "Hello, John. There is something I think you should know. I have your sister and mother."

Well, shit. The only good news is that I wouldn't have to go searching around for them. If that could be called good news.

If there was one thing I could deal with never hearing again, it was Sol's voice. On the phone, in person, on TV. But I knew that I couldn't just run away, not anymore, not with my family in jeopardy.

Sol once had my sister and thought she was nothing but a helpless girl. This time was different. Sol knew her power, knew she was a threat. He would treat her much differently. He wouldn't just let her slip away. Not ever again.

My hand was forced. I knew the risks. I had to go. Sol called me, told me the odds, and nonetheless, it was time.

"Then I guess I'll be seeing you," I said, disconnecting the call before I had to hear another word from him.

Pip was in her room. She spent a lot of time holed up in her room. I didn't know what to do but give her space. Still, I had to talk to her.

I knocked, gently, and after a few minutes, she joined me in the kitchen. I told her about the call. "Pip, I know this is all a mess, beyond belief, and I don't want to go back there any more than you do, but he has my mother. And my sister. For that matter, he must have Naima again, or else how could he hold Holly? Which means he has her son, too. Four people who don't deserve any of this. Will you help me?"

Pip stared at me, unmoving, leaning up against the spotless silver of her massive refrigerator. "I'm sorry, John. I can't," she said.

"You have to!" I shouted, the fire inside me blazing in an instant. "I need you!" I wanted to tell her that none of this — her apartment, her income, the damn silver fridge — would be possible without her powers. And her powers were needed in action, out in the world, not closed up in her room. But tact prevailed and I didn't say any of those things.

Still, I looked at her with an intensity and with a burning need, and she met my eyes. For a moment, that old Pip bravado flared, and something else… Anger of her own? Was she remembering me from the moment I leaped into the air and cut off her arm? The strength behind her eyes was like a dare.

And then Pip hung her head. "You may be right. It's probably something I'm supposed to do. It's the *right* thing to do. But *damn it, I can't!*" Her shoulders drooped and she seemed physically beaten.

I waited, wanting an explanation. When she remained silent, I didn't know what else to do. It was probably wrong, but I shouted at her: "Why?"

"*Because*, okay?" she yelled back. "Just *because*."

"Bobby," I said, this time quietly. Not a question.

Pip turned slowly back to me, looking into my eyes with her own, red and wet. "I can't do this anymore because he's gone," she said. "I just wish I could have told him how I felt, and not been so arrogant. So foolish." She shook from the anguish and sorrow.

Seeing her that way, my anger dimmed, but I still felt compelled. I would say my final piece, but one way or the other, I was going. The spite I had for Sol, the anger over Bobby's death, was like bile that wouldn't stop erupting from my stomach. There would be no peace until this was done. "I don't have a choice," I said. "I can't leave my family with *him*."

"I know, John. Of course."

"Last chance," I said, not really begging so much as demanding she change her mind.

Pip stared at me with eyes so serious that I held my breath. "The only thing that ever made me capable, that ever made me believe in myself, that made it so I could *do* these things — these *superpowered* things — was *this*." She pointed to her heart. "And now, it's broken."

* * *

Silently, I zipped high above the busy streets, returning to the city Sol ruled, dressed in the stretchy black clothes Pip had provided, this time all alone.

Flying unseen, like a deadly arrow just below the clouds, I watched the people of the city go about their evening tasks, as if Sol didn't exist, as if life were normal. But I felt something. I was too far up to fully read any one person's mind, but a general feeling floated through the night nonetheless.

Fear.

The city's inhabitants shopped, ate, worked, played, maybe even danced, sang, who knows. But all of it was tainted with fear. Fear of Sol.

And the son of a bitch had my family.

Here I was, coming back to try to be the hero. Why me?

I realized slowly that any one of the people below me could be a hero. Looking down, I saw a dark-skinned woman in a business suit, walking briskly. She looked resourceful and strong. Why wasn't she a superhero? Then there was the child walking with his father, hand in hand. The child scanned the crowd as he walked, with more curiosity than anything else. *I bet he's strong, too. I bet he could be a hero.*

An older woman walked slowly and stiffly down the street, carrying a bulging plastic bag. A much younger man stopped beside her and said something, perhaps offering to help. She nodded but continued on her way, able to do her daily chores all by herself. I bet she could be a superhero.

But, there was this one thing. They couldn't.

And I could.

Yet I hadn't. Not enough. And that brought the old rage back in full force. My belly blazed with a fire that only the permanent death of Sol might quell.

It was time.

Time to change.

I came to think of my fire as the manifestation of Sol inside me, as if he were the reason for my rage. I didn't know if I could be a true superhero. But I knew I was going to find and kill Sol. Or be killed myself.

Either way, the fire would finally go out.

An image of Bobby appeared in my mind, him giggling just after performing the hammer trick — that ridiculous thing we did when we first found out we had powers. Put your hand out on a hard surface, get something equally hard in the other hand, like a hammer. Then swing. Poof! Magic! Your body sluices you out of harm's way! In my mind, Bobby looked so pleased with it all. So happy. He didn't know where it all would end up.

When was the last time I really tried something new with these powers? I thought. I couldn't remember. *Is it really fair to think I know everything already? I don't even know how Holly does what she does. What is it that I* don't *know?*

Bobby and I had spent so much time just trying to figure things out when we realized we had powers. Now I walked around like they were luggage. Something I ported from town to town, day by day. Damn it.

What if…?

What if I could stretch my abilities? What made me have a distance limit for my mental control? A few hundred feet. Why?

Zipping through the sky, I looked down at the people below me and selected a guy at random and I reached out. I just wanted to see if I could connect with him.

Just gauging by sight, I could tell he should be significantly out of range of my power. Still, I tried.

Nothing.

I pushed harder with my mind, stretching out, clenching my jaw as I strained to make the connection from such a distance.

Nothing.

The man walked down the street, completely unaware that I floated above him in the dark. Maybe it simply wouldn't work. *The distance limit is real*, I thought, cursing at myself for being a fool. Angry at myself.

But, damn, I wanted it to work. I wanted *something new*. I got so pissed.

"Stop!" I yelled out loud, in frustration and rage.

And the man stopped. Just for a second.

After a heartbeat, he continued on his way.

Was it me? Was it coincidence? Did he just hear me? The city was full of noise, from every direction. I didn't think he could hear me, so far above. Did he feel my command in his mind? I had to know. I reached out again, allowing fury to flow through my mental command like lava down a mountainside.

Stop.

And the man stopped, abruptly.

Turn around.

The man turned around.

Walk.

He walked. It worked…

I had to try something else. I floated upward, soaring to the top of the nearest tall building. The man became just a dot in my vision. Sucking in air, I felt myself fill with anger. Then I pushed it all out, stretching toward the man far below.

Stop.

Once more, he stopped.

I laughed out loud, my hair whipping in the wind like a maniac, perhaps a thousand feet in the air. Then I reached out to the man one last time. *Turn around. Go home or wherever else you were going. And forget about this.*

Far below, the man turned and began walking again, heading away.

I hung in mid-air, thinking. *What else can I do?*

There was only one answer. I would never know what I could do until I tried. And I knew just who I'd like to try a few things on. Edgy things, maybe violent things. Using anger as a fuel — a *directed* fuel — seemed to have opened new doors.

And that meant only one thing.

It was time to pay Sol another visit.

6

I circled Babilu Tower, with my eyes closed. Too far away for Sol to reach me, assuming he was compelled by the same distance limit that had ruled me for so long. My mind was reaching out, searching.

Where are you, asshole?

I fueled myself with anger. Feeling my way through the night sky, my mind began to map the penthouse suite. It was as if I could see inside the building, but not in regular colors or dimensions. I could feel the structure of the walls, the floor. I felt objects of shape and mass that I realized were furniture. But people? I couldn't feel anyone.

I squeezed my eyes shut and pushed in deeper, letting fury power me, its heat amping up every detail. I felt the outline of the elevator, its doors resting closed on the top floor. The desk and the waiting area. The gleaming, polished floor. And the two huge wooden doors to Sol's inner sanctum. My mind slid through the doors as if they were vapor, and I was back inside.

Scanning, scanning… walls and floor and furniture… and — wait! Something irregular at the desk. A form. I focused all of my mind onto the form, while my body continued to circle in midair around the building. The form took shape, but something was off. It didn't have the rigid lines of the walls or floor.

Then it moved.

It was *him.*

I could *sense* Sol.

And best of all, he seemed to have no idea I was there. Controlling the anger, I used it to fuel another thread. I reached into the irregular shape, digging with my mind.

...Soon he will come, though the trap is already in place...

My eyes snapped open. Sol's voice had been in my head. For a moment, I faltered, not sure what had happened. Then I realized that *I* had put Sol into my mind. Or, more precisely, I had put myself in his.

I looked at the large, floor-to-ceiling glass windows on the top floor, now knowing that Sol sat just inside, unsuspecting.

"Soon?" I muttered to myself aloud. "So wrong, *old friend.*" I chuckled, an echo of Sol's own laugh. "Not soon. *Now!*"

With all my rage and power, I thrust myself forward, directly toward the glass windows. In my mind, everything slowed down.

And I thought of atoms.

I remembered something I had learned in science class — that atoms are mostly composed of empty space. It gave me a crazy idea. What would stop me from passing through just the empty space in that glass window, while leaving the nucleus and the electrons alone? If my atoms' parts could just zip past the window's atomic parts, I'd be inside and no one would be the wiser.

I loved how clever I was!

I pushed myself, to what felt like an unbelievable speed, flying head first, directly toward the glass.

As I reached the moment when I would sluice my body, not in a fluid style like normal, but literally atom by atom *through* the window and into Sol's penthouse, I smiled.

I knew I would achieve my *coup de grace* — and I would walk through walls!

An instant later, I did it.

The glass window exploded into pieces as I slammed into it with ridiculous force and speed.

Well, shit. That didn't work. Not one bit.

Inside the penthouse atop Babilu Tower, I stood amid the remains of a wall of shattered glass, half-dazed. I had a microsecond to consider what went wrong. *The thorns. The things that give me power…* I thought. *You idiot! They're cellular, not atomic.*

Damned science, I thought.

Sol stood behind his desk, startled. "John?"

Instantly, I reached out, and instantly, he put up his guard. I was faster. I reached into Sol's mind and saw his distress, his surprise.

He wasn't ready for me. Not yet. Whatever trap he'd been talking about wasn't laid yet.

Dumbass, I thought, with a grin.

I leaped. My mind dove further into Sol's while my body jumped toward him. I reached out, knowing that he would sluice out of the way. My anger was power, and I sought to overwhelm him. But he resisted. As I grappled, he struggled. As I tried to control him, he sluiced and slid, trying to get free. Unless I could do something to short-circuit his abilities, Sol might still overcome me, despite the surprise. He pushed to move above me, and I resisted. *What can disarm Sol, the world's nemesis?* I thought there was something. Something from the stories he told me when I was half-awake. I tapped into his past.

Something…

When I was half-conscious from the gas, his words had slid off me like water down a rocky outcropping.

She…

Not just any *she*… Her name was *Ramona.*

That was it!

"Ramona," I said out loud.

Sol froze. "What?"

His confusion was enough. Tapping my fire, I dug deeper into Sol's mind, looking for Ramona… and I found her face. Smiling, young, and happy. As it sprang into my mind, so must it have sprung into his. Sol's defenses collapsed and as I wrapped my mind into the spaces of his brain, I wrapped my arm around his throat, tugging backward. With the paralyzing force of power plus memory, my mind held his and denied him his abilities. I didn't bother continuing to struggle with him physically. There was no sense in trying to harm him — his body would just avoid anything I could do. Still, I had other plans. As gently as I could muster — to avoid his body's nature defenses — I dragged Sol backward like a lifeguard saving a helpless swimmer.

I reached into his mind a little further and sought direction. Finding it, I guided his body to the elevator and down a few floors. Left, follow the hallway. A Way of the Sun guard sat there. Sparing only a fraction of mind power, I put the guard to sleep, slumping him over his desk. Then beyond, to a door.

The equipment looked alien from the outside of the door, but I didn't stop to think about it. Still holding Sol by the power of my mind over his, I led him to the table that looked the same as how I had left it — straps undone, two gas tanks and a mask conveniently beside. I willed Sol's body to walk itself over and lie down, then I happily strapped him in and placed the mask over his nose.

There was only one guess I had to make. Which gas would put Sol to sleep, and which one would kill him?

Because, for the moment, I wanted the bastard alive.

I choose one, admittedly not completely at random. The red skull and crossbones stickers on the second tank were sort of a dead giveaway. Get it? *Dead* giveaway? All right, fine.

I spun the nozzle of the first tank, and waited.

The whooshing hiss that followed sounded blissful — such a contrast to the horrible, gut-wrenching feeling I'd had the last time I heard it. I let the stuff do its own sort of magic and watched Sol go limp. With my mind still in his, I could feel his resistance give way. Still, I waited. I had to be sure.

Although it was frustrating not to act, I stayed for nearly an hour. Sol was a boogeyman, and my fear was that, just like in the final scene of every horror movie ever made, I would turn around thinking everything was finished and he would leap into the air to stab me though the gut.

Finally, the fire inside me acted as a sort of a calming agent. A reassurance. I left, closing the door behind me.

While I had been in Sol's mind, I probed for answers. Where was Holly? Where was my mother? Where were Naima and Sharif? And where, dammit, was my *belt*?

His mind complied.

The belt, as it turned out, was in a drawer in that very room. Despite the fact that my weirdo superhero suit had no belt loops, I curled the old double-belt around my waist and fastened it with a grin.

Then I walked back to the elevator to make the trip downstairs, knowing I had to be careful. I needed Naima for what came next, but

I couldn't get too close to her, couldn't risk losing my powers. I had to rescue Mom and Holly, and I knew everyone was being held together, so that Naima cancelled out Holly's abilities. Luckily, I had found a way to push my powers even farther than I thought was possible, so I had a plan.

That is, until I started to feel strange.

No! Shit!

I turned to run, away from the elevator. I could blast out a window, get far away, anything. I willed my body to zip through the air, smash its way out of trouble, but nothing happened.

Behind me, a bell dinged, and the elevator doors started to open. And I knew Naima was there. But apparently not alone.

I heard my mother gasp. "John!"

"I *told* you to keep quiet!" a male voice growled.

Turning back, I saw a man in dark clothes — Way of the Sun — smash the butt of a rifle into my mother's stomach. With a cry, she fell to the floor. Blood dripped from her open mouth, and she clutched at her abdomen.

Not again! I thought. She hadn't ever really recovered from the first injury. Mom was only human, after all. Powerlessly, I watched her pant, trying to regain some strength, some ability to stand. She couldn't.

Still, the most disturbing thing I saw in the elevator wasn't what happened to my mother. It was the look of pure hatred on Holly's face.

7

Some time later, Sol had regained a few things. His powers, his swagger, and most importantly, the upper hand. As soon as I was taken by his lackeys, they set him free and gave him fresh air to breath. Fueled by power, it wasn't long before he was back to normal.

We stood once more at the top of Babilu Tower, and he spoke to us. "I am *very* glad to have all of your here this evening, all together. Just as I had hoped." As if reflecting my mood, dark clouds rolled by in the night sky above us, muting the world, allowing only an occasional star to poke its dim light through.

Along the wide expanse of the roof, we stood in distinct pockets. On one end, Sol and Margrethe, who had joined the party. A few male and female Way of the Sun thugs stood with them, guns draw. On the other end, a much larger group of Sol's goons surrounded me, Holly, Mom, Naima, and Sharif. Holly sat in an unfamiliar wheelchair, something Sol's people must have provided.

With Naima only inches away, my powers, and Holly's, were as distant as the pale stars, and the array of guns pointed toward us presented a very real, fatal threat. They didn't even bother to take away my belt. After all, in my state, it was just a belt.

Holly continued to throw daggers at Sol and his henchmen — sorry, henchpeople — with her eyes, but without my abilities or hers, there was no way for me to talk to her.

We were helpless again. And Sol was pontificating. Again. "This evening will be something of a ceremony — a culmination, if you will. So it's only just that we should be together. The *superhumans*." Sol smiled, his hair gently waving in the breeze, like the fronds of a palm tree at the beach, not disturbed so much as enhanced. He looked perfect, as usual. Pressed cream-colored shirt, dark pants, and his typical hipster loafers. "I'm actually not fond of the word *superhuman*. Would you like to know why?"

He didn't wait for my response, which would have been, *No, and please keep it to yourself. No one gives a crap what you think, jerk.*

Instead, he continued.

"Did you know that the term *woman* is derived from the phrase *wife-man*? Literally, *the wife of the man*. I have no doubt that feminists for generations have rued this fact. It must be no short source of frustration, when you are trying to advance the equality of the sexes, to realize your entire gender is named merely as a relation to the other side. So, similarly, I find issue with the term *superhuman*, because the very foundation of the name labels us as *human*. The *super* part is merely hyperbole. But I would make the case that we are more than human, more than even super — or superior — humans." He paused, eyeing Margrethe at his side before glancing at me, then Holly. "My friends, we are *gods*."

Although he stood across from us, he managed to make it feel as if he stood over us, with his arms splayed out to each side emulating a religious pose. I scoffed, but then caught myself. *I* thought Sol was full of crap, but around me, the Way of the Sun — dozens strong — all dipped their heads in deference. Sure, I had questioned whether I really was human anymore, but never once did I consider myself a god. *They* actually bought his bullshit.

"Margrethe, John, and Holly. Together, we make up the most powerful collection of living creatures this planet has ever seen. What other name than *god* applies? Yet we are not equal, no, indeed not." Sol chuckled again, and my skin crawled. "I have faced death and returned. John, you have as well. But Holly? Margrethe? You ladies have some work to do." He said it like a polite, charming joke. It pissed me off. "And it is unfortunate that our other friends Pip and Bobby cannot be with us this evening."

That made me flinch, and Sol caught it. "Ah yes, I suppose Bobby Graden will not be joining us ever again. I nearly forgot." The lie of Sol's nonchalance fueled my anger, and I seethed at him. In response, he turned and stared into my eyes. "Let Bobby serve as proof to us all. Even a god can die."

As Sol let his words soak in, we stood powerless before him and the many Way of the Sun who steadfastly held us at gunpoint. His meaning was quite clear.

"John, it gives me particular pleasure that you returned. I really wanted you to see *this*, my crowning achievement." Sol gestured grandly, suddenly preening around like some lord or king.

"What are you talking about?" I spat. Anger was there, but with no power, it was pointless, wasted anger.

He grinned at me, emitting that awful chuckle. I clenched my fists. "Do you recall what it is that I wish to be?"

"A jackass? If so, then congratulations! You succeeded a long time ago. Now, can we all go home?"

Sol's smile froze a little bit, but he shrugged aside my comments. "For a very long time, I wished to be *eternal*. And thanks to you, John, I have achieved that goal. You killed me, yet I returned. But do you know what? I think that eternity is no longer enough." He paused, looking toward Margrethe with glee in his eyes. "Although I cannot be killed, I do not believe I can stop myself from aging. And, to be honest, I do not know what will happen to my powers with the passing of time. Will they remain? Will they grow? Or… might they diminish? And that — *that* — would be unforgivable. To allow *me* to diminish, especially when there is a way I can avoid such a fate."

"Let me guess, you've found the Fountain of Youth," I interjected.

Sol stopped, looking at me with an almost apologetic expression. "Almost, John Black! Almost." He returned to his pacing, and I realized that — second only to his chuckle — I hated the pacing, too. "You see, I *have* found something. Something that can give me an eternity of youth." Sol walked closer, but only slightly, not daring to come into the sphere of Naima's influence. He stopped, staring directly at my sister. "I do not need a *Fountain of Youth.* No, I have something much, much better. With you, Holly, I can produce life itself."

Holly's brow furrowed and she fidgeted in her chair.

"You leave my daughter alone, you bastard," Mom said, although she lacked any sort of real confidence. Mom sounded like a shell of herself, her normal assurance and strength overtaken by fear that her family was soon to be destroyed. Her voice was pained and weak. She looked pale. The blow she had taken in the elevator, combined with the injury from that day at our house… had they done permanent damage?

Seeing Mom that way, as Sol quipped and smiled, my anger continued to brew. What was this game he was playing? Holly made giant monsters, and tiny spiders. Of the two, it was obvious that Sol would prefer monsters.

Did he mean to overrun the earth with such creatures? What would the world become if Sol made a dozen of them? A hundred? What would stop him from making thousands?

Humanity itself would be destroyed.

"I see your thoughts, John, my old friend. And your fears are confirmed. With Holly, with her ability, I could take over the entirety of the world and destroy every human obstacle in my way."

"She'll never help you!" I shouted. Turning toward my sister, I hissed. "Holly, whatever he says. Whatever he does, you *can't* help him. You can't!"

Holly looked at me with confused eyes, then glared at Sol. It was clear she had no desire to be complicit in his plans. *Good. Just hold on, Holly. We'll figure something out.* There was no answer, of course. She couldn't hear the thoughts trapped in my head.

"John," Sol said, in a tone that sounded like an amused schoolteacher. "Your sister doesn't have to help me do anything at all. I don't expect her to be working by my side." He chuckled again.

"What then? What's your deal?"

Sol nodded to Margrethe, who in turn nodded toward the many Way of the Sun around us. Guns that were loosely pointed our way were suddenly aimed directly at us. Bolts slid and safeties toggled off. This time Sol looked at my mother. "Mrs. Black. Andrea, if that is acceptable to you. Would you please roll your daughter forward, slowly?"

"I won't lift a finger to help you," Mom said, still clutching at her stomach with one hand.

Sol rolled his head back on his neck, frustrated. "Fine," he said. "Kill the boy." Guns shifted to focus on Sharif, who immediately cowered behind his mother.

"No! Stop!" Naima shrieked.

Sol snapped forward. "I will say this for the last time. Andrea Black, roll your daughter toward me, slowly. And Holly, hear me carefully. If you try to do anything — anything at all — once you have powers again, my people will kill your brother and mother. I, meanwhile, will use my own powers to pull you and Naima close to each other once more, and when your powers are gone again, you will die next. So, you must decide. You have free will. Make your choice. Do as I say, or…" He raised one palm, her options clear.

Everyone froze. Holly's face turned from anger and hatred to uncertainty. She turned toward me and spoke out loud. "Johnny?" It was both good and terrifying to hear her use that name again.

Sol interrupted the moment. "Mrs. Black, do it *now*." He rolled his hand around, gesturing for her to hurry.

Mom's eyes were feral, shifting endlessly in all directions. I knew what she was thinking, even though I couldn't read her mind. She needed to find a way out of this situation, for all of us. But there was no way out.

Slowly, and in pain, she rolled Holly toward Sol.

"Well, then," he said. "Finally, we can begin."

8

"Holly, listen to me," Sol said, walking right up to her wheelchair. "I know you can access your powers again, and that means you may do whatever you wish. Your decision. You know the consequences. Deny me, and someone dies. Attack me, and death rains down upon you all. Will you do as I say?"

Yes, Holly said.

I was used to hearing her voice in my mind, but I realized something unexpected. *Everyone* could hear it now. My world shook.

She's getting stronger, I thought.

Yes, of course, John, she replied, to me, but in that way where everyone heard. *Isn't that what people do? Grow up? Get bigger and stronger?* A flash of annoyance crossed her face before she turned back to Sol. *What do you want from me?*

My sister was ticked off.

The building shook, just enough that we all felt it. Holly's anger on display.

Sol wagged a single finger at her. "Ah, ah… none of that, or else we have a problem, Holly. Are you able to control yourself?"

Yes. Just hurry up.

"Very well," Sol said. "I want you to recall the moment when you made the Gorgols. When you made *life*. And then, when you are ready, I want you to slowly and carefully try to do it again."

Holly shook her head, just a quick tic-like gesture. *You're in my head.*

"Yes, my dear," Sol said. "That is quite the point. I plan to *learn* from you. From you, I plan to learn the secret of creating life."

So you can do terrible things? Holly said. *You have no idea what it's like. I* created *those monsters, and they killed people. I don't even know how many people they killed. I'm responsible for that. I'm a murderer.*

Mom fell to her knees beside Holly's chair. "No, honey! Don't think that! You didn't mean—"

Stop, Mom. It doesn't matter. I did it. That's all. Holly slowly lifted her head toward Sol. *And now, you want to do it, too? Slaughter people like animals? No, worse. Crush them like ants.*

Sol grinned again. "Well, you know what they say. If you want to make an omelet, you've got to crack some eggs."

The building shuddered again from Holly's residual anger.

Sol *tsked* her. "Last chance, Holly. No more little earthquakes. No more debate. Ready?"

She didn't back down. Instead, my sister appeared to puff up. Despite the fact that Sol was an adult, standing over her, and she was a girl in a wheelchair, she was defiant, strong. *I'm ready, Sol. But are you?*

He looked stunned, but recovered quickly. "You have no idea how ready I am, young lady. Now, if you would, go ahead. I am quite anxious to learn more. Show me the way. Show me how to create life."

It doesn't work quite like that. I have to make a doorway first.

Sol nodded, barely holding in his excitement. His teeth gleamed like he was a lion sizing up dinner. "Show me," he repeated.

Mom lurched forward, reaching out for the handles on Holly's chair, tugging backward, away from Sol. "Don't do it, Holly! You can't!" A gun-toting thug pressed himself between Mom and the chair, then shoved the business end of the weapon toward her, knocking her back. Instinctively, I jumped for them, and another guy clocked me in the back of the head, making me see stars. Getting hit that way, feeling pain. It was so… odd.

I turned back toward the guy who hit me, not meaning anything more than to look, and he hit me again. Hard.

I went down, not just seeing stars. I was seeing universes, friends. Without my powers, I had been practically brained, twice, in rapid succession. I don't recommend it. I fell to my knees and the world spun.

Sol waited until the scene settled down. "I will warn you both that another outburst of this nature will not be tolerated." He gestured toward my mother. "Remove her, away from her daughter. No need to keep her near our friend, Naima, of course, as Andrea is merely human." The man dragged Mom away from Holly and behind Sol, to a place where he held her at gunpoint. "Now, Holly. Begin."

No, Holly. Don't, I thought, willing my mind to reach hers, but to no avail. I stared at her intensely, as if my eyes alone could connect with her mind.

And they did.

No, not that way. My powers were well and truly gone. Naima remained close by. But my eyes could read Holly's mind.

The slight flush of her face, the way her eyes flitted back and forth nervously. But most of all, it was the little pull at the side of her mouth.

Oh my God.

At that moment, the tiniest of gestures made reality come crashing down on me. All the things Holly had said to me, that I never truly heard or understood. Or that I refused to let sink in. Now, I had a revelation about my sister, and nothing was ever going to be the same.

She wants *to show him what she can do. Finally, somebody respects her for her power, and she* likes *it.*

9

The look in Holly's eyes made me want to shout out, tell her she didn't need to prove anything to anyone. But my mind was scrambled from the hits I had taken. And it probably would have been pointless, because Holly didn't hesitate.

Without warning, her body lifted into the air, and she hovered several feet above her wheelchair. *I am Shadow Ghost, Sol*, she said. *If you hope to learn from me, you'd better pay attention.*

The Way of the Sun closed in, guns raised nervously.

Sol raised a hand, urging them to stay calm. But his focus remained on Holly, only on Holly.

Just then Holly's attention shifted from Sol to the open air between them, and a small swirl of black appeared, sort of like a puff of smoke. It seemed to churn or spin, making a wispy circle maybe an inch or two across.

I could see from Sol's face that he was concentrating, watching the spectacle while reading the inner workings of Holly's mind, trying to see *how* she was making it all happen.

The black circle grew to six inches across, then a foot. Sol looked confused. "Wait, Holly. Hold it there. I need to see — *there*! The source of this construct in your mind. Continue."

Holly obliged, spinning and enlarging the circle of smoke between them. Slowly, it grew bigger, and behind it, Sol's eyes grew wider. "Yes! I am beginning to understand!" The circle continued to expand, a disc of dark vapor turning in space. It was a dark evening, but the city, like all cities, was aglow with light. Although the rooftop was dim, we could all see just fine. In fact, the clouds worked to reflect the city's light back down toward us.

But the black, smoky disc didn't reflect any light at all. As it got larger, it seemed like it was a true black hole, eating up anything that came too close, even light itself.

A grin spread across Holly's face as she made the circle bigger still. Three feet, six, more.

"It's incredible," Sol said, his mouth hanging open, a man enraptured.

"No!" I shouted, struggling forward on my knees. The man behind me struck me again, hard, driving me down. My vision blurred and it hurt simply to think. *I've failed you, Holly*, came into my mind, burning through the pain.

Finally, the swirling mass reached more than 10 feet in diameter and stopped growing. It's bottom edge touched the surface of the roof, while its upper edge loomed above the maniacally grinning figure of Sol. Every eye stared at it, every person stunned to silence. Except one.

"*Yes*! I see! I see!" Sol stepped forward, jubilant, holding his hands aloft as if he were praying to the infinitely black disc in front of him. Holly's grin widened. "I have it now! I have the ability to *create life*! And with this, I shall become death, destroyer of worlds!"

For one hideous moment of pain, I blinked at Sol. What else could he need or want? He'd won. He had achieved everything there was to achieve. Eternal life paired with the ability to create life itself.

Sol was truly a god. How else could you describe him? Yet I knew, too, that he would be a vengeful god. A terrible god.

I imagined that in hundreds or thousands of years, with Sol still living, scriptures would be written about him. The Way of the Sun, the Word of the God Sol.

Nothing could ever possibly stop him again.

Least of all, me.

I sat back on my heels, my hands holding the sides of my head which throbbed with blinding pain. I couldn't even form words, except for the word *no*. Even that felt pale.

A shriek rang out behind Sol, and my mother leaped forward, shaking past the thug with the gun who tried to stop her. She cleared the few steps before anyone could reach her. Before Sol could even turn around.

The gun behind her was raised, aimed. I saw it all in slow motion. I knew the trigger would be pulled and my mother would die. I knew it no longer mattered. That we would all die, at the hands of the God Sol. I admit it. I despaired. I lost hope. After losing so much else, finally, the worst had come to pass.

When the gun fired, I was motionless.

My mother reached Sol, her gesture seeming futile, childish. A baby — no, an insect — raising its hands to fight a god. Impossible. And yet, with those two raised hands, she pushed.

The bullet struck her in the center of her back, propelling her forward, possibly even augmenting her push.

Sol's body sluiced out of the way of Mom's shove, but in doing so slid too close to Holly's black hole. His arm passed into the darkness and was gone.

Two sharp gasps tore the air at the same moment — from Holly and Sol, both wide-eyed, staring at the swirling mass. Something was wrong, very wrong.

Mom staggered back, one hand raised to her chest. I could see red oozing between her fingers. She fell.

Just as light seemed unable to escape the turning black disc, neither could Sol. With one arm lost inside, it held him, and he turned, flailing, his look of victory instantly turned to panic.

I tried to understand what I was seeing. Had Holly trapped Sol? No, she seemed stunned, too, struggling in her own way.

Sol pulled back, but the circle reacted, sucking him in a little farther. He tried again, with every muscle, every ounce of his power straining against the black hole.

For a moment, time seemed frozen.

Then, after a heartbeat, Sol was sucked completely inside, too quick to groan or sigh.

With a whoosh and a thunderclap, the disc winked out of existence. Holly dropped heavily back into her chair.

And the God Sol was gone.

10

The world fell into an almost complete stunned silence, but one person had the presence of mind to act. Margrethe.

"You — grab her!" she shouted to one of the Way of the Sun, gesturing for him to drag Holly back into the sphere of Naima's power-deadening influence.

Holly didn't resist. She slumped in her chair like someone had socked her in the gut. No, worse. Something very bad had happened. I couldn't even tell if she was still breathing.

I strained through my fuzzed, pained head to look sideways, and found Naima near me. "Naima, please. Move away. Let me regain my powers. Please." I couldn't even get up off my knees.

She glanced at the guards holding their sleek and dangerous guns, then at her son. "I can't, John. They'll kill us. They'll kill *him*."

I just needed enough power. Enough to clear my head. Enough to get me away from Naima, to give us a chance. I had beaten Margrethe before. I knew I could do it again, but not without my powers.

"Surround them," Margrethe called out, still on the other side of the rooftop. "If anyone tries anything, shoot them. Except her." She pointed at Naima. "Keep her alive and near the others, at all cost."

The Way of the Sun, Sol's devotees, surrounded us. A few of them dragged the unmoving form of my mother back until she was near us, so they could watch everyone at the same time, in a group on one side of the rooftop. They dropped Mom in a heap beside Holly's chair, and I saw so much blood.

I tried to speak. "Mom?" *Are you okay? Talk to me, please!* I wanted to say those things, to go to her, but even turning my head brought on immobilizing nausea.

Along the distant horizon, the sky seemed lighter. Morning was coming, although with the dense cloud cover, I expected it to be a slow, dull process, with no sudden rays of light filtering down on us.

Meanwhile, Margrethe was doing something with her mind, closing her eyes and reaching out.

It looked like she was searching for something.

No.

Searching for some*one*.

Finally, her eyes opened. “I’m not going to pretend to understand what happened here, but I don’t care. Sol is gone. If he comes back, we’ll all deal with that when it happens, but until such time, *I* am in charge. And that means we’re going to do things a little differently.”

To the side, I saw Naima cringe and pull her son closer. “If Sol is gone, as you say, then let us go. This is over.”

Margrethe raised one hand sharply. “Not hardly.” She was, after all, the Norse God of Vengeance, or at least that’s what I liked to call her. “There is a debt that must be repaid. Now that we’re done with these experiments, we can move on to the final act.” Margrethe turned to me. “Now, John Black, you get what you deserve for what you did to me. For how you took Petrus from me.” She smiled, slicing one finger through the air in a gesture to the gunman behind me. “Now, you get to die.”

I felt the cold steel ring of a muzzle press against the back of my head, and I knew there was nothing I could do. “I’m sorry, Mom. I’m sorry, Holly.”

Although I would die, it seemed I had already lost my family. Holly remained motionless, doubled-over, catatonic or worse. Mom was bleeding out. It wouldn’t be long.

“Now you know exactly how I felt,” Margrethe said, her face stone solid with determination. She nodded. “Do it.”

I heard and felt the gun cock.

And then I, too, was covered in blood.

11

I rolled to the side to see the man behind me gurgle and spit viscous red blood. The long metal blade of a sword protruded from his stomach.

I know that sword…

Margrethe blinked in confusion, but in an instant she was back in charge. "Everyone — shoot them! Kill them now!" But her words were cut short.

A red flash whizzed past overhead, skirting Naima's power-dampening circle and instead focusing on the other side of the building. With a crash like a meteor landing, the object slammed into Margrethe, and the two forms twisted, rolled, and sluiced around each other, sliding to the far wall of the rooftop.

Pip had come. *Pip had come!*

The two bodies rolled and then leaped free from each other, and there she was. Pip, ablaze in her red outfit, weaponless but ready, faced off against Margrethe. The blonde woman seethed and jumped to attack, but Pip dodged, striking out with her foot in a sharp kick as Margrethe passed. The blow only accelerated Margrethe's passage, but as she reached the wall, she pushed off it and flew into the sky.

Pip shot like a bullet toward her target, and the two fought high above us, alternating strikes in a fluid motion. They were eagles soaring above, tearing and clawing at each other, spinning around with their wings clipped, before separating and arcing back into the air.

I rubbed at the side of my aching, almost broken head. "Naima," I whispered. "You *have* to find a way to get away from me. I have to help her!"

Naima's eyes flitted side to side, at the guns so close and leveled at us.

But… on the far side of the building, by the door that lead back inside, there was motion. A couple members of the Way of the Sun put down their weapons and turned away, taking the opportunity to escape. Their leader, their precious Sol, was gone, and their second in command had her hands full. It was decision time for some of them, I suppose. How committed were they, after all? Without Sol, I think the decision became a lot easier.

After the first two defectors, another one turned and left, then two more. The ones surrounding us began taking notice, not leaving us, but turning their heads away from us to witness the desertion of their comrades, or watch the fighting above.

Without warning, Margrethe and Pip crashed back down to the rooftop, tumbling and turning over each other. A blur of fists and feet tried continuously and missed, or at best landed a glancing blow.

For a moment, they slid apart and stood, facing each other. Margrethe's hair flew free of her braids, making her wraithlike and terrifying. Meanwhile, Pip was panting from the exertion, looking notably more tired than her opponent. Margrethe took the moment not to attack, but to turn and drop off the side of the building.

Is she running away?

Near the door, more Way of the Sun departed. Apparently, they felt their new boss was deserting them. Two of the thugs near us lowered their weapons and sheepishly headed for the exit, although many still remained. Too many for Naima to risk action.

Pip ran to the edge where Margrethe had disappeared and looked down.

Directly into a trap.

From below, Margrethe flew upward, holding two tanks of gas, one on each side. Apparently she'd taken the moment to zip in and grab Sol's stash, the same gasses that he'd used on me. The nozzles of both tanks had been snapped off, causing them to erupt their contents directly into Pip's face.

The knock-out gas *and* the deadly gas.

Pip staggered backward, coughing, falling over, covering her mouth and nose. There was an assortment of building materials stashed against that side of the rooftop, and she dropped behind them, disappearing from my view.

"No!" I shouted, although it came out as a sort of weak and groggy puff of sound instead.

Margrethe hovered, holding the tanks until they were spent, letting their gasses mix and float down over Pip where she lay. Then, their contents exhausted, Margrethe turned and tossed the tanks into the far corner with a crash.

Standing over her fallen foe, Margrethe wiped strands of hair from her sweaty brow.

Just then, a thin line of metal rebar jutted up at a sharp angle, stabbing at Margrethe. Her body sluiced around it.

Behind the blonde woman, Pip jumped up and continued the thrust, even as Margrethe's body sluiced and dodged. Taking the offensive, Pip pulled back the metal bar and then swooped it around in a deadly circle, using all of her powers to make the blow fast, precise, and strong. Margrethe's head barely had time to slide out of the way, and her body rolled to the side, but Pip wouldn't let up. She hacked and slashed and sliced and stabbed at Margrethe, and there was nothing the Norse woman could do but evade.

Over and over and over again, Pip struck. I could see her hair was damp with sweat, her face red, but she wouldn't stop. Her breathing was labored, no doubt a lingering effect of the gas she'd inhaled. Still, she continued. Another blow, another slice, another thrust. Margrethe dodged again and again.

Finally, Pip slid her hand to the center of the rebar and began to twirl it, a nightmare of deadly, spinning steel. Tens or hundreds of blows pelted Margrethe, and she was overwhelmed. She turned, rolled out of the attack, and leaped into the sky.

Without a look back, Margrethe fled, soon becoming nothing more than a speck in the distance, heading toward the rising sun.

12

Pip tossed aside the metal bar with a loud clang, and dropped to one knee.

Near us, the Way of the Sun who were left held their ground. One nodded to some others who were arrayed behind us, and from that group, a couple split off and pointed their weapons at Pip.

Bad idea, I thought at first. Then I saw how tired she was. She didn't look like she could even stand.

"Come on," the leader said. He gestured with his gun. "One of you push the wheelchair. We're moving. Now!"

Someone grabbed me under the arms and began to drag me. The Way of the Sun pushed Holly and pulled me, and Naima was urged forward with threats. Slowly, our group closed the distance with Pip. Mom was left behind, discarded.

My mind ached. So many things. So many.

I wanted to shout out to Pip, warn her to move before Naima got too close.

I wanted to go to Holly, see if she was okay.

I wanted to run to my mother, do something. So much blood. Was she still alive?

And I was so, so sick of these people with guns.

Too many things. Too damn many things.

In the deep mud of my mind, fire burned.

Pip, in her exhausted state, either didn't realize the danger approaching or couldn't do anything about it. In moments, I feared, the slowly moving group of me, Holly, Naima, and Sharif, prodded on by goons with guns, would be too close, and Pip's power would slip away. Then all would be lost.

Come on, Pip. Do something!

She remained on her knees, panting but otherwise frozen. Unable to act. As if the simple act of breathing was all her body could do.

Then her neck twitched, just the slightest amount. I couldn't say for sure, but I think it was the first vestiges of Naima's power touching Pip and deadening her. It must have amplified the exhaustion she felt. Pip's body shuddered again. If she was so worn out *with* her powers, what would she be without them?

As if realizing this truth, Pip reached out one hand toward me.

And suddenly I found myself flying through the air, the two thugs supporting me coming along for the ride. My body was pulled directly toward Pip's, then over her and to the far side of the building. I crashed into the wall with the two men still holding my arms.

Just before we hit, I realized what another blow to the head might do to me in my already diminished state, and I cowered.

But the wall didn't hurt. In fact, the pain and dizziness in my head started to fade, at first slowly, and then the remainder of it blasted away, like an explosion filling my mind.

I reached inside myself, and I found my powers.

Pip, now completely spent, dropped so that her hands had to support her upper body.

In the millisecond before hell would erupt, I surveyed the rooftop. Holly was still slumped in her chair, Mom lay dead or nearly so across the roof, and Pip was being surrounded by the Way of the Sun and their guns, along with Naima's power-killing ability.

As the power coursed through me, it touched something inside.

Fire.

The powder keg within exploded. And I stood.

With a flick of my hands, the two goons next to me were sent in opposite directions, crashing into the walls of the roof so hard they probably lost teeth. Then I gestured and the two holding guns on Pip were tossed aside like rag dolls, over the side of the building to their deaths.

The leader of the group pushing Holly called out. "If you try to hurt us, we'll kill her!" He raised his gun toward my sister, touching it to her forehead.

It reminded me of how we used to touch our foreheads together, our way of connecting, even before she could talk.

But it perverted that gesture in a way that enraged me.

"Go ahead," I said, spitting venom. The anger filled me, and my power raged. I could sense everything. If I wanted to, I could read every thought. Feel every heartbeat. Know every action before it happened. I felt the entire space around me, down to the smallest gnat flicking in one corner, down to the cells in my body. I glowered at the man holding the gun. "Do it."

"Gladly," he said. "One less of you damn freaks. Somebody should give me a medal for this." With a sneer, the man pulled the trigger and a blast of sound erupted.

At the same time, I reached out, finding the bullet with my enhanced mind and holding it steady, locked inside the barrel of the gun. *Equal and opposite reaction*, I thought. With the bullet frozen, the gun and the man holding it had to accommodate the explosion that had occurred within. They were tossed backward, a kickback many times stronger than anything the thug had ever expected. He fell back, tumbling over himself, the gun clattering to the rooftop. Then he looked up at me in utter terror.

I grabbed him with the power of my mind and tossed him aside like a forgotten toy. As he plummeted out of view, I heard a voice. "John! Stop! Don't do it, don't make yourself as bad as them!" It was Pip.

Her voice cracked into the hard shell of my rage, weakening it. But anger still remained, and men and women still held guns on my sister, on Naima and Sharif. And my mother was dead.

I leaped into the sky to hover above the rooftop like a force from the heavens. "The rest of you," I said in a commanding voice, made stronger and louder and deeper and more compelling by the power within me and by my sheer anger. "The Way of the Sun is finished. Drop your weapons and leave. Leave and never let me see you again." I looked over their faces, one at a time, memorizing them each. "Do it now and I will spare your lives. But if any one of you tries anything, *all* of you will die. If one of you tries anything in the future, *for the rest of your lives*, all of you will die. I see you all and I remember you. Make your decision now, and hold to it, or I'll make it for you."

Immediately, the remaining dozen or so threw down their weapons and ran for the door, pushing and shoving past each other to escape. With no one left to fight, I lowered myself back to the rooftop.

And in an instant, I was a terrified little boy. I rushed toward my mother.

Falling beside her, I searched for something, any sign of life. I crashed down so heavily that at first I didn't even think to use my powers.

She's dead! "Mom! Please! Wake up!" I said. Tears came, but I smeared them away. "No. No, you will not be dead."

I reached inside for my powers, and fueled them with rage, pushing them to the limit. Then, with my mind, I reached out.

I was no doctor, I had no medical knowledge or skill at healing, yet I persisted.

And I found something: hope.

My mother was, miraculously, not dead. She clung to life by the thinnest of threads, showing me once more how she was the strongest person I will ever know. Amazed, I dug deeper.

Just show me what's wrong. Let me try to fix it.

And I found the problem. No, *problems*. There were several. They stood out in my mind like white blazes of light amid the neutral background. One blazed the brightest — the gunshot wound. The bullet had torn through her flesh, from back to front, shredding one of her lungs. Lower, another ragged glow of white showed me internal bleeding around her stomach. And beside that, another spot, duller but still emitting white light — the injury from back at our house, when the Way of the Sun had broken in and hurt her. She'd suffered for so long.

But still, I was no doctor. How could I help her?

I tried to use my power to close the wounds, like I was playing a doctor in a movie. It was pointless. One part of her body closed and another opened. My mother unconsciously groaned at the shifting strains and pain.

"It's not working!" I shouted. "I don't know what to do!"

My mother was going to die, right before me. Of that, I was sure. I couldn't fix her. I didn't know how.

It was over, and I hated myself for it.

13

Still raging, still reaching out with all of my power, still trying to put my mother back together, I flailed. For every positive step I took, something negative happened. For each healing action, something else fell apart. She was going to die. I simply didn't know how to stop it. Maybe it was impossible. Maybe no one on Earth could have saved her, not even the best team of doctors.

There was nothing on Earth that could save my mother.

That's it.

If nothing on Earth can save her, then it's time to try something that isn't from Earth.

"Naima! Come here fast! I need you!" I shouted.

From across the rooftop, she hesitated. "But John —"

"Please! No arguments, come quickly! I need you here!"

I could tell she still didn't understand, didn't want to comply. But she came.

As Naima approached, all the mighty powers I had seeped from my body, like water down a drain. I lost my connection to my mother, and once again, she simply appeared to be dead.

Was I making a mistake? Should I have kept trying? Would I ever again see even a glimmer of life within my mother?

There was no time to hesitate.

My power was gone, but still I needed something. I swiveled my head, looking, searching. Thankfully, my powers had completely fixed the concussion or whatever else had been wrong with me, and I could think straight.

There.

Pip's sword still protruded grotesquely from the gut of a fallen Way of the Sun thug — the same one who had brained me, several times. I ran to his body, finding no sympathy in myself for the dead man. Rolling him over, I put a foot on his torso, then pulled Pip's sword free with both hands.

"What are you going to do?" Naima sounded horrified. After all, she had seen me toss gun-toting thugs to their death. With a sword in hand, who knows what I might do.

"Just stay close," I said. I crouched next to my mother, leaning over the bloody wound, then raised the sword with one hand. I held out my other hand, and pressed the blade of Pip's sword against my forearm. The irony wasn't lost on me — Pip's sword cutting my arm, as I once had cut hers.

I slid the blade across my flesh, yet I had become so accustomed to my abilities that I expected nothing to happen. Or worse, that my skin would simply sluice, and everything would be for naught.

That wasn't the case.

With Naima close by and my powers a distant memory, Pip's sharp blade cut cleanly through my skin, drawing a red line across my arm. And, damn, it hurt.

Pushing harder, I made the opening deeper, and red blood began to flow. I clenched my teeth at the searing pain. At first, the blood simply ran down my arm, but soon enough poured out in a steady trickle.

I held my arm above the exit wound in my mother's chest, letting my blood fall into hers.

How much? How much?

Without my powers, the pain ached. I let more and more of my blood pour down upon my dying mother.

How much?

I couldn't know. Not exactly. But I started to fade, to become dizzy. I couldn't pass out — there was something else I had to do.

I lay my arm over my mother's body, our blood flowing together. "Naima," I said in a weakening voice. "Run. Get away from us now. Please…" And I put my head down on my mother, waiting.

It would either happen or it wouldn't now. There was nothing else to do.

Naima began to move away, slowly at first, then faster, going back to her son.

Do it, you thorns. If I've ever needed you, it's now.

My own power came back, first a flicker, then a blast of light and energy, restoring my body. The cut in my arm closed itself, my cells knitting themselves back together. I tossed Pip's sword aside.

Once more, I reached out into my mother, sensing her. The white blazes remained — all three of them. And her tendril of life was dimming. Her heart barely beat, blood barely flowing.

That's the problem, I thought, and with my mind, I pressed on her heart, pushing blood through it. Again, and again.

Then I saw sparkles.

I didn't understand at first, never having seen them this way before. The thorns.

There were thorns in my mother's body, and they were spreading. Once it started to happen, I released the pressure on her heart, watching it start to beat on its own. The white blazes dimmed and grew smaller.

I was watching the thorns in my mother's cells heal her body.

I don't know how long it took — a few minutes or a few hours — I was simply transfixed.

And when the white blazes were finally gone, she opened her eyes. "John? How?"

I smiled, although a stark reality hit me hard in that moment.

I just made another superhuman.

14

A while later, with Naima far enough away, Pip healed herself, too. Her cells did their special work to tackle both the negative effects of the gasses, and the tremendous exhaustion of using her powers so hard and so long. Slowly, she was restored. When she approached me, I could tell she was weary but better. "Where is he? Where do you think he went?"

Sol. I glanced at my sister, still knocked out, or seemingly so. Mom had recovered enough that she sat, propped against Holly's chair. We were a motley group.

I didn't really want to contemplate what it meant. That Sol had disappeared into Holly's portal, or doorway, or whatever it was. It didn't feel good to me. Not good at all. "No idea. I'm just glad he's gone." At least the second part of what I said wasn't a lie.

"What now?" Pip asked.

"What do you mean? It's time to go home."

Pip glanced toward the other side of the rooftop. "Taking them with us?" She pointed toward Naima and her son.

Well, crap. I hadn't thought about that. I had no doubt the government was still looking for Naima — hell, they'd most likely be happy to capture and study us all. But Naima was their safety net. An insurance policy. Just in case the superhumans got out of hand. "I have no idea what to do with her. And right now, I'm pretty tired. Why don't we stop trying to save the world for a minute and just ask Naima what she wants?" I rubbed the bridge of my nose.

Pip nodded, smirking. "Finally a good idea comes out of that thick head of yours."

"Thick head? Really?" I feigned anger.

“I thought you were done with the rage stuff,” Pip said abruptly. “What happened?”

I sighed and hung my head. If there was one person I would forever be embarrassed to talk to about my anger, it would be Pip. At least her powers could reattach the arm I cut off. But how could I explain it? Most likely the way everything gets explained. With a bunch of words that tumble down like a waterfall until maybe enough has been said to allow understanding. “I found out something, by accident. It feels like there is this fire inside me. And my powers, they seem to increase — no, that’s not the word… It feels like they grow, extend, when I use that fire. It makes me more powerful. By a lot.”

She thought about that for a moment, unsure. “And this fire is what makes you so angry?” Pip asked. I nodded. “Interesting. But listen, speaking from personal experience, your fits of rage get a little over the top.”

“Sorry,” I said. It wasn’t enough, but it was all there was.

She shrugged. “Now that we might have a little free time, can you do me a favor?”

“What’s that?”

“Work on it. See if you can tap the fire, without becoming the raging angry asshole that no one likes. Fair?” She stared at me, eyebrows raised, waiting.

I guess she meant that as a serious question and not just an insult. Could I do it? Could I use the fire and not the anger? I had no idea. “Sure, yeah. Well, at least I’ll try.”

“All right.” Pip raised her voice to call to the others, still across the rooftop from us. “Are you all ready to leave?”

Naima stood by her son, unsure. “And go where?” she asked.

“Excellent question. Where would *you* like to go?” Pip said.

“Back home,” Naima said in a gasp. “Back to our normal lives and away from all of this. We didn’t ask for this. *He* didn’t ask for this.” She hugged Sharif closer. “*I* didn’t ask for any of this.”

Pip shook her head. “There’s no going back. The world knows about us, and about you. That means some people will revere you. Others will fear you. And some will try to take you and use you. Because there are all sorts of people, and all sorts of reasons, and not all of them are good. So, given that, given the new reality, where do you want to go?”

Naima stood thinking, confused. “If we stay with you, we would be safe. But I take away your power…”

“Right, which kinda nullifies us protecting you.”

“And if we leave, we’re on our own.”

“Not quite,” Pip said. “I still want to help you. I can’t come near you without losing my abilities, but that doesn’t mean I can’t help you. It just means I can’t help you *directly*.”

“Okay, thank you. Really. What do we have to do?” Naima said, a tear of happiness welling in one eye as Sharif looked up at her.

“Let’s talk about that,” Pip said with a wink. “But first, let’s get off this damn rooftop. You — take the elevator. I’ll…” She made a flapping gesture with both hands. “Meet you downstairs, north side. I’ll be over in the park. We can find a place to talk there. I don’t mind sitting without my powers for a little while so we can make some decisions. Power can be exhausting anyway.” And with that, Pip jumped and flew in the air, then looped around and down. With a blur of red she was gone. Naima and Sharif walked to the door and went inside. As she passed me, my powers left me once more, and I realized then how much I hated that sensation.

Then there were three.

“Mom?” I said.

“Yes, Johnny?” She still seemed tired, but her strength was rapidly growing rapidly. In that moment, I wondered what Mom would do. She’d been the odd one out in our family for some time. Now what?

“We should go home,” I said. “Is Holly okay?”

“I don’t know. She’s breathing, but she won’t talk to me. Physically, I can’t tell that anything is actually wrong with her. She was just *out*, but she’s coming back.” Holly was still slumped over, but breathing. I couldn’t see if her eyes were open. “She’s tired. I think everyone is tired. You look tired, too.”

“I am,” I admitted.

“Then let’s get out the hell out of this damn city. We just need to get the car.”

“You drove here? Where’s our car?”

“Not *our* car, we came in — oh, no!” Mom raised a hand to her face. “Marcos!”

“What? What is it?”

“He was captured first,” she said. “I haven’t seen him since they brought us here.”

“Then maybe he’s here, too.”

For a while, we searched, me using my new ability and trying real hard to keep the fire from brewing into real anger. I sure hope I seemed calm when Mom looked at me.

Marcos was locked up on the 67th floor, unharmed, except for an aching back. “These chairs are *not* ergonomic!” he said, rubbing at the curve of his lower spine, when we finally broke him free.

He was so dramatic about it that for a second I almost believed he’d been through more than us.

Mom just gave him a patient, knowing smile.

15

The building wasn't completely deserted as we left, but darn near it. News had traveled fast. Leader gone, second in command run off, tons of armed thugs dispatched or AWOL. It was enough to break up the band pretty thoroughly.

I held the wide, glass door as Mom pushed Holly through. Holly glanced up, and maybe even gave me a tiny smile. Progress.

Before the four of us had even crossed the open space to the street, Pip returned.

"Where's Naima?" I asked as she fell in beside me, Mom, Holly, and Marcos.

"Being taken care of. That's all you need to know right now." She smiled, though her eyes sparkled with deviousness.

"It's 18 blocks till the car," Marcos said, unasked, holding up the keys. We found them in a bin of his possessions just outside the room where he was held.

Everyone froze. Eighteen blocks of walking? I tilted my head toward Pip. "Well, Red Hope. You wanna save the day, or me?"

She snorted, reaching out and taking the keys from Marcos. "Please. Are you even old enough to drive?" Then came a whoosh, and a red streak disappeared into the air.

Thirty minutes later, the car pulled up with Pip driving. "Sorry. Traffic," she said.

"How did you even know where the car was, or what it looked like?" Marcos asked.

"Corner of 43rd and Alabama," Pip said, before suddenly blushing red. She put one index finger to her temple. "Oh sorry. Read your mind."

* * *

The miles slid by, streaks of green and brown and grey. *Nothing in the world is really ever black and white*, I thought.

I sat in the middle of the back seat, with Holly on one side and Pip on the other. Marcos drove and Mom rode shotgun.

As a small sign of her improvement, Holly seemed glad to be rid of the wheelchair Sol's goons had provided.

What will the world look like without Sol? I thought. *I mean, truly without him?* The first time I killed him, peace lasted only weeks before the Gorgols came out of the sea, and Jake Weissman appeared. But this time… what was next? Margrethe was free, but was she the type to try to conquer cities, like Sol? Or would she just pursue some future revenge on me? My bet was on revenge, nice and cold.

And Mom. What did the future hold for her, now that she was… different?

My mind wandered as we flowed along the almost endless expanse of the highway. After a time, I almost dozed.

Until I realized Holly was looking at me.

You okay, Hol?

I… Yes, John.

Are you sure?

I don't need you to worry about me, John.

I'm not doing it because I think you can't handle yourself. You're my sister, Holly.

Sure, she replied.

Holly?

Yes, John.

Is Sol gone? I was terrified of the answer. *I mean, that was your doorway. Where did Sol go when it sucked him in?*

She didn't answer.

Holly? What's on the other side of the doorway?

John, do you know every detail about your powers? Where they come from and why? Why they chose you? Or me? Or Sol?

No, Holly, of course I don't know all that.

Of course.

I hissed a small sigh, exasperated. *What's your point, Hol?*

Just that you don't know. And neither do I. I don't know exactly where Sol went. Or Gorgol Alpha, for that matter. Maybe they're both in my head. Or maybe they've been destroyed. Or maybe I sent them across the universe.

I wanted to believe they were both destroyed. But could I just go on faith? That was hard. Real hard. *Holly?*

What is it, John? She was getting annoyed.

Is Sol in your head now?

Of course not.

Are you sure, Holly?

Give it a rest, John. The only thing inside my head is me.

She said it calmly, clearly, forcefully. And I really wanted to believe her. But her eyes didn't seem so sure.

Maybe I did believe her. Maybe.

Until she blinked and looked away.

THE END OF

ON A BLACK WIND BLOWS DOOM

but

JOHN BLACK WILL RETURN

in

IN THE BLACK VEINS OF THE EARTH

Author's Note

Keith Soares

By day, Keith Soares runs an interactive game, web, and app development agency. But by night, his imagination runs wild. A fan of authors such as Stephen King, Robert Heinlein, Arthur C. Clarke, Brandon Sanderson, Justin Cronin, and Andy Weir, Keith writes stories of science fiction, the apocalypse, fantasy, revenge, and horror. He lives in Alexandria, Virginia, with his wife and two daughters, who are all avid readers.

Subscribe to the Keith Soares New Releases Newsletter

Get release news and free books,
including private giveaways and preview chapters.

Sign up at KeithSoares.com

Like Facebook.com/KeithSoaresAuthor
Follow Twitter.com/ksoares

PLEASE CONSIDER leaving a review where you purchased this book. Reviews are the best thing you can do to help an independent author like me, and even one sentence about your thoughts is enough.

Thanks in advance!

— K.

Made in the USA
Columbia, SC
20 May 2021

38291486R00212